Jayne Lytle

Jayne Lytle

EUROSWYDD'S CAVERNS

Thanks for the support, Nick!
Enjoy –
Dawn

MINI ACRE PRESS

an imprint of

STREAKING DONKEY BOOKS

For information address:
Mini Acre Press, an imprint of Streaking Donkey Books, 71 Mason Road,
North Stratford, New Hampshire 03590.
www.geocities.com/streakingdonkey

Book and cover design, cover and interior illustrations by Dawn Frost

ISBN: 978-0-615-18840-9
1. Science Fiction—General. 2. Environmental Conservation. 3. Spirituality

Printed in the United States of America
First Edition

To Dawn for her unflagging support, skilled cartography and unbelievable patience and skill in finding logic within the – to me – incomprehensible world of computer technology.

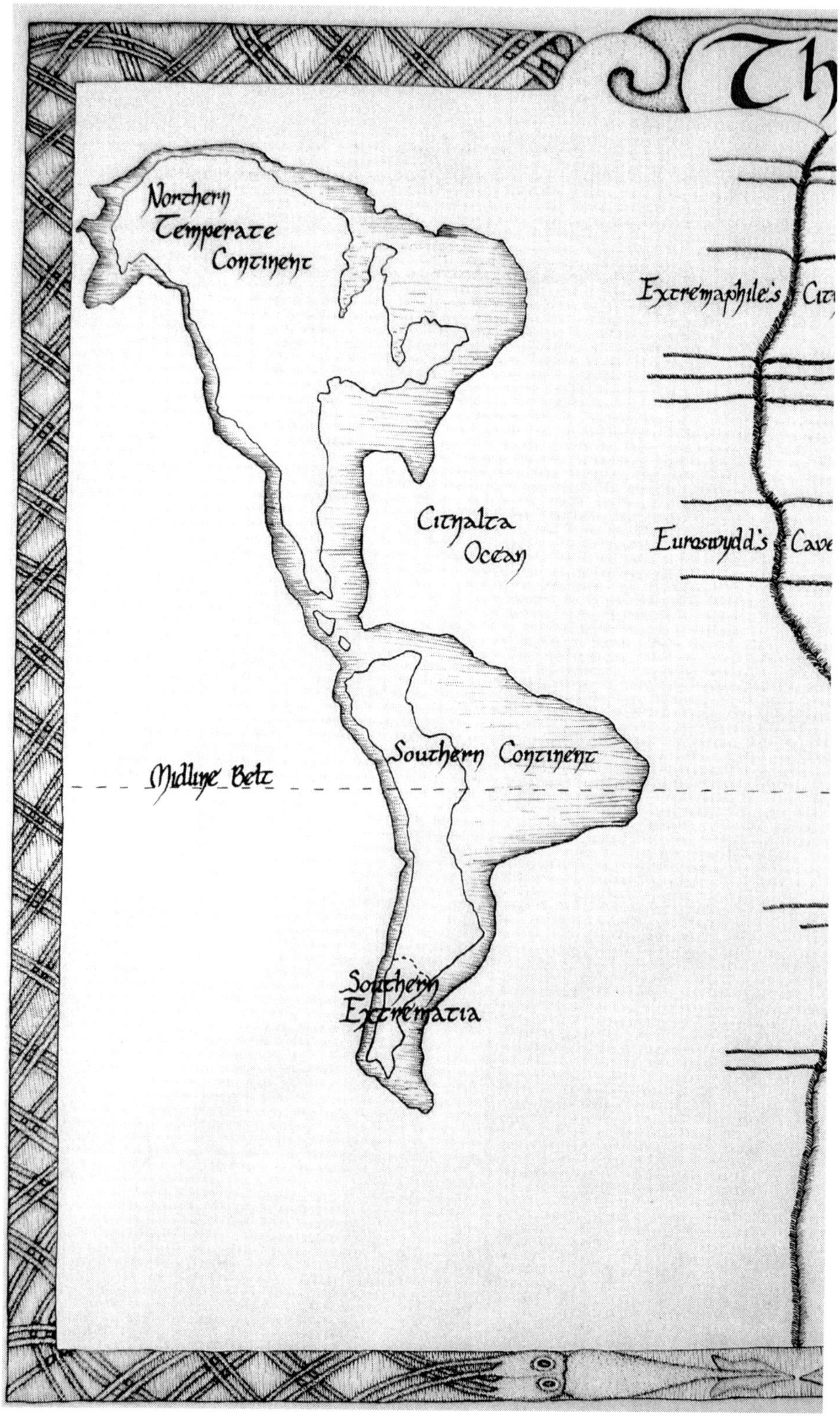
Th
Northern
Temperate
Continent
Extremaphile's
Cit
Citnalta
Ocean
Euroswydd's
Cave
Southern Continent
Midline Belt
Southern
Extrematia

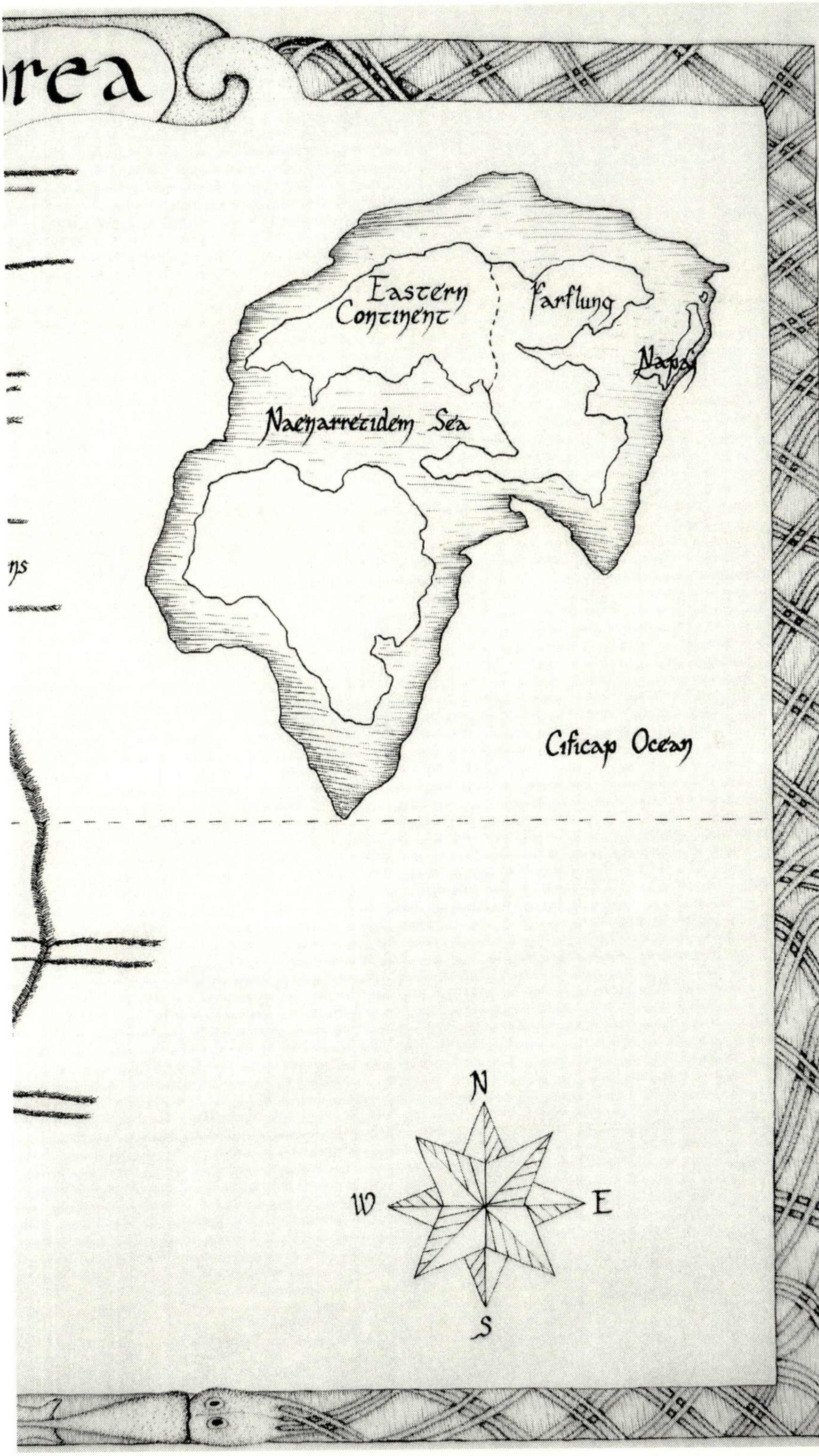
Eastern Continent
Farflung
Naenarretidem Sea
Cificap Ocean
N
W
E
S

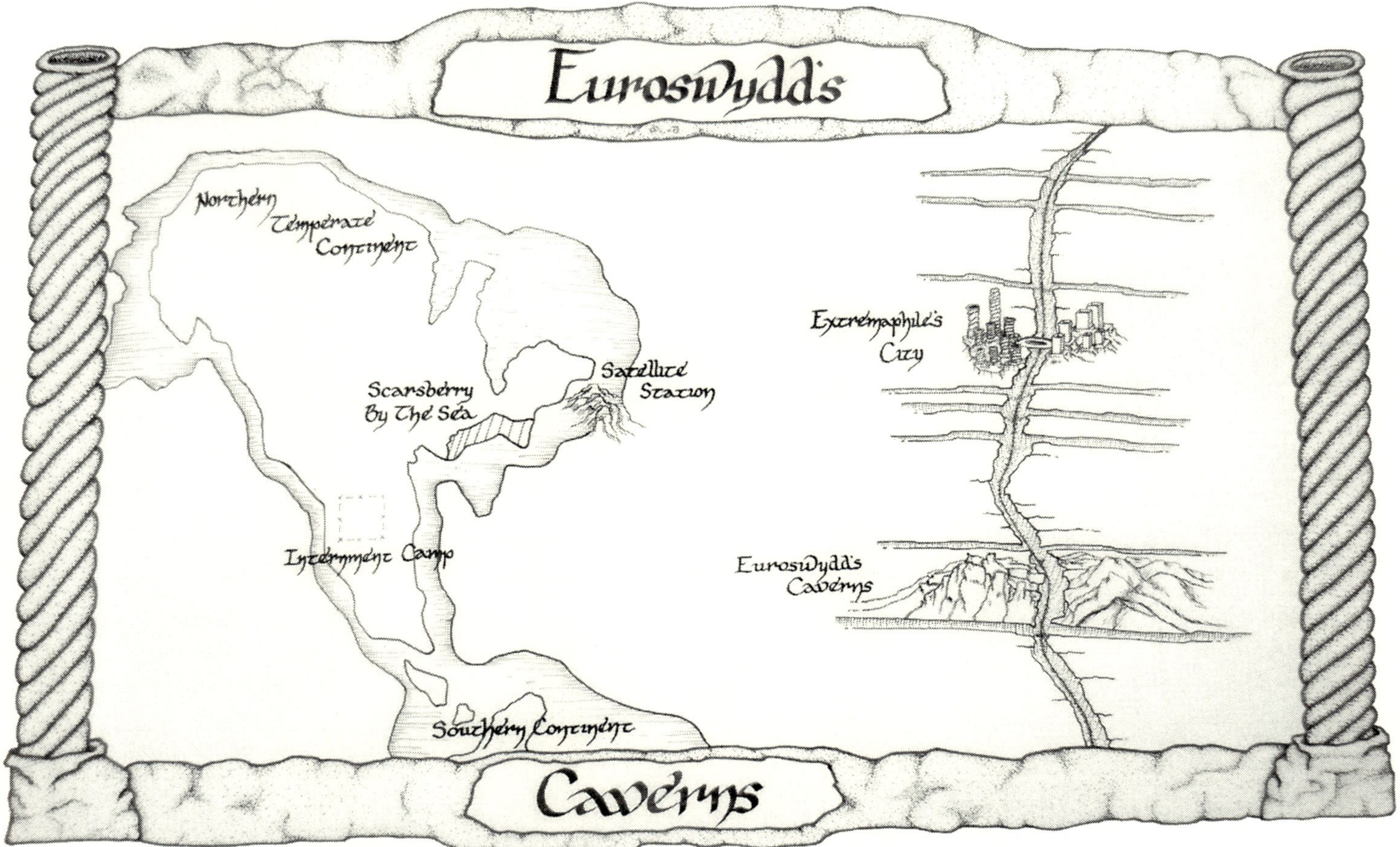
Euroswydd's
Northern Temperate Continent
Scarsberry By The Sea
Satellite Station
Interment Camp
Southern Continent
Extremaphile's City
Euroswydd's Caverns
Caverns

CONTENTS

APPENDIX

PART I

THE THREANS

PROLOGUE

Accepting the inevitable rankled. For what felt like millennium she'd tried to get her message across but pitifully few had taken notice. Experiencing disease, debilitation, anger, frustration engendered depression, denial giving way to eventual acquiescence, she'd followed the stereotypical route traveled by those suffering life threatening afflictions.

Initially the enthusiastic optimism inherently fueling birth's such as hers had reflected the positive expectations for her future growth. Opportunities had abounded, she'd managed to diversify, recover from adversities, learn one of life's most important lessons—that as change provides opportunities for growth so too does it provide moments of angst before clearing the path of inflicting detritus. Overall she'd blossomed and flourished.

In those days blue sky mirrored color in the lapping waters below, framed bulging peaks rising through alabaster haloes, set off brilliant prismatic displays of spreading petals. Nightly fireworks, expressions in orange, magenta and red, tempered into a black veil interwoven with twinkling diamonds cocooning vibrant, diverse, slumbering life forces. At the time it had seemed those days would never end, now it seemed they would never return.

The reflection she presently beheld through haze clouded eyes was barely recognizably the glory that had once been hers. In the galactic grand scheme of things her chronological age wasn't synonymous with a lethal decline in function but then death and destruction befell living Beings without regard for such timelines.

Stereotypically a tilted lowering shake of the head accompanying such platitudes as, "what a shame he/she died so young; how awful he/she was <u>only</u> how old when they passed?!?" exemplified the societal aversion to premature shortening of an expected lifespan. Conversely death at a venerable old age was greeted with an accepting, knowing nod and such platitudes as, "well he/she certainly had a good long life; he/she had a good run", seemingly offering kudos for a job well and thoroughly done. The former platitudes would be mouthed at her funeral.

She rarely tried catching a glimpse of what had once been the all encompassing blue unfurled overhead. Reduced to ever decreasing smidgens of color edging between grey swathes, the expenditure of unrewarded effort was too costly. Her energy sapped by the overwhelming of toxins infiltrating her system leeching into every nook and cranny of her Being needed to be conserved for more crucial activities.

Not many understood the full ramifications of what was happening to her. It had taken decades for a competent diagnosis to be realized. Now having reached it no one seemed willing to endure the changes pursuing a solution necessitated. The medical experts reiterated the usual dictum, "if you don't catch it in time, in the early stages, there's very little that can be done. Once the disease has progressed to a certain stage treatment is a waste of time and money. It's basically just a waiting game until their time is up. Keeping the patient quiet and comfortable helps preserve quality of life."

As far as she could tell, based on the actions or lack thereof of the experts assigned to her case, the great preponderance of opinion adhered to the concept that it was too late to even bother with quality of life issues. At least as far as she was concerned.

Sometimes behind, then beyond
An ephemeral emulation
Wisps to consciousness

1

SHADOWS ROUSED

1.

The cadence of her granddaughter's footsteps enticed Mrs. Random from the embrace of recollection. Smiling she set the journal on the table beside her chair.

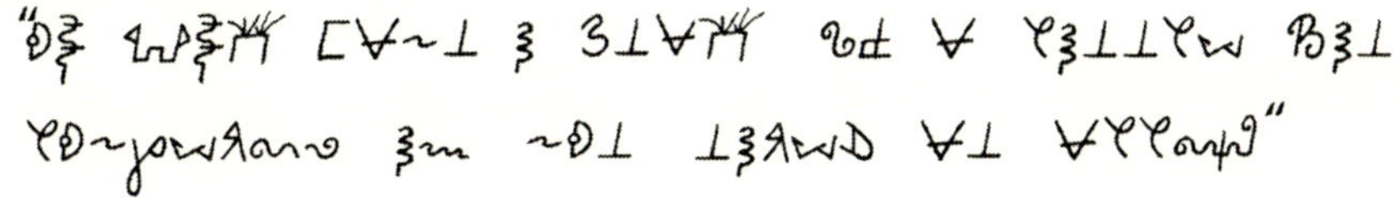

"You know I want you to practice speaking in the language of the Ancients," she said her look of disapproval offset by the gentleness with which she stroked the light brown curls of her granddaughter, "and don't give me that look. There will come a time when you'll thank me for making you remember the tongue of your ancestors.

Sighing Elva switched to the same dialect as her grandmother, "No one pays any attention to that old stuff—anyway it's all in the library if I'm ever bored enough to want to read about it." Squirming into her grandmother's lap she looked up at the lined face framing clear blue eyes and white wisps of hair, those not confined by the paisley scarf, dancing in the evening breeze. Reaching up to touch the lips less lush now than in her youth, Elva added, "Oh tell me a story grandma it's been ever so long since you told a really good one. And before you tell me I'm too old for such rubbish I asked Daddy and he said he hopes I'll never be too old for storytelling."

"He would say that I spoiled him with stories when he was growing up." Laughing Mrs. Random settled back into her rocker, "I will tell you a story but it's a long one and you have to promise me you won't fall asleep during the telling of it."

"You mean this is one I haven't heard before?" Elva leaned back against her grandparent.

"That's right, and it's a true story although there's times when it'll seem like fiction. Now hush and let me begin."

2.

An interesting if antiquated read the classic novel, *Journey to the Center of Threa*, explained transitions the movie left out. While entertaining as a unit and offering examples of the bravery and imagination exemplified by explorers of the 19th century making such an adventure a personal reality wasn't on Jinny's list of things to do before she died.

Such thoughts occupied her mind as, somewhat prone to claustrophobia and above all else not eager to trip, plunge, drop or otherwise catapult over any precipice invisibly yawning in the darkness she continued her fumbling efforts to navigate. Anyone who's ever been on one of those guided cave tours can relate. At some point or other the guide douses all lights providing sightseers with the disconcerting sensation of being plunged into an impenetrable black void. Jinny's worst such experience had occurred encased within steel confines dropping into Dabslrac Caverns. As soon as the elevator door clanked shut the beaming operator flicked the light switch. The mile long downward plunge lasted an eternity in the absolute blackness.

In spite of her recalcitrance, one foot continuously preceded the other while her hands acted as navigators of a sort. Pressing too hard on the invisible walls resulted in nothing more than cuts and scrapes but when the vertical—presumably—forms were caressed with a gently, gliding touch she could achieve some directional sense and move further along the downward sloping path.

The tunnel, for so she supposed it to be—although they could have been following the parameters of a cave—had, for some time, been prompting them to move inwards away from the violence on the surface. Punctuating the sound of their breathing and the plop, scrape of footfalls were the increasingly muffled sounds of explosions, pops and crashes. The nauseating swaying of the ground beneath them had lessened then stopped as they'd shuffled through the initial grayness into the blackness now encasing them.

Becoming a gradually increasing presence a pulsing, misty, rutilant-grayness outlined by darkness hung in the distance. Did it swirl towards them or were they just plodding towards it? A hand clamping down on her shoulders dispelled her reverie.

"Get a move on Jinny . . . this is no time to be daydreaming or whatever you're doing."

Realizing she'd come to a stop she pointed at the suspended mass, "We don't know what's happening up top and we've got to find a safe place soon. I wonder if that mist means we're getting to a water source. I don't smell anything bad." She said turning to the person behind her, "Do you?"

"No, can't we use our lights to see where we're going? I don't know what's up or down or sideways anymore."

Turning from Jinny, Lileas answered the questioner behind her, "We don't know what we're going to have to deal with up ahead . . . we need to save all the resources that need regular reconstituting to remain functional until we have absolutely no choice left but to use them. We also don't want to give ourselves away to anything that might be in here. Just keep a hold of my shirt and follow along." Then to Jinny, "Let's keep moving and find out what that mass up ahead is."

Voices muted into the darkness behind her as once again Jinny inched her way forward. No sulfur smell or other types of odor reminiscent of chemical residue wafted from the glowing, misty vapors. So how to explain the ever increasing emanation of light? Could a fissure from above have opened? Ahead of them was sunlight streaming down? It certainly didn't have the yellowish glow of sunlight but what? And had there been enough time for the storm clouds to dissipate?

Aromas hard to place, yet comfortingly familiar titillated her senses. Simultaneously she breathed in the unique salty, low tide, cleansing aspect of the coast, vying for recognition amongst the scents of fall. Those cool, crispy, decaying, leafy forest fragrances in tandem with associations aroused by an electrically fresh, clear damp scent similar to that which pervades once a thunderstorm has cascaded through. Was there any chance this was all simply a dream?

The path edged into air beneath her feet precipitating a tumble onto hands and knees. The "WOW" behind startled her head upward. They'd reached a Chamber. Filled with huge stalagmites and stalactites whose waved creases and crevasses—minerals glinting and glowing in the emanating warm reddish/yellow radiance—appeared as would a legion of royalty awaiting the arrival of their most honored guests. Cream colored dirt webbed precipitated mineral forms continuously reshaped and grown ever so gradually as time, measured in drops of water, inched along. Some encompassed widths of eight feet and more, with lengths of fifty to one hundred feet. The soft glowing light silhouetted these giants and their more diminutive relatives against a backdrop of colorfully veined walls, a tapestry in delicate tendrils of greens, gold, silvers, blues and reds woven into the stony background. A large body of water, perhaps a quarter of a mile in circumference glistened wetly several hundred yards from the entrance. Bodies swarmed around then past, as still crumpled on the Chamber's floor, Jinny soaked it all in.

A hand descended before her face, moving up and down in the manner of someone trying to attract the attention of a person in another world. "Are you going to help get camp set up or are you going to sit there staring around forever?" Laughter and Lileas's alto voice cracked the fuzzy nether world that had captured her powers of movement.

"I'm going to help, of course I am. I'm just dazed by everything that's happened." Rising to her feet she entered the chamber. Within and amongst the huge presences the angular profiles of the sculptural deposits softened in the luminosity. Now more reminiscent of benevolent guardians, bastions of long enduring fortitude and security than craggy, jagged, architectural marvels emulating the inviting but generally stiff postures of royal greeters, the cavern's persona seduced.

Forcing herself to concentrate on the tasks at hand she dropped her pack with the others before turning to see what needed to be done.

"I'm going to see if this water is useable." Hans headed towards the lake with the Sampleometer. This tool needed only a tiny drop of any liquid to ascertain then print out that fluid's components. In this case it would tell them whether they could drink the water or whether it was pure poison beyond redemption. Sometimes with just a few modifications water can be made drinkable but not always and their supply of treatment chemicals was much depleted.

In the days before the Upheavals every household had had at least one Sampleometer since even treated water touted as safe was suspect. There had been lots of money to be made from supplying people "treated" water that hadn't been. Both the suppliers as well as the medical profession, which included the pharmaceutical companies, lobbyists, and health care professionals, if not held to the strictest guidelines, fudged on the specifics.

A Senior official indicted for fraud commenting on the situation to a reporter had succinctly described the mindset of the times, "It's regrettable but just the agreed upon way of the world. Them or me, survival of the fittest and all that."

"Wow, this tastes wonderful; come over here; you've got to try this. I've heard that water could be this pure, but I've certainly never seen any." Hans, eyes agleam, his body vibrating in excited wonderment, held some of the liquid in his cupped hands for Jinny to sample.

"I've never tasted anything like it. Ambrosia must have tasted like this." Jinny reached for more.

"Yes, and a few hundred years ago the streams and such on the Surface were filled with liquid like this." Scratching his head, "I wonder how this came to be here and how it's stayed so pristine."

"And since this is fresh water how come I thought I smelled salt water before?" Jinny added.

"Are you guys going to drink and gab or help us over here?" Lileas's voice accelerated from the campsite a strong stone's throw from the lake.

"OK, OK but you've got to try this stuff it's out of this world!"

"Soup's on; come and get it while it's hot, or should I say lukewarm," Morna announced from the center of camp, "and bring some of that ambrosia with you."

3.

Hans joined Morna behind the serving table—an elongated slab of rock they'd set up for the purpose. Jinny, after filling a jug with water, joined Derek, Orla, and Mab grabbing plates and cutlery, anticipating their first relaxed meal in weeks.

"This feast is brought to you by On the Run Productions, some re-hydrated victuals to assuage all your hunger pangs and really long for Mom's home cooking." Hans's rendition of what he continually proclaimed to be the humorous banter of the 20th century spawned a ripple of laughter.

"Hans, you make me feel less like I'm on line for food at a homeless shelter and more like I'm in the observation clinic at a psyche ward." Mab declared reaching for a glass of "ambrosia".

"Ah, it may not be the most accurate statement you ever heard but it made you and everyone else laugh. Next . . . ." Spoon in hand, Hans turned to his left and the next empty plate.

Five minutes later the clanging of silverware on metal camping plates—most of the blue speckled variety—combined with the crunching, smacking and grinding of avid chewing swelled, drenching even the innermost recesses of the Chamber. Intensity dwindled each wave boomeranged back to the source, dissipating in flight. The hibernating shadows experimentally roused.

"Oh, that feels good." Lileas stretched to her full length of 60.5 inches, yawning widely. "A full stomach and nothing to do but sleep. I'm going to bed."

"Shouldn't we decide who'll keep watch while the rest of us sleep?" Orla's words mimicked the stop button on a remote control.

After dinner cleanup activity ceased and heads simultaneously swiveled in her direction. Their full attention captured, she continued, "So far we haven't seen or heard anything threatening but what if others survived and are already down here? If they're here and hiding from us they may be unfriendly. I'm not comfortable thinking of us all snoring away without some sort of guard in place."

"Yeah, what if they're just waiting for us to go to sleep before they attack us?" Derek asked.

Sighing Jinny said in a resigned voice, "I suppose you're right although I can't honestly say that I want to." Looking around, "Does anyone have a timepiece that still works?"

A particularly severe electrical storm, the impetus for their descent into the depths where they now found themselves, had wreaked havoc with their timepieces. The less temperamental wind-ups had long been relegated to the realms of antiques and what the modern timepieces lacked in character they made up for with accuracy and convenience, or so the advertising had proclaimed. The modern timepieces were little more than digitalized magnetic blips representative of passing seconds. Early models, susceptible to the persuasions of ionized particles churning within electrical storms, had been replaced with revisions believed to be impervious to natural phenomenon. The storm causing all their timepieces to malfunction had been of an unprecedented electrical magnitude not deemed—by the experts—to be physically possible.

"Mine is running, but I don't know how accurately. I've no way of knowing if it's running fast, slow or what." Mab stared at her timepiece, holding it away from her as if it were about to explode. "The second hand has been moving in a clockwise direction at least since we got here. Is anybody else's doing the same thing?"

"That's weird, mine just started up . . . mine isn't doing anything . . . mine is going I wonder when that happened . . . it wasn't a minute ago." A cacophony of pronouncements filled the chamber. Everybody either shook their timepieces or stared at them speculatively.

"OK, let's take the ones that are running and put them together on this table. We'll set them all for the same time and see if they all move at the same rate."

"What if they don't?" Morna's question to Jinny edged out the scraping of seven watches being placed on stone

"We'll cross that bridge if we come to it. Let's go with the positive and hope that the magnetic disruption didn't break the watches but simply caused them to malfunction until we got out of its field of influence." Jinny replied. "If the watches are working again how about we set up a twenty-four hour time frame so we can have morning, noon and night. Some sense of a normal time frame will help us a lot." The listeners nodded grunting in agreement. "Let's have two hour shifts for each of us to watch out for trouble tonight." She turned to Lileas, "Would you take the first watch with me? We'll come up with a list and surprise everyone when it's their time to guard. I'll sit with you through the second one."

"Sure, sounds like a plan." Everybody returned to the business of after dinner cleanup uncharacteristically disinterested in commenting or complaining about the arrangements.

4.

In the months spent traveling together the group had devised ways of providing for themselves with a minimal amount of fuss and muss. Their solution to various essential cleaning and storage issues had entailed converting several large canvas bags into multi-purpose containers through the addition of bamboo ribbing followed by applications of a waterproofing agent. The bags folded for ease of transport, were lightweight and each a different color. Designated for drinking water the green trimmed vessel now bulged with "ambrosia" while soapy steam rose from the yellow accented washbasin filled with dinner dishes awaiting scrubbing before transferal to rinse water in the purple embellished container.

Upon completion of their assigned chores each person disappeared into a sleeping bag draped with blankets as insurance against the possibility of chill. Soon each mound, an elongated multi-colored arched expanse of cloth framed against the brownish cavern floor, gave vent to symphonic whistles, snores and gurgles.

Contentment can be as simple as a feeling of security, a full tummy and a warm bed Jinny mused pulling a tattered chambray shirt over her faded yellow t-shirt. Watching Lileas brush her shoulder length brown hair before securing the string she used as a tie Jinny sighed gesturing towards the reddish curls on her head, "I really wish I could let my hair grow but if I don't keep it short it looks like I'm wearing a clown wig."

"Yeah, well hair that actually adheres to gravity's laws and doesn't float out from the head when it gets long isn't all that easy to deal with either, believe me. Mine just hangs straight down unless I spend a lot of time working with it, something I haven't been able to even consider for over a year."

Laughing, forefinger to lip Jinny cautioned, "Sshhh, we should be quiet. Let them get some sleep."

"Do you think we're safe here?" Lileas quietly asked after they'd set the watches and sat down, their backs comfortably pillowed against limestone etched by years of moisture erosion. Stretching out threadbare blue denim clad legs, wriggling her toes in their worn leather sandals before extending bare arms upward, stretching the seams of her grey t-shirt she continued. "These lights are something. It's like there are fixtures in all the nooks and crannies of this cavern."

"And the ceiling too," Jinny said, her sage green eyes gazing upward, "it seems to emit from the rock itself. It's rather quiet and comforting, never thought I'd say that about an unexplainable light." She continued, chuckling, "I think we're as safe as we've ever been since this began. But you know it almost seems too perfect. I guess my cynical side has really developed these last few months."

"Yeah mine too." Uplifted head moving back and forth as would a metronome, Lileas transected the rock above them, café au lait eyes surveying for answers, "But what is it with those lights . . . I've never heard of lights shining without some sort of power source, whether it be solar, bioluminescent, incandescent or whatever. What do you think is providing that source? Is this some type of trick? I feel very comfortable here and perversely that makes me feel paranoid. Sometimes I wish I could just shut my brain down and not think at all." Shaking her head Lileas stopped to draw a breath.

"I wonder what's going on below the surface of that lake. Do you think there's fish there? I wonder if this light can support plant life? Could it be photosynthetic?" Jinny waved her hand toward the liquid expanse melting into the shadowy horizon. "Certainly doesn't look like it but maybe within the waters of the lake? Or maybe beyond what we can see of this cavern. It seems to go on forever."

"It would be really cool if there were fish and plant life, particularly if this winds up being a safe haven for us. We could just stay here." Yawning, "How much longer do we have . . . . I can barely keep my eyes open."

"We've got about another hour," and in response to Lileas's groan, "let's make up the guard schedule for tonight, that'll help keep us awake. Tomorrow we'll explore the cave and see how far back it extends.

Release from fears . . .
Entice and leads towards
Possibilities
Ahead through the gloom

2

IMAGINE A PLACE

5.

"I can't believe it; I almost feel relaxed." Even Mab's voice was different, softer, less like flint on rock. "I really should just cut this all off; I can never keep it out of my face." She said flicking her freshly restrained blond pony tail.

"That's what twelve hours of sleep, no sign of imminent danger, and a nice big breakfast will do for you." Stretching to his full height of 119 inches, Hans looked around the camp. Rumpled sleeping bags littered the Sleeping Ledge. In his twentieth year, Hans exemplified the stereotypical sculpted blue-eyed characteristics of TV news anchorman renown. Blueberry hued coveralls framed the blond braid descending just past his shoulders and flowing beard. Incongruous with such cold weather clothing, his feet displayed leather sandals whose straps were now hemp cording. While Jinny had laughed at his insistence on naming the area where they'd set up their sleeping bags she'd agreed with the basic Threan need to name, identify or otherwise clarify areas of their lives.

"And it helps when you're trying to guide someone to a place!" had been Lileas's contribution to the previous night's discussion regarding nomenclature.

He'd just finished—escorted by the opportunistic chickens and ducks—carrying dishes and cookware to the washing bag where Morna now readied them for the next meal. Orla and Mab were gathering dirty clothes, plunging them into the red bag already bulging with soapy water.

"Where are we going to dump the grey water?" the question came from Hans. "It's wonderful to be able to do dishes and wash clothes, not to mention ourselves, but where are we going to put the used water so that we don't harm the lake and the rest of this area? Cave ecosystems like this are particularly fragile, especially those protected from outside sources."

"Yeah, he's right; I remember learning how fragile cave ecosystems are from school and watching documentaries on television." Derek said. "The slightest disturbance can disrupt their equilibrium."

"I was just thinking about that. Come over here and look at what I've found." As soon as everyone was gathered around Jinny continued, pointing at the depression in the Chamber's floor. "Couldn't we put the grey water there until we come up with some way of storing it and maybe using it for plants? It should percolate through the rock and back into the water table."

Reverentially one and all silently peered down into the depression. Stepping back the six arrayed before her reminded Jinny of her three cats. The image of them all peering down off what had once been her home's elevated front porch, huge question marks of tails and rear ends strained upward, body weight supported on crouched front legs, ears pointed forward and downward, all attention on a small creature invisible to any but the riveted cats, came to life in her mind.

Why do such images pop into my mind, Jinny asked herself . . . and why at the most inopportune times? Given the gravity of the situation it was unlikely her companions would appreciate her take on the hilarity of their postures. They were sure to glare at her if she suddenly burst out laughing for a no good—at least as perceived by them—reason. Yet she just couldn't keep such images out of her head. Some people said it was imagination and she should develop it—like she had any control, which was the problem!—others told her to grow up and act responsibly. Can't I be responsible and have fun too, was her oft repeated unresolved query.

At the time of these events Jinny's talents at discernment weren't yet fully developed. Self described as "flashes of things", she acknowledged the dangled teasers tantalizing just beyond conscious encompassment, but wasn't able to realize any clear meanings. She once told Lileas she felt as though something or someone was either in close proximity or that she was somehow missing a very tangible—if only the constraints would release—something.

Look down, look down, focus on the here and now, Jinny repeated to herself absentmindedly patting the two canine heads—

one sable, the other a blending of browns, whites and blacks—nudging her palms. The bowl like depression seemed to be etched from a porous substance resembling beige lava. Reaching a depth of perhaps four to five feet the pockmarked depression displayed rings of muted color in much the same way one sees solid material form when its liquid carrier evaporates.

"Unless one of you objects I say we put the grey water in here. But I don't want the water used for any purpose until we find out what's been in here before. There's no telling if toxins are present or not. " Looking at Hans, "Can I ask you to test the materials on the side of this today so we know exactly what it is?" and as Hans nodded she continued to everyone, "We don't want to get into any more trouble than we're already in."

Somewhat ironically Jinny maintained she was considered the "leader" of these displaced Threans. Not a person to seek out positions of authority, preferring to live her life unencumbered by others, she often bemoaned the fact that doing the "right thing", when it presented itself as necessary, seemed to have been a trait incorporated into her mental and physical molecules through genetics. The Upheavals that had been occurring and the resultant change in their lives had created the necessity for someone to take on the role of leader if for no other reason than it offered some semblance of familiarity. Most of the group had been old enough to have part time jobs before their lives so drastically changed and as such had been under the direct authoritative umbrella of parents, teachers and bosses. So rather than let anarchy reign she'd stepped in when it became apparent that no one else could or would do the job effectively.

As Hans left to go get the equipment necessary to test for toxins the others waited, looking expectantly at Jinny.

"OK, who hasn't got a job to do?" Suspicious, most claimed possession of a task, then groaned when she continued with, "The rest of us are going exploring." Fending off the protests with laughter and raised hands, "I'm kidding; we'll all take turns exploring and doing the chores. But I do want to make sure we keep an eye on our stuff while others canvas the area. It just wouldn't do for us to loose everything and the animals need to be cared for."

As if in agreement the donkey, Olivia, heehawed curling her lips back and moving her head up and down for emphasis. She was the Jesus Christ clad version of a donkey with a grayish coat, white muzzle and the black "cross" stretching from withers to ears and back towards her rump. Her erect ear tips rose just above Jinny's sixty-four inches. The cats—one black the other a grey tabby—gazed from lounging positions on the now folded sleeping bags.

"You know exploring may not be all that interesting. Whoever stays here may have more fun." Lileas observed.

A chorus of "Uh Huh's and yeah right's." cut short her remonstrations.

"Let's split up into groups of two and I guess one of one. We'll go around following the walls of the cavern and when there's a tunnel or concerted indentation one group will take that until it ends."

"What if it doesn't lead anywhere?" Derek grumbled.

"Then you'll come out and take the next available one." Jinny said.

"Since our watches are working," Hans suggested, "at least they're all keeping the same time; shouldn't we decide what time it is and set up a twenty-four hour cycle?"

"Yes, what time does everyone want it to be?"

They decided on 1000 hours and set their time pieces.

Circling the lake in a clockwise direction all but Hans and Orla—who'd remained behind to take the first camp duty—eagerly anticipated the first substantial outreach from the tunnel. The team of Morna and Mab had pulled the short straw and would be the first to venture into the unknown.

They returned soon after broaching the first tunnel.

6.

"Anything interesting? What did you find? That was quick." questions peppered the two who, breathing heavily from their run to catch up with their comrades, talked around and about each other's words, "The light is beautiful and the colors of the rocks . . . well I guess they're filled with all kinds of minerals, was spectacular but it only ran about a quarter of a mile before it ended. There was plenty of dripping water. This is definitely a living cave. I've never seen anything like it."

The group continued for another five miles and all but Jinny and Lileas were exploring a tunnel when an opening gaped prompting a simultaneous turn to the left. The tunnel's ceiling twinkled with faceted stones, sophisticated as cut diamonds. The passing walls, in style reminiscent of those created by the ancient Threans indigenous to the Northern Temperate Continent, resembled a sand painting. Rivers of aquamarine, saffron, crimson, mauve, ocher and azure blue, its appearance would have seemed contrived had not the magnitude and flow defied the perception of being a creation stemming from Threanoid hands. Worn as if from a parade of use, the patina seamless and tawny beneath their feet—reiterating once again the question of whose feet, paws and/or hooves used this system buried miles below Threa's surface—the footpath led them forward. Not a sharp edge to be seen or felt, nothing to trip over, it was like a relaxing Sunday walk in the park—reminiscent of times gone by when there had been peaceful Sundays and glorious parks to stroll in.

Looming in the Cave rock an entrance beckoned. Entrance being the only way to describe the structure Jinny and Lileas now stood beneath and between. Above their heads a straight beam of wood, recognizable as mahogany, stretched until its horizontal five foot length met with twin beams of similar ilk, vertically fortifying the left and the right. The doorway appeared to be one continuous unit, the footings of its ten foot height disappearing into the rocky ground. Actually it didn't so much disappear as melded with the molecules of the rock. The surface of the wood displayed whorls of time volunteering its life story illustrated as years of deprivation, endurance and opulence.

What really grabbed their attention lay beyond the doorway. Within this Chamber of modest proportions, perhaps only 300 to 400 square feet, a wealth of technological equipment gleamed. On the walls there were what appeared to be computer monitors or screens.

Not similar in design to those familiar to Jinny and Lileas these were flush with the stone walls. A metallic grey edging—extending outward from the wall as would a picture frame—surrounded each black rectangular visage. Measuring approximately two feet by two feet, these electronic displayers were arranged symmetrically, reminiscent of artistic endeavors hung in galleries awaiting review. Knobs displaying unfamiliar symbols protruded from the rocky wall seemingly placed at prescribed intervals. These dots of varying color and symbol positioned strategically between the screens left the areas above and below the screens devoid of anything save the naturally formed rock protrusions.

Filling most of the room from the center on out were several long tables placed in a pentagonal pattern, end to end. Each exhibited more knobs of unknown significance delineating screens whose installation found them flush with the surface of the tables. Within the boundary of the pentagon the computers rose above the tables appearing as a conglomeration of slender drawers, each molded atop the other.

A general hum enveloped the room and the same soft, warming light emanated from not only the ceiling but in transmuted shades and hues from the various machines in the room. An orb sat on one of the tables. Impossible to tell if it was glass, a synthetic version or some derivation thereof, close examination revealed delicate veining manifesting all the colors of the rainbow lacing through its clear form.

7.

In the times prior to the Upheavals—the name the seven members of the group used to describe the Surface phenomenon—believing in Aliens had become less and less of an aberration and more of an accepted possibility. Given the events that had transpired over the previous months not one of them scoffed at the hypothesized existence of advanced life forms inhabiting other planets. The rational of infinite space, while a hard concept for the Threanoid brain to wrap itself around, had been accepted by one and all long before the Upheavals began. They'd all agreed that if one could accept the reality of other galaxies, why not accept the reality of other Beings from worlds within those galaxies!

The familiar persona of the technology spawned chemical releases generating nostalgic surges of comfort and security in both women. Jinny later recounted how she'd felt that movement on either one of their parts might cause it all to vanish.

Eventually the necessity of discharging carbon dioxide and refueling with oxygen moved them both. Lung expansion didn't cause the technology to dissipate into nothingness so, as if of one mind, the two moved deliberately and very slowly forward, hands protruding before them, palms down. Outstretched fingers touched solid surface and it stayed in shape. The room was real and lights now flashed where Lileas appeared to have touched a control panel. A screen relinquished its dark visage to figures vibrating with movement.

Configured as toys they clearly lived, breathed, walked and yes . . . talked to each other. The skeletal figure laughed and drew from a pipe. A puff of smoke appeared as does steam above hot pavement after a cool rush of rainwater sears its surface. The puff hung, suspended in dissipation, merging with invisibility as the skeleton sent another to take its place.

The middle figure, a donkey standing upright, walked in bipedal fashion sporting a pronounced proboscis. The third individual was a knitted clown. His features and entire body language emanated an aura of peaceful, delighted charm. In fact, a most benevolent, kindly aura flowed from all of them.

One after another other screens came to life, neutral black giving way to colored images. Several showed sea creatures swimming and interacting, the inner life of a greenhouse grew on one screen while others showed a wealth and diversity of terrestrial animals living in habitats of various climatic regions.

Then there was—as Jinny and Lileas related later—the most puzzling and mesmerizing of all. Some of the screens displayed currents of color which—and they both agreed on this—emanated emotions. Against a background of changing glows exhibiting all colors of the rainbow and if you can believe it more forms of light—white, golden, silver, bronze swirling into blues, greens, reds, and yellows—vibrated and pulsed.

"We must be in some kind of command center. Do you think it's been abandoned or are we being monitored right now?" Jinny ended the silent, astonished gaping they'd shared for close to half an hour by her watch.

"I don't know, but I want to find out what this is all about. I don't feel threatened by this—just curious and comforted. Isn't that bizarre." Lileas moved towards the screens, her eyes glued. "Do you think this is real; happening right now; are these some type of camcorders recording live or do you think these are pre-recorded programs like the sort that used to be on TV?"

"Somehow, don't ask me to give you a good, logical reason, my gut reaction is that this is all real and we are watching events occurring elsewhere. Just don't ask me where. That could be the undersea world of our Planet on that screen, but they," she pointed at the figures, "certainly aren't from Threa."

Lileas pointed at another one of the screens, "I've seen some of those creatures on documentaries and some in books. I actually thought those," her finger now on the screen she mostly obscured the scarlet eyed passenger pigeons their blue headed, grey backed, claret breasted feathers glowing, "were extinct."

"I did too." Both moved betwixt and amongst the electronic machinery assimilating the imagery displayed in the walls. The horizontal screens embedded in the desks, smaller versions of the ones in the walls, remained darkly blank. Knobs, colored and displaying identical shapes as those found on the walls, protruded from control panels residing in depressed channels extending the height of each screen. As with those screens placed in the walls, the areas above and below were devoid of electronic decoration.

"Should we go get the others or should we try to see if there are more rooms like this or what?" Lileas asked, but before Jinny could respond, Derek, Morna, and Mab appeared. They stood mesmerized in the doorway until Derek pointed at the screen displaying the donkey, skeleton and knitted clown. "Look at them. They're walking, talking and acting as though they're alive! I guess all those renditions of Aliens we've seen were wrong." Shaking his head he continued, "They look like toys, yet obviously they're not. Look, a screen within a screen. They're talking to another Being . . . he looks like an old grey donkey . . . at least his head does; I can't see his body."

The Beings were in a room closely resembling the control room occupied by the five Threans. Similar screens, controls and symbols suggested a link between the two.

"Take a breath will you . . . hey, be careful what you touch. We don't know what this all is. Don't break anything. Derek, I swear you're a bull in a china shop." Lileas looked pleadingly at Jinny, "Let's see what Jinny has to say."

Addressing the recently arrived trio Jinny explained, "We really haven't found out much more than you can see for yourself. These appear to be screens that show real life happenings rather than staged productions, but where or what we have no clue."

Derek's attention now redirected Lileas chimed in, "We don't feel threatened by them, which is odd. If you stand still and just take it all in you'll feel the most enjoyable calm bordering on total security. It's almost like being a child again . . . you know . . . when you don't know that bad things can happen and your parents provide you with anything and everything you need?"

"Not to interrupt this whimsical philosophical conjecturing but what do we do now? We're miles below the surface of an unstable planet standing in what looks like the control room of some sort of Alien species." Mab said. "Shouldn't we go back and tell Hans and Orla about this, maybe make sure they're OK, then figure out what to do next?"

"Well I for one can't relate to total childlike security, let's get out of here before we get zapped or something worse. I've had enough for one day." So saying Derek turned on his heels heading out the door. A quick look at the screens showed they'd all returned to their previous black unrevealing status. Morna, Mab, Lileas and Jinny looked at one another, shrugged then followed in Derek's wake through the entryway.

An hour of steady walking passed before the lakefront campsite came into view.

8.

"You look exhausted. Did you find anything interesting?" Hans helped relieve them of the now empty water and food bags before handing them the steaming bowls of food Orla had prepared.

"Let them eat first." Orla said left hand sweeping wisps of straight auburn hair from her sweaty forehead. The lessons she'd learned about cooking, preparing food for her three brothers and two sisters when they were all still together as a family, were coming in handy now. Brown eyes glued to her friends, she watching them spoon stew into their mouths. Lasting only a moment her solicitous expression spread into a grin as she asserted. "Then we can grill them!"

Later, sitting in a circle, having relayed all that had happened on their expedition Hans asked, "So what should we call that room?"

"Yes, that's the most important consideration right now." Mab leaned further back against the rock she was using like the back of a chair. "Let's not worry about who or what might be monitoring us or worse yet be responsible for what's been happening on the Surface. No, let's make our Priority One the naming of the room." Throwing her hands up in the air, she looked at the circle of faces.

Chuckling, Morna poked Mab's shoulder, "Well then what about the All Seeing Chamber."

Mab glared, her usually green eyes glinting steely grey as she minced, "*Fine.*"

"Mab does have a point and we're going to have to address the issues she brought up soon. But for tonight let's just not go there." Lileas said. "And we do need to name things so that we all know what we're talking about."

"Sleep it is." Hans said stretching and yawning. "I'm wiped and it looks like Derek's already asleep."

All eyes focused on Derek who now slumped to his left, leaned against a stalagmite his narrow lips ever so slightly separated. His nose the most prominent feature of his small boned, indeterminate chinned face was partially hidden by cascades of wavy black hair. A faint snore gurgled from him as they went to their sleeping bags. No one set any alarms or suggested guard duty.

No on saw the movement of Shadows who came to hover around the homeless Threans. Tenuously extending slivers of dimness as though intending to caress, none seemed able to traverse the last few inches needed to actually touch the prone bodies. Each thwarted equidistant from the intended target it was as if force fields were in place. In unison the extensions reincorporated within their primary forms before wafting away into the tunnel leading to the All Seeing Chamber.

Nomadic travails
Put upon as circumstances
Ever seeking the security
Of home

3

AMENABLE HOUSING

9.

"Geothermal vents may be supplying a lot of this moisture. The caves we're used to, the ones closer to the Surface, get their moisture from seepage and runoff and they don't have steam rising from fissures in the floor and walls," Lileas's voice faded as she looked up, "or the ceilings."

Lileas often pursued answers in the realm of conjecture, her thoughts doubling back and around on themselves as would a series of cutbacks make it possible to eventually navigate a particularly severe gradation. Used as she was to her friend's way of clarifying baffling situations Jinny smiled silently, returning to her diary. Her clarifying methodology necessitated the writing down of all observations in hopes of reaching a viable conclusion.

The days spent working through and around the various tunnels and passageways mapping and exploring had produced more puzzlement than elucidation. How to rationally explain the warmth, light, water and food occurring naturally so many miles below the surface of their Planet? Wouldn't the location necessitate synthetic production of these fundamentals? Certainly the indigenous mushrooms, lichens, and mosses required low light conditions but what of the rest? Alcoves containing gardens filled with beans, squash, tomatoes and leafy veggies resembling kale, radicchio, red, green and purple lettuces, and edible flowers such as nasturtiums, pansies, herbs, grasses, and grains seemed to receive liquid requirements through a system of hydroponics but how to explain the flourishing of photosynthetic processes without the presence of a sun? Vigorous, bountiful growth cascaded over containment perimeters. Did the light so warmly glowing from fissures contain the necessary wave lengths? Was this natural evolution at work or some more contrived device? And who or what was responsible for it all?

Within the fresh waters of the lake grew an abundance of plant life but not until finding the first storage larder did it become apparent that the aquatic vegetation was edible. This storage alcove sealed off from the rest of the Cavern area, its outline obscured by moss growth, escaped notice until "discovered" by the pets. Apparently carrying out explorations of their own Jinny had found them feasting on dried produce after one of them had—it was presumed—inadvertently released the locking mechanism holding the door shut. Contained within a selection of dried seaweed and kelp, dried fruits including apricots, pears and apples and dried vegetables jammed the shelves. Flour, seeds and spices rounded out the inventory. The symbols on the packages, identical to the ones in The All Seeing Chamber, didn't clarify anything.

All the amenities a living Being could ask for existed without the edifying answers as to why or how. And how could the temperature be so comfortable? Most root cellars hover in the undeniably chilly fifty degrees Fahrenheit range, most caves complexes as well—so what made this one so different? Had they, as Morna had jokingly suggested, been transported into a self-sustained living area operating beyond their level of knowledge and perhaps even mental sophistication to comprehend?

Morna's comparison of their situation to being on a Science Fiction show where the Threans are swooped off by Aliens into a hitherto unknown galaxy and exposed to a different system of life, while farfetched, seemed almost plausible given the current lack of edifying information. Sighing Jinny put her pen down shaking her head. The hoped for answers hadn't come.

"So you're saying you think the steam coming from the contact of water with the magma is supplying the humidity. Why then aren't we bathed in it? We've seen a little steam coming out of small side caves but not what you'd expect from a vent of that type, not if it were close anyway. And what about the temperature . . . we're not boiling."

"I don't know Jinny I'm just trying to go with what I know to be possible. Maybe vents opened years ago, helped create this space, then plates moved again and they partially closed. I'm also puzzled as to how this area seems to have escaped damage during the recent quakes." Lileas walked around peering as if making sure to not miss the answers that would surely pop up out of the surrounding rock.

"Geothermal vents support life that functions by means of chemical synthesis rather than photosynthesis. I wonder if the light sources are the result of evolutionary process. Life this far below the surface of the sea was pretty much ignored by most scientists. Space exploration being more popular than sea exploration I guess it's more than possible that things like this exist and we wouldn't know anything about them." Lileas smiled patiently as Jinny continued expounding, "Maybe this left these areas free to evolve. Most of our scientists for all their claims of interest in seeking new knowledge still presented conclusions not as part of an ongoing stream of continually gathered information—always leaving the door open for new revelations—but instead as a *fait acomplie,* the finite dead end to the discovery road. Then time would pass and they'd come up with a change or such and proclaim *that* new factoid to be the definite result or answer to the puzzle."

"I know, I know," now caught up in intensity of conviction Lileas added, "and they certainly didn't leave their minds open to the possibilities of variant means of acquiring energy and processing it by living Beings below the oceans. So much was written and conjectured about it with respect to Outer Space. I wonder at the rational of focusing billions of dollars on discovery then restricting the parameters to the area beyond our Planet when we had such a wonderful classroom surrounding our continents. It's funny, those not victims of the constraints imposed by culturally dictated plausibility, like the writers of programs the ilk of *Star Trek* and

Farscape, were much more forward and dynamic in their thinking than actual scientists who proclaimed such an interest and ability to think outside the box!"

"Yeah, but I do wonder if even they would have had come up with anything like the scenario we've been through these past couple of years!" Jinny observed, replaying events in her mind's eye.

10.

She and Lileas, unsure as they'd been of exactly what was going on when people first started to disappear, had spent a lot of time discussing their thoughts and feelings on the changed way of their world. Less self sufficient than their contemporaries of just a century before they and all Threan children had still been housed, clothed and fed within the parental wingspan well into their twenties. As their parents found themselves being shuttled to and from various corporate buildings under the auspices of attempting to utilize labor in a more efficient way, the "kids" had been forced to fend for themselves with ever increasing frequency. Some days adults picked up before seven in the morning had not been dropped off until after ten that night. Leisure time had become a thing of the past.

Although forbidden to do so, both Jinny's and Lileas's parents had related stories of time spent in interrogation in addition to the eight hour work days. All adults—those Threans over the age of twenty-five—had been subjected to the interrogations, but none of them could figure out why. As told by Jinny's parents a subject would be escorted into a room and left there for hours with reading material, a TV set or sometimes games to play. Other times they would be ushered into a room and made to take written tests which questioned how they would react if placed in various hypothetical scenarios. The interrogation process ended after each person underwent several days of verbal examination concerning particulars of their life.

Paradoxically every aspect of conduct and personal reactions to every situation encountered during each individual's previous years of living seemed to be contained on pages housed within manila folders. An individual questioned about something he/she had no memory of or didn't believe they could or would have been part of precipitated a referral to these paper files. The interrogator's finger sliding down the page would stop briefly before horizontally reaching some notation or other, then a video screen would appear and a short digitalized filmstrip would clarify the situation. Using such antiquated organizational means to store information had seemed in step with the overall peculiarity of the entire invasive process. It was as though the interrogators had been training cameras and other recording devices on them their entire lives. That the interrogators had been training cameras and other recording devices on them wasn't a surprise but why were they questioning the citizenry about it? What were they looking for?

Dulled by a lifetime of "Big Brother's" heavy handed manipulations the populace had endured the treatment, hoping for a speedy return to a life of normalcy. Then the disappearances had begun.

11.

"Where do you think all those people went—what became of them?" Lileas wondered, not for the first time.

"I don't know; we don't even know if it wasn't some sort of genocidal death camp mentality thing. Remember those internment camps? If it hadn't been for our pets we would never have escaped." Jinny shuddered, thinking what might have happened if their animals hadn't come looking for them. Improbable as it sounded, after gnawing through the fence surrounding the camp they'd found where their Threans were being housed.

Afraid the animals would be hurt if discovered by their captors the seven detainees had planned and managed to facilitate an escape three months from the day they'd been bundled into the bus that had delivered them to Gated Community #3. Once free of its confines they'd headed back to their home town through the all pervasive turmoil.

Contrary to what they'd expected Threankind's sophisticated annihilating machines didn't seem to be the causative agents of the destruction. Instead it seemed to have resulted from natural events, storms of cataclysmic proportions, earthquakes and floods. Traveling the fifty miles back to their home the devastation had increased as storm intensities decreased. Seemingly the waves of demolition had passed through already and were advancing in multiple directions, continually extending mayhem's parameters. Needless to say the escapees found neither their parents nor any other living Threans. After briefly viewing their old homes they'd continued traveling.

Initially subsisting solely off the canned food littering the landscape necessity had eventually prompted experimentation with the edible offerings of the forests and nearby ocean. Building materials combined with other mangled, twisted necessities of life as lived by the advanced sophisticates of the not-so-distant past. Such was the abundance of once functional remote controls, Ipods, Blackberries, plasma flat screen TV's, notebooks, cell phones and other electronic devices that the crunching sound engendered by stepping on the bits and pieces had quickly blended seamlessly with the other unremarkable daily sounds.

Travel hadn't been in a straight line but along the path of least resistance. Frequently the movements, rumblings and crashes of the various natural calamitous lashings had made travel impossible.

After several months, feeling they'd outdistanced the calamities and resulting damage, they'd moved into a community of houses whose unkempt, dusty, jaded appearance lent credence to their having been long abandoned. The four foot by six foot welcoming sign, faded black letters still standing bold against the white background, had proclaimed the name of the town to be Scarsberry By The Sea.

Mansions replete with carriage houses, tennis courts and boathouses stood out amongst the houses of lesser stature gracing the avenues. Deemed dwellings of lesser stature by comparison only, none would ever, by any stretch of the imagination, be described as hum drum. Their ornate construction encompassed many rooms and each had a four car garage. Clones, these three-story houses came replete with gabled roof, multiple balconies, and numerous upper story bedrooms easily identified from the street level by their characteristically curtained windows. Downstairs, glassed French doors opened into spacious dining, living, den, hobby and library rooms. Complete with alarm system accoutrements whose controlling pads, no longer recipients of electricity's nourishments, now appeared as garish decorative objects lifelessly gracing the front portals, their arrays of red and green lights sparking now and again, briefly, when struck by a ray from sun or moon.

Scarsberry By The Sea's retail shops had contained little of practical use to Jinny and her six companions. Stocked with the luxuries of the financially secure, and it should be added in keeping with the grandeur of the houses, a rather high level of financial security, there were no food supplies—what little there had been already consumed as evidenced by torn wrappers, broken glass and the like—and very little serviceable clothing. The many shells of restaurants, art, café, gourmet, gift and antique shops stood as skeletal reminders of a past era of opulence. The previous inhabitants of Scarsberry By The Sea had apparently been the sort able to leave the providing of their most basic daily needs to those not as financially fortunate as themselves. That these providers were expected to shop for necessities suitably removed from where their patrons interacted was suggested by the lack of stores equipped to comprehensively and economically supply life's needs within the town's limits. The nearest grocery, pharmacy and department stores were eventually located ten miles away hulking on an acreage of black asphalt padding. The surrounding residences—apparently of less sturdy construction than those found in Scarsberry—weakened by the Upheavals and no longer recipients of constant upkeep, were crumbled remembrances, fragments of past structures.

Nearly a year passed before things had become dicey once again. This time having a proprietary feeling towards their homes they'd tried to stay. Eventually the ground shaking beneath their feet, buildings simultaneously falling and being blown away, bits and pieces tossed in the winds accompanying the torrential rains, they'd been forced to acquiesce to their sense of self preservation.

Hans had declared it was as if the Gods of ancient times, those who controlled all the natural forces, were at war with each other and their efforts to outdo one another were comprehensively annihilating everything.

This most recent evacuation had brought the group to their present location which Jinny conjectured to be somewhere below an island complex off the Northeastern Coast of the Northern Temperate Continent. Of course as Orla pointed out, not one of them knew exactly which direction they'd traveled since broaching the entrance to the Caverns. In reality they could be below the Continent or out underneath the sea, yet another ingredient to add to the stew pot of unknowns.

Days passed, the soft lights glowed, food abounded, and no specific threat revealed themselves. The Chamber with all the screens, computers, levers and symbols purred benignly. No other water source save the lake in the entrance Cave came to light. Swaths of steam continued snaking out diminutive nodules tucked discretely from discriminating sight but save for the guess of geothermal activity no other causative agent came to light or was hypothesized. Setting up various camps enabled contact while avoiding the time and energy expenditure of daily trips to the main camp. Questions continually peppered Jinny's and everyone's consciousness. Giving credence to the plausibility of water tables beneath the Surface logic proclaimed that given current planetary circumstances they be bulging with liquid rather than hollow grottoes. Furthermore those areas had been only a few hundred feet below the upper crust of the Planet. Every tremor and quake would be felt at such a shallow depth and they felt nothing. The puzzlement of it all was enough to make ones head spin, Orla proclaimed, just like the child in that movie *The Exorcist.* Mab posed the theory that they'd somehow accessed the *Twilight Zone.*

At week's end Jinny suggested they consolidate their equipment, leaving much of it in the ASC (All Seeing Chamber), and head back to the main camp to compile the collected information.

12.

"You know this may sound silly but it's nice to have all of us sleeping in the same place again." Mab said pausing while drying the dishes. Looking around she smiled, "I feel all warm and fuzzy. It must be hormones or something."

"Actually I feel the same way. So I don't think its hormones." Hans chuckled looking up from his task of washing the dishes. "In a way we've become a family unit and it's comforting to have everybody 'home'."

Dishes and other chores completed they crawled into their sleeping bags, Jinny purposely neglecting to bring up the issue of guard duty.

Waking up thirteen hours later to full light intensity she initially resisted replacing the languorous well-rested, relaxed feeling one gets after a thoroughly satisfying sleep with the heightened awareness of full consciousness. Clearly not alone in her desires the yawns and other sounds particular to newly awakened Threans reverberated throughout the Chamber. Finally willing her eyes open Jinny looked around. Derek, Morna and Mab although awake were still in sleeping bags while Lileas, Orla and Hans ambled indecisively about the camp. Lileas seeing her opened eyes came over and nudged the bag with her foot.

"Come on you sleepy head . . . it's time to rise and shine!" Jinny's retaliation created a wave of laughter as, her ankle firmly held in place, Lileas neatly tumbled to the ground.

Several hours later after the animals had been cared for and breakfast finished Jinny suggested, "How about a meeting to decide the best course of action from here in, say about an hour . . . 1115?" Six bobbing heads confirmed agreement.

An hour later the gathered semi-circle looked expectantly at Jinny.

"I assume that we've been filling each other in on what we all saw and I know everybody has been in and able to look over the ASC." A chorus of yeses and nodding heads signified everyone's affirmative response.

In Jinny's remembrance the meeting progressed as most meetings do. The proverbial dance around the crux of the vital issues encompassed cutting in by someone going off on a tangent, another succumbing to personal pet peeves and individuals expounding rather than a succinct elucidation of thoughts. She'd summed up the salient points with her closing words.

"Then it's agreed; we will have a satellite camp here at Ambrosia Lake, good choice of names Orla, while the largest group camps at the ASC. This way we can keep an eye on things here as well as try and figure out exactly what's going on in there. Since we're all going to take turns at each location, everybody will start out at the ASC. Things should be OK here for a couple of days and this way no one feels slighted."

Again a general nodding of heads and rising somewhat stiffly from sitting positions the task of packing began. By the time they reached the ASC there was only time to unpack then eat before settling in for another night.

13.

"Hey, they're back on the screen. Looks like they're having a meeting of some sort. Remember the other two times we saw them on this very screen? They'd get up and not come back and we were really puzzled . . . well they're back in their chairs; this monitor must be set right on those chairs, and they must have to be in them in order for us to see them when they're in this room," Lileas shouted excitedly unable to control herself.

Looking sleepily around Jinny wanted to start chuckling but didn't. Lileas had awakened the entire slumbering camp with her excited shouting and everyone was attempting to wake up and figure out what all the fuss was about. Hans and Mab reaching for the weapons no longer laid out at night as they had when threat seemed more imminent, leaped instantly to their feet. Morna grumbling rolled over to return to her dreams while Derek and Orla glared at Lileas asking if she couldn't have waited until a decent hour to let them know that the mysterious group had reappeared on the screen.

"After all we can't hear them and even if we could we can't understand what they're saying." Derek complained.

"Oh stop being such a fuddy duddy, these are the first life forms we've seen in months and these three may be the answer to everything. I wasn't sure we'd be able to get them again. But there they are." Triumphantly Lileas swept her arms towards the monitor.

"Yes, *there they are,* and what should we do? Wave, shout, jump up and down?" Derek glared scathingly at Lileas and Jinny who'd abandoned her sleeping bag to get a closer look at the figures, "Shall we admire them like a quality painting or what? How does seeing them help us?" Stomping off to the lavatory area he left the rest of them staring at the screen watching the three Beings clearly conversing with one another. Even Morna had roused herself into a sitting position.

"You know he does have a point; how are we going to communicate with them? They certainly don't seem aware of us.

Their connection with this is either one way, off or broken." Morna's freckles stood out against her pale face—a redhead's skin—hazel eyes still having trouble focusing.

"Maybe they don't have any reason to pay attention to this connection. Perhaps they think there's no one left up here." Orla's arms reached high above her head as if in stretching she could increase her 62" height.

"Yes and maybe they are the ones trying to kill everything off. Do we really want to announce ourselves to them?" Derek was back.

"No we don't, but if we could somehow access their conversations, understand their language then we could figure out whether they are friend or foe." Jinny suggested glancing at Derek.

"So we should continue with the plan we decided upon at the Lake." Lileas proclaimed, "And they're gone again. Well that does it for me. I'm going bed."

A candle's beacon . . .
Sputters, flutters, glows
Then flames
Grown as faith marches along
Seeking release
From oppression's grasp

4

EXPLORATION

14.

"Why can't you ever make up your minds and stick to it? Let's be fair to everyone, you say, be democratic, have meetings all the time. Well what's the point of all these meetings, if we're not going to follow through with what we voted for?" Derek glared at one and all. "Yes, as you said Morna, it's a good idea to be open for change if the situation warrants but how has this situation changed?"

Jinny sighed. Her parents had been right there *was* one in every crowd and Derek was most definitely their one. His cloak of contentious behavior while shielding his self from susceptibility to assault created unwieldy behavioral issues difficult to accommodate into the otherwise balanced social interactions of the group. The most notable problems arising when they'd each agreed to take on the responsibility of specific tasks, emulating the commune lifestyle their ancestors had successfully followed before the inception of the Mechanized Age.

Implementing the system shortly after arriving in Scarsberry by the Sea, Derek's unreliability when it came to anything strenuous or essential had necessitated revision. With the understanding that failure to complete any chosen tasks would result in punishment meted out in the form of task reassignment devoid of any request input on his part Derek had been allowed to choose from a list of nonessential daily chores. Revamped in this manner the system had worked well until they'd been routed from their domiciles.

Initially rambling through in the pre-dawn hours Threa's surface had rolled and bounced. Not the stereotypical functioning of earthquakes of old where massive plate movements initiated a concerted heave followed by a series of smaller shifts spaced over a period of days and/or months. No, this had been akin to being on a welter of ocean waves, deep trenches etched between the expanding heights.

The first few days of their return to nomadic existence had passed in a haze of misery. Black clouds had pelted, showered, then pelted again. Rain, sleet, icy hail balls the size of onions insinuated, melting into every nook and cranny of their Beings. At times the winds and the objects embraced within those tempestuous currents had swirled with such malignant venom it forced the evacuees to seek immediate shelter. Setting up structures had proved fruitless, the winds gusting all attempts to smithereens. Huddling behind tree trunks, rocks or under overhangs had provided their only relief from the confrontational weather. Then the seas had begun rising.

One morning finding it lapping within several feet of the campsite, they'd blamed exhaustion and gloom for failing to realize the sea's close proximity when setting up camp the night before. As the day progressed, and in spite of the inland direction of their steps, the distance between them and the water decreased, elevated apprehension further incising the lines on all their faces. Displaying a determined will, the seas had continually striven to catch up, seemingly loath to leave their presence as a small child follows afraid of losing security. Rests called off, travel had continued as steadily as possible.

The following day a rocky incline had offered escape in altitude. Safely atop the rise they'd traveled onward, the seas frothing upward, foamy fingers leaping. No longer questioning the inland progression of the seas, they'd simply plodded forward. On the fourteenth day of their retreat, Mab, looking for a private place to relieve herself, had entered the mouth of a cave.

Their first night indoors in a fortnight had been spent enjoying warmth and safety free of intrusions from any animal, atmospheric or aquatic forces. The next day they'd begun the descent that took them to the Cavern of Ambrosia Lake and subsequently the All Seeing Chamber.

Making the decision to go blindly down into the depths had been surprisingly easy. Unanimously agreed upon that life on the Surface was being rendered impossible and following a discussion revolving around the possibility of the sea levels rising high enough to wash completely over land masses it was the general consensus that placing themselves as far as possible below the Surface could increase their chances for survival. Another hypothesis posed by Orla and bandied about suggested the possibility of the tunnels being extensive enough to reach other Continents.

And it wasn't such a far fetched idea. Numerous studies undertaken to clarify how Threankind had spread over the Planet had never resolved the issue to everybody's satisfaction. One theory posed the idea of catacombs far below the Surface that offered paths from one area of the Planet to another but the idea had never been proven. Lileas did remember—she'd had a friend who loved diving and cave diving was his specialty—that there were areas of caves that while located below the level of the prevailing seas were only partially filled with water.

15.

The sound of Hans's voice disrupted Jinny's reminiscence, "So what do you think? Should we all camp here with one or two of us going back to pick up supplies when we need them or do you still think it would be better if there was always someone camping at the Lake? The supplies we found in those enclosures don't need guarding. They're obviously storage units left undisturbed at least long enough to be obscured by moss growth. The gardens haven't been cared for any time recently and they seem to be growing just fine. If a couple of us stop by every few days or so it may be more attention than they've received in a long time." After pausing a moment, giving each a glance as if offering any who might wish it the opportunity to speak, he continued, "The other consideration is safety. We don't know what this ASC is for, who set it up, how to work the machinery in it or anything! There is some measure of safety to be had in numbers not to mention the fact that if someone back at Ambrosia Lake ran into trouble we'd have no way of knowing until it was too late to help."

"It's true that we have no idea who set this up, or for that matter who they are." Though nearly six inches shorter than Hans, Orla's exuberant personality generally made her seem taller than her actual physical manifestation. The energy of that exuberance was focused towards the screen where once again the clown and donkey had appeared, "But my instincts tell me that we're safe. I don't think they're anywhere close and anyway they certainly don't look threatening."

"What's so comforting about that little skeleton dude?" Derek clenched his fists glaring into her brown eyes, his face reddening, "How do we know they aren't Aliens planning on killing or experimenting with us! What about all those stories of UFO's pulling people up into their ships then examining them by putting things up their noses and other invasive, painful things?"

"OK, OK, calm down. Let's try and figure this all out. We don't know anything except the concrete obvious." Looking around Jinny tried to keep from smiling. Sometimes Orla's hair took on a life of its own and there were now auburn hairs standing upright, bobbing with her every head movement. "This room could have been created by our government and been operational for years without public knowledge."

"Then how do you explain them . . . oh great, they're gone again!" Derek's voice pitched higher than normal.

"Maybe it's a show, a fictional depiction of something. Maybe it's been set up to fool spies; maybe it's none of that and we'll never know; maybe we should just stop trying to speculate, settle in, get to work and actually figure it out instead of wasting time."

"I think Mab's right. A show of hands please, how many for staying together here, setting up camp and sending a couple of us back every so often to get supplies and check out the lay of the land." She looked around at the group as Lileas, Hans, Orla, Mab and Morna raised their hands. Looking at Derek, "well that's it then, we'll stay together and camp here."

Derek stormed off. Shaking her head and again sighing Jinny approached him narrowly avoiding the yellow, curled and clustered bristles of an airborne brush, "You know there's going to be times when you will be part of the majority and you'll get your way. Do you think you'll really want to watch those that disagree acting like two year olds?"

"Oh shut up and go away. You're not my boss or anything. I may just get up and leave anyway." Derek grumbled.

"Fine, you're free to go but keep in mind you won't be able to take any supplies with you. No food, cooking utensils or anything. Remember when you suggested that we adopt that way of thinking right after we arrived in Scarsberry? Dissenters shouldn't be allowed to compromise the survival possibilities of the larger group, you said. Remember how you maintained that the larger group had the right to the comforts since they would have the better chance of survival?" Receiving no reply and knowing that some men, in a similar manner to cats, will only follow a course of action if it appears to be "their" idea Jinny joined the others in setting up camp.

Soon suspended sheets and blankets delineated seven cubbyholes in a cavern area adjacent to the All Seeing Chamber.

16.

"How are we going to go about figuring out what this machinery is and how to work it?" Orla asked during breakfast the next morning.

"I think the best *modus operendi* is to ask those of us most familiar with computers and such, aka the electronic geeks, to look the equipment over. Lileas, Hans and Mab, I think you three have the most extensive knowledge don't you?" Jinny asked looking from one to the other eyebrows raised. Definitely not a candidate to do initial or other examinations of anything computer or digitally related, her interests relating to such machinery focused solely on productivity, she preferred to leave the intricacies of the technological functions providing the service to others.

"OK," Mab said as the three nodded at each other, "we'll be glad to examine and provide an inventory of what we find."

"Thank you," Finishing quickly the trio left the breakfast gathering to assemble the diagnostic equipment. Managing to save some of their evaluating equipment and pick up others as well as scavenging bits and pieces of electronic hardware during the time spent in Scarsberry had been a group obsession. The evacuees far reaching plans, once over the mere survival aspect of it all, had been to reestablish links with whoever else might still be living on the Surface. Knowing it to be irreplaceable they'd carried all the salvaged electronic equipment with them on their journey to the Caverns.

Several hours later watching the busy puttering around the array of tables brought a smile to Jinny's face. Lileas, Mab and Hans looked like happy little chipmunks, first motioning here with a Skeltograph then there with a Guggenmometer. Chirps, beeps and whirs emitted steadily from the diagnostic machinery interspersed with the sporadic, blurted exclamations from the diagnostic team. "Wow, that can't be; well, would you look at this; what the @#$?!? and humph's".

"Hey, get those jades over here and help me." This plea directed at Mab from Hans.

"What . . . you're blue orbs need the help of the green-eyed, blond haired bombshell?" Laughing Mab came over to stand by Hans. Within an inch of his height, she filled out a cotton t-shirt its message long faded away, worn blue jeans not quite extending over her ankles and a chambray shirt. Well used but intact leather sandals separated feet from rock. Friends since early childhood they could—and did—talk to each other about everything.

"Look at this," Mab said pointing at the monitors on the wall.

"It looks like some form of runes or hieroglyphics." Peering at the marks and tracing them with his finger holding it just above the lines, "I don't think those are pictures so they wouldn't be hieroglyphics but they could certainly be representative of letters in an alphabet put together to form words then phrases . . . just as runes are." By now Hans was just inches away from the wall, "I'm really beginning to think that some group from another planet created this equipment and set up this room. That or our government or some governmental conglomeration was much more advanced than we thought. Either way this is REALLY COOL."

"It doesn't bother you that these Aliens, if that's who or what created this may be the cause of the devastation on our Threa?" Derek had come up behind them.

"No, because I don't think they did. Don't ask me to give you a solid reason why, but I feel that these people are friendly and if anything they've tried to help us."

"Oh great, not you too!" Derek said, backing away from the two. "We could get killed because you, Jinny and Lileas *feel* they're benevolent. Well I'm going to put my efforts into constructing weapons, just in case your *feelings* are wrong." He finished with a triumphant about face before crossing the threshold of the ASC into the rocky corridor beyond.

"What was that all about?"

"I never understand what causes him to go off like that. You'd think he'd calm down now that we seem to be in a safe area. For the time being anyway." Mab responded to Morna's question then looked at Hans. "You knew him before all this began didn't you?"

"Yeah he started showing up at the stables I worked at just a few months before everything went wonkey." Hans said eyeballing Derek's retreating back. "He certainly seems to love animals but his people skills are dismal and his temper seems to be on a shorter and shorter fuse. He was always somewhat mysterious about where he lived and never talked about anything but the stables and what was going on in the moment. I can't say I liked him very much then but he didn't drive me as crazy as he does now."

"Maybe he came from that foster home all the NIMBE's were in such an uproar about. You'd think they were housing ax murderers the way all the grown-ups carried on." Morna suggested. "Being one of those kids could certainly make it difficult to develop healthy social skills."

"Yeah maybe, but we all have our baggage to deal with. I'm not willing to take his on too. He's wasted enough of my time." Hans pronounced turning back to the screens displaying much of nothing on the wall. "I'm going back to work."

Shrugging her shoulders Morna side glanced at Mab before following in Derek's wake out the ASC.

A few hours later Jinny found them hunched over printed expulsions from the various diagnostic apparatus.

17.

"Can this be written in some sort of code? I can't understand a word of it. All these symbols and none of them recognizable." Mab's voice sounded tired.

"I don't know what to tell you. These diagnostic tools are highly sophisticated, the most advanced of our society. This little Skeltograph functions in much the same way as the x-ray machines of old. No harmful rays are emitted and while its sensors don't pierce flesh the way Superman's vision could, it reliably exposes the innards of electronic equipment enabling diagnosis and repair without dismantling complex machinery. Nicknamed the Third Eye," Hans pulled a small piece of black metal tapered at one end displaying two inch long prongs on the other from the Skeltograph, a three by five inch seeming resurrection of the disposable camera popular in the 20th and 21st Centuries on Threa, "this optional diagnostic tool when plugged into the Skeltograph functions to further disseminate and clarify its visual findings. The Guggenmometer acts in the capacity of a Universal Translator. Probably the most intricately designed and far reaching of all this diagnostic equipment it's able to decipher the multitudes of symbols and languages programmed into it. What makes it really unique is its ability—and before these Runes it had a perfect record—of tackling and clarifying those new to it. Basically it could decode just about anything it came across, making its inability to make heads or tails out of the inscriptions and descriptions found in the ASC that much more puzzling and a little bit frightening." Hans wearily piled the papers with their illegible scrawl on the table. "All this information and we're no closer to understanding than this morning. I'm tired; let's call it quits for today. Maybe tomorrow that screen," pointing to the one that sometimes showed the Aliens, "will have those Beings on it and maybe that will open something up. I just don't know."

At that moment of discouragement Morna popped her head into the All Seeing Room, "There you are; we were wondering where you'd gone." She nodded at Jinny before addressing the other three,

"Are you guys done for the day? Every time one of us came by to check on you, you were all so immersed we were afraid to interrupt."

"Yeah we're done." Mab said in a low, tired voice. "We can't figure out any of this." Waving at the reams of paper covered with illegible symbols.

"Oh . . . " Morna looked at them quizzically. "Well I'm sure you'll figure this all out eventually, one way or another." Holding up her hand and directly addressing Hans, "I know it's much more complex than I realize; I really don't know what I'm talking about and we don't have all the time in the world since we don't know what 'they' may do to us." Smiling now, "Look I know it's frustrating but we've set up camp in a little cavelette next to the ASC and we have dinner ready. Come on, drop the day's frustrations and relax."

"You mean don't bring our work home?" Lileas punned.

"Yeah, that's it. We're safe right now and you're tired after working on this all day. Let's enjoy a peaceful night and you guys can pick up tomorrow where you left off today. What d'ya say?" Morna looked expectantly at the half circle of faces before her.

"I suppose you're right; what'd you make us for dinner?" Mab asked as they headed towards the newly arranged campsite.

"You'll see. We spent the day finishing setting up. It's pretty snazzy if I do say so myself." Morna waved them into the Chamber.

18.

"Wow, you guys have been busy!" Complementing the sleeping cubbyholes a central communal area invited. "This looks great . . .

and you've got both of the stoves assembled. It's like having a professional kitchen here in the depths!"

Their appearance reminiscent of the wood burning stoves used before the Mechanized Age the cooking stoves operated using a non venting system of friction. The heating elements—four, two inch diameter curved foot long cylinders, per stove—housed particles that when prompted rubbed against each other. Increased rubbing intensity equated directly with increased heat production and higher cooking temperatures. Additional fine tuning of heat levels could be facilitated by turning the levers controlling the moveable supports able to lift and lower the cooking implements. The particles or Enterprisers—named after the Threan who discovered them—were stimulated into action by turning a crank handle in much the same way the first car engines were started.

Aromas of garlic, rosemary, cilantro, squash and beans emanated from pots gurgling and steaming on the stoves. Rocky slabs laid end to end provided level expanses for food preparation and serving. Slightly removed from the kitchen area the "bags" used for cleaning and refreshments leaned against rocky formations. Seven seating spots created using the configurations of rock worn smooth over time promised comfort reclining.

"You've even laid out rugs!" Lileas exclaimed admiring fragments of multi-colored weavings framed by the dun colored floor. "It feels like a home instead of a camp. Candles!" she said seeing them glowing from the nooks and crannies around the Chamber.

"Yeah, we don't need them for light but they sure do a lot for the atmosphere! The animals have their own area just through there"

Jinny pointed to a screen of material which opened into a sizeable Chamber. Within the Chamber the chickens, ducks and donkey, Olivia, each had an area to call their own. All the animals had the freedom to roam at will but during the night each liked to have their own little cubbyhole to bed down in, just as their people did. The chickens preferring elevated sleeping quarters had "high rise" nests. The cats and dogs slept amongst their Threan caretakers.

"OK, now that you've seen it all I'm starving, let's eat!"

Next morning a meeting convened directly following breakfast.

"More and more evidence seems to point to the fact that all this," Jinny waved her arms around expansively, encompassing the equipment in the room, "is the product of Beings from somewhere else, presumably another planet."

"Yeah, what have I been saying!" Triumphantly Derek puffed out his chest. "I knew it."

"Yes, Derek you're probably right; however, we have to be sure and I don't want to jump to the defensive here. We don't know if they mean us harm or not.'

"Have you noticed what's happened on the Surface lately? It hasn't exactly been a picnic and I for one am going to defend myself against these creatures."

"Yes, well as I was saying, based on the findings of our examiners it seems logical to assume that a group from off-world built this. It also seems fairly reasonable to assume that it was done recently . . . say within the past hundred years or so. Before the Upheavals scientists doing studies on newly discovered empty caverns felt they'd been emptied recently. According to them the depletion of natural resources such as oil created lots of new underground cavities, some of which imploded and some of which remained empty pockets."

"So the theory is that this used to be filled with oil or something for millennium until society sucked it dry? I don't remember any oil drilling in this area of the Northern Temperate Continent. And what about all the steam . . . I don't remember hearing about that so close to shore. Of course I'm assuming that we're near the shore." Hans scrunched his face as when puzzled or experiencing difficulty in remembering something.

"No there wasn't but I read an article just before we were taken to the Internment Camp that presented an interesting theory. Posing the hypothesis that many of the oil cocoons were interconnected, it conjectured that emptying the crude from some areas had caused oil in others to migrate out. You know gravitational pull combined with the propensity of liquid to flow into voided spaces. Maybe that action also opened up some type of venting." Mab shuddered. "It's kind of eerie to think about catacombs of big empty spaces crisscrossing underneath our feet. I know it's silly but I can't help comparing them to giant sinkholes. You know the kind that suddenly appear and swallow everything up."

"According to a friend of my parents who worked for the government, it was becoming more of a problem than the general populace realized. That was why the studies were being funded. They were trying to keep it hush hush to avoid a panic reaction.

People just didn't get how interconnected the areas below our feet were; it took them long enough to get an inkling of the interconnectedness of everything on the Surface." Morna said. "Remember when the garbage thrown out into the coastal waters off the Eastern Continent's coast washed up on the western side of the Northern Temperate Continent?"

"Yeah, wasn't *that* an uproar and a half. Everybody wondering just how could they DO such a thing to US. Like we're above it all. I'm sure our esteemed governing forces did worse to them and others." Orla chuckling continued, "No one could get it through their thick skulls that the stuff as it existed had to fill space somewhere and somewhere is connected to the way back to them."

"And getting back to our issues here," as a group they could really get off topic, shot through Jinny's mind as she steered the conversation back to the problem at hand. "How do we want to approach this equipment? Pretend we never found it, turn it on and hope for the best, or turn it on and have a set plan of what to try and find out."

Morna contributed, "We can't just pretend we didn't find this; what if we can do something to stop what's happening to our Planet? What if we can persuade whoever built this to help us?"

"You must be nuts," Derek declared. "I for one don't see any reason to let these Aliens know we exist and I don't want to talk to them. They're different and strange and who knows what they might do to us. They're probably ugly green slimy monsters that spit blue."

Ignoring Derek, Orla said, "I also think we should fire these babies up and see what we can find out. If there's any chance of rescue or resolving this situation we need to take it."

"I think that's true and what an opportunity; we might possibly communicate with Beings from another planet. How can we not try and do that?" All heads but Derek's bobbed in agreement with Lileas's enthusiasm.

"What about those things that look like remote controlled toys we saw on that screen?" He pointed at the now blank screen. "Where are they? Another planet? Huh?"

"Let's vote. I suggest that our next step be to download any files still not done—of course whether we'll understand anything or not is still up in the air—and familiarize ourselves as best we can with the operations of this equipment. Perhaps we'll be better able to try and communicate with them." Jinny said also failing to acknowledge Derek.

"I second that motion and would add an addendum. I think we should put a watch on the screen where we saw the figures and if they reappear observe everything about them. They don't seem to be able to see us and don't seem aware that they are being watched. Perhaps some of our equipment can tell us something about why that is. We also may be able to tell," Mab looked at Derek, "if they mean to harm us or not."

"I second that." Orla said.

"All those in favor raise your hands." Six hands including Jinny's went up. For the sake of formality she asked, "All those opposed raise your hands." But Derek had already risen and stormed away.

Mab, Morna, Hans, Orla and Lileas seemed to take that as the end of the meeting until, "Wait! Wait! We need to set up a schedule for watching the screen in case those three come back." Jinny's words sat everybody back down.

"I'm going to set this up so Derek isn't involved, so dividing twenty-four hours by six gives each a four hour stint."

"Why don't we put a sheet up and have people sign up for a time period they'd prefer. That way there should be a minimum of fuss." Morna suggested. A chorus of yeses and that's a good idea approved her suggestion.

As the meeting broke up Lileas came over to Jinny, "What are we going to do about Derek? He just doesn't want to cooperate. I'm afraid he'll try and wreck the equipment or sabotage our efforts in some other way."

"I've been wondering about that myself. He's flying off the handle more quickly and with more frequency than when we were in Scarsberry. I wish I knew why. "

"What do you suggest we do?"

"For the time being just keep an eye on him. People like him need something to fuel their aggressions, something like drugs or alcohol or an ally. As long as there's someone watching for activity on the screen I think he'll refrain from doing anything really drastic. I may even ask him to go back for supplies as a way of getting him out of our hair."

"What if he disappears and never comes back?"

"Then that's the choice he makes. We aren't in any dire need and won't be for some days yet. If he doesn't show up someone else can bring back whatever's needed."

"What if he refuses to go?"

"Then he will have to appear before us all and there will be a vote as to what punishment to mete out. Remember our set of rules?"

Chuckling, "You don't miss a trick do you?"

Jinny just smiled.

Comforting familiarity pillows
As into the clearing
Manifests the intrigue of
Four Unknowns

5

THE FOUR UNKNOWNS

19.

"We're wasting our time watching this screen. It's been two days and there's been no sign of those creatures." Derek rasped.

"What do you care? You're not taking any of the watches; all we asked you to do was get us some fresh supplies and you haven't even shown any inclination to get started on that." Orla rasped back.

"Actually we don't know for sure if they've been there or not. Each person that's had the night shift has said they've dozed off from time to time." Jinny intervened. "We're all tired and trying to catch up on food and sleep. It's going to be at least a few days until we're back to being ourselves, then we can be more reliable in our observations. For now let's just do what we can to the best of our ability. We don't seem to be in any danger; there's enough food and water not to mention peace and quiet to sleep in."

"Harrummph, I guess I could go to Ambrosia Lake tomorrow. It'll be nice to be away from everyone and by myself for a change. I can do things the way I want to."

Of course you can, Jinny thought to herself as aloud she thanked his retreating back. Derek turned to look at her before disappearing behind his privacy curtain. Shaking her head at Orla, Jinny shrugged her shoulders gesturing resignation with an uplifting of her hands, palms skyward before turning and going over to the screen where Mab was giving up her watch seat to Lileas.

"Do you think those of us watching the screen at what we've designated as night are missing seeing the Aliens because they're asleep? Maybe we've got it backwards and the night is really daytime and vice versa. Maybe they're in a different time zone altogether. Maybe they're vibrating at a different frequency and we can't see it. Kind of like certain animals being able to hear different frequencies." Lileas continued, "I would really like to see those Beings again. They're fascinating, and I want to experience their emotions as best I can through the screen."

"It's possible that we have the twenty-four hour cycle upside down but by the same token we don't know what kind of a cycle if any these Beings may be using. And if they are vibrating at a frequency our eyes can't see then how do you explain what we have seen?" Lileas kept her eyes glued to the screen as Jinny talked, "They may not use the room with any frequency; we've just got to keep on watching."

"Do you think we have any chance of surviving all this? We're, I don't know, how many feet below the surface of Threa, the target of some sort of malevolent forces clearly bent on annihilating every sentient Being not to mention Threankind's structures and the only Beings we've seen so far resemble toys." Sighing Lileas continued, "I just wanted to have a normal life without any great incidences. I guess that's out of the question now."

"I'd say so."

"They're on the screen! They're on the screen! Everybody come look!" Lileas's shouts stopped Jinny halfway to her cubbyhole. Impossible to differentiate within the ensuing maelstrom which of the five sleepy Threans tripped, fell, entangled, or snarled as they swarmed in Jinny's wake toward the screen.

20.

They really do look like stuffed toys Jinny commented to herself. At least two of them did. The third resembled a skeleton, not the kind used in medical schools or as Halloween embellishments but a Day of the Dead folk rendition. In the process of showing the two other animated Beings how a small device attached to what looked like a very thin, long, black hose functioned, this Being displayed digit dexterity and mobility of joint movement. The knitted clown, intently concentrating on the skeleton's explanation, was dressed in a pair of blue shorts and mauve t-shirt. The third Being in the room was a donkey. Surprisingly adroit—at least to the Threans watching who viewed him as a donkey of lengthy trunk—standing on his hind hooves and using his front as if they were Threan hands—he was picking up and handling objects with the manual dexterity usually associated with having fingers, most particularly an opposable thumb. This adroitness most particularly evidenced itself when the skeleton unraveled the hose handing one end to the donkey whose left extremity manipulated the object much the same way Threans used to twirl plumbing snakes, feeding them down pipes to do away with clogs. By far the most flamboyantly attired of the trio he wore a mint green silky scarf, puffed in well set folds from the lapel of his paisley shirt covering his lower neck and filling in the gap left by two unbuttoned top buttons. Short legs filled out the cream colored shorts topping his green mesh shoes. In style resembling those originally designated for beach wear, their open weave material allowing for water flow in and around while protecting from nibbling crabs or sharp rocks, soles tough enough to protect tender feet but pliable enough to bend and conform to the surface topography being traversed. The knitted clown stood taller than the donkey and skeleton whose heights were similar.

"They really do seem to be alive, but what are they doing?" Orla stabbed the silence.

"Look at that, there's another one; it looks like he's sticking his head through a window." Mab pointed at the screen which now showed another donkey. This donkey, grey and white with the usual upright ears and wearing glasses revealed his head and a bit of his neck through what looked like a window opening into the room the other three Aliens were in. While his spectacles emphasized his academic appearance—stereotypically ascribed to a Being of eminent intelligence—the twinkle in his dark eyes banished any resemblance to a stodgy old codger. As the skeleton rolled the hose into its container, this gentleman—a term that seemed to fit him—was nodding his head and moving his lips seemingly expressing approval.

"Wow, look at them. We're looking at a screen with images coming in from somewhere out there." Morna's arms waved upward and roundabout, "We don't know who or where any of this is. But I will bet you anything none of this is some covert project our government was involved with." Her tone expanded with awe.

"Yeah just think, we get to see Alien creatures and we can't take advantage of it in any way since no one's left for us to tell." Derek's comment disrupted them all.

"Derek, just shut up or go away or something. We're all sick of you and your negativity. We may have the opportunity to make contact with another world and if you can't see the coolness in that perhaps you should just go back to the Surface and leave us alone. I for one am tired of pussyfooting around you to try and keep the peace!" glaring Hans finished his tirade before rejoining the others already returned to viewing the figures on the screen. Derek huffed and puffed a few times but ignored sat down and watched as well.

Animated, smiling and laughing the three Beings were now seated and conversing with the fourth one. From time to time pieces of paper were passed from one to the other then shown to the donkey with the glasses. Occasionally one or the other of the four wore a look of severity, the kind associated with the thinking or realization process.

"So what do we do now?" As taken as she was with watching the scene unfolding before them, Jinny still wanted to make sure they took advantage of every opportunity to get as much information as they could from this event.

"What do you mean? Did you want to try and see if we can somehow establish contact with them? We haven't really had a chance to figure out what switch and/or button does what yet. I guess we could try activating them and see what happens." Mab looked apprehensively at the machines.

"No, I don't think we should wildly go about activating the electronics. For all we know we'll do something that these Beings will view as antagonistic and they'll retaliate. No, I don't know quite what I'm looking for. I just don't want to loose these images. Somehow they seem a beacon of safety and security." Jinny's voice reflected her frustration, "Oh I wish I could be receptive to the FULL message at times like this!"

"I agree they don't seem to be malicious Beings. I think we should watch them for now and take in all that we can from observation. Then we'll take the data we've managed to amass so far regarding the machinery here and try and figure out what might be the best way of approaching possible communications with them. Maybe if we could do it in such a way that they don't realize where the signal is coming from?" Morna suggested.

"I think we need to go one step at a time. Let's observe and take any notes we deem appropriate." Lileas suggested, "Then our next step will be to try and decipher the readings we've made on this equipment. When we arrive at the next juncture we can decide what to do from there."

"What does everybody think of that?" Jinny asked. Distracted sures, yeses, and OK's emitted from Threans more interested in watching the screen than deciding what to do once the show was over. Lileas pulled out her drawing pad her pencil flying across the page. Jinny wrote into her notebook, continuing her writings. The others sat imbuing themselves with the visual emanating from the screen.

21.

Revealing images for another hour or so the screen eventually succumbed to blackness. The Beings hadn't left, in fact they'd still been talking. Similar in fashion to the plague of TV reception before the advent of digital connections the picture on the screen had begun fuzzing and shifting. Precipitation in the form of grey/white snow grew to blizzard conditions. Jinny remembered watching historical documentaries detailing the crudeness of early TV's and the technology used to transport the images from one place to another. Very often, in those days, if there were electrical occurrences somewhere on the signal's path, or just simply high winds, the signal would be garbled and the result a fuzzing and shifting picture on the TV screen. The observers remained transfixed for several minutes after the blizzard gave way to blackness as if by moving they would negate any possibility of the picture's resurrection. Eventually all leaned back looking at one another.

"We need to figure out how to work this stuff." Hans nodded towards the control panels, absolutely beside himself with eagerness.

"I don't care what it takes. This is way bigger than anything I ever hoped to be a part of."

"So you didn't get any feelings of negativity." Jinny asked.

"No, absolutely not. Didn't you all feel comfortable with them?" Hans looked around.

The ensuring chorus of yeses, and a few they're cutes and let's get to work made Jinny smile. She felt a very strong pull to the Beings but wanted to make sure that they had a consensus before delving any further. Looking around she saw more enthusiasm on her comrades faces than she had in a long time. Realizing they were all looking at her expectantly she smiled and raising her arms up said, "Let's get to work."

Broadscope the mind,
That clasps at this.
Evidenced possibilities,
If we but have the
Facility to appreciate.

6

UNRAVELED HERE AND THERE

22.

"Who wants to go next?" She asked holding up the clam shell. In an effort to quell the Threan tendency to interrupt when someone else was speaking the Ancients had used a common object to designate the speaker. Whoever held the quahog shell—or whatever was appropriate to their culture, inland dwelling North Temperate Continent Natives had used a corn cob—had the floor and no one could speak without permission or unless the shell was handed to them. Before the Upheavals began several of the group had been regulars at Native North Temperate Continent New Moon and Full Moon Ceremonies where they'd been introduced to the practice.

Living in Scarsberry By the Sea they'd incorporated this method as one of the ways of smoothing over any tensions that might have otherwise splintered the group. Shells were in abundance and corn for the refugees meant kernels out of a can, so they'd picked the quahog as a means of indicating a speaker.

"What if anything did you two come up with?" walking over to Lileas and Hans, Jinny handed an off-white and purple hued quahog shell to Lileas.

"Still nothing definite. We've been trying to decipher or break or come up with some pattern or rhythm to these runes but so far they're still incomprehensible." Lileas handed the shell to Hans.

"I don't have anything in particular to add to that, except that I don't want this to get shoved under the proverbial rug. I can't give you any kind of time frame regarding how long it might be until we can understand what's been written but I feel that we should keep trying. It could open up so much for us." Hans rose and handed the shell to Morna.

"We think we have the inner workings of the control panel figured out. We've drawn sketches of which buttons and switches control what functions and have made a copy so everyone can have it. Of course this is based solely on the readings of the Skeltograph and we've not been able to test anything out. I guess that will come when we try it out for the first time." Hans held his palm open for the shell as Mab raised her hands and Morna nodded at her to speak.

"You can get that from looking at the results of something equivalent to x-rays?"

"Even though the alphabet that these people use has, so far, eluded our abilities to decipher, the inner machinations of the electronics are far less obtuse. Don't get me wrong, it's very sophisticated—quite impressive actually. They seem to have mastered the art of the miniature and don't have anything under those covers that's not absolutely necessary. We've been able to follow the connections, look at the computer and digital chips and figure out how the leg bone attaches to the hip bone and so on. From our extrapolations we've hypothesized which switches will control which specific screens, monitors and the components that send the images to them and what doesn't have anything to do with them."

Orla took the shell from Morna, "While we are now pretty sure we know the connections between the screens and the computers capable of operating them, we don't know the full extent of the network. We followed the pathways present in this room so the next thing to figure out is how to follow those extending beyond without turning everything on and possibly giving our presence away. One of the interesting things we did figure out is that the computers appear to be set up to receive signals sent at variant tempos. Each seems to be configured to receive waves of signals coming in at contrasting intervals. Instead of having a set up whereby one 'tunes in' to a particular frequency—similar to tuning a radio in order to pick up a specific radio wave from a selection of offerings—these are setup to receive only one specific type of frequency. It's almost as though they have different units to pick up signals—frequencies—from air, water and perhaps other physical conductors such as maybe rock, sand . . . who knows. The conduit could be anything, at this point there's no way to tell. It just seems to make the most sense given what these electronic setups are telling us." She handed the shell back to Mab.

"While it may sound as though this type of technology is more primitive than ours we don't think that's the case. Our sensibilities have been programmed to think of big and more complicated as being better. It would appear that simple and extraordinarily sophisticated is the key. If our theories are correct—even partially so—this form of communication is far beyond anything Threans have even imagined in the most progressive Speculative Fiction of our times."

"Why is that?" Derek hadn't waited for the shell but he had raised his hand. No one chastised him as Mab nodded at him to speak.

"Because we think they are equipped to receive signals that we don't even know exist. Signals that may be transmitted through or by rock, or lava or the dust on the tail of a comet—I know what we're suggesting may seem fantastical but why not? It would also facilitate their being able to have a group meeting of members from various different cultures, environments and/or dimensions at one time. They wouldn't have to be on the same frequencies or transmitting through the same medium, because they would be using screens and signals specifically designed to transmit that signal or different vibrational frequencies. We also don't think there's any lag time in a setup like this. Wouldn't it be nice to have a conversation where you didn't have to guess whether someone was done talking? Or could see the recipient of the conversation clearly as though sitting in front of you?" No matter the electronic advancements made on Threa the voice stream had never jibed with the mouth movements.
"Remember how clearly the images of those four Aliens were? And one of them seemed to be in a different location than the other three.

Couple that with auditory as clear as the images and well . . . wow!" Awed she handed the quahog shell back to Orla.

Smiling at her friend's reaction, "This is pretty cool but for our immediate needs we've figured out which receivers we think are connected to areas on this Planet. We did this by assuming that any connected to Outer Space would be capable of receiving the minutest of signals. So the screens that seem set to receive signals traveling through an atmosphere or water we hypothesize are the ones with the wider receptors set to pick up transmissions coming in at a more forceful strength setting than those moving basically unhampered through space. Now again I know this sounds a bit confusing but let me try and sum it up as simply as possible. This a new technology so bear with us. We're hypothesizing that in order to have signals arrive simultaneously these Aliens created a system whereby the speed with which the signals travel through various media could be controlled to such a fine degree as to be able to guarantee immediate image and auditory exchange. The settings and hookups we've found with the Skeltograph support this supposition." Mab and Orla looked around at their rapt audience.

Reaching for the shell Jinny said, "I guess there's very little doubt that there's life on other planets. They must be, at least some of them must be, quite a bit more advanced than us. There's that nudging question regarding other dimensions too. I guess the Billion Buck question now is when do we try this equipment out?" Jinny held up the shell and Lileas reached for it.

"I think we should proceed with care but we definitely need to proceed. Perhaps we need to figure out an escape route before we start turning things on, just in case whoever we wind up contacting isn't as magnanimous as we might hope."

23.

Hans again held his hand out for the shell, "What kind of escape route could we possibly come up with that would thwart the sensors of such an advanced group of Beings? I would imagine that if their technology is as advanced as we think that escape would be pretty much impossible."

"We don't know what we're dealing with; we don't know if they have bases on Threa or if they have to travel to get here or what. I for one don't want to miss an opportunity to make contact with Beings from another world. By the same token I'm not naïve enough to just assume that because we feel comfortable with a few of their images on a screen that all of them will inspire the same confidence. Look at how diverse Threans are. Some of us are kind, compassionate, broad-minded individuals while others not so much. The extremist would just as soon annihilate anything they haven't seen before, are different from them and/or don't know anything about. Perhaps there are members of this Alien society who reflect the same diversity of attitudes as we have—or had—here on Threa. I think we have to keep that in mind and come up with whatever we can think of to try and minimize any possible danger to us."

"You're both right," Jinny said as soon as Lileas paused for breath. "We don't know if we're opening Pandora's Box or not by activating the machinery in this room. I guess it behooves us to plan what to do in case of some sort of attack. How should we go about it?"

This rapid fire exchange had occurred without the passing of the shell which Lileas now accepted from Hans. They all watched as her head slowly lowered and staring intently she rotated the quahog as though drinking in every facet of an intricate sculpture. Finally raising her head she spoke, "Sorry for taking so long but I was just thinking of when I was a kid and what the dog trainer told us to do in order to impress our new puppy. The dog learned quickly and would perform beautifully as long as someone was in the room with her. But as soon as she was left to her own devices she did whatever she pleased. The trainer suggested that we do things like squirting her with water or throwing something in her direction and/or creating loud noises."

"What does this have to do with the present situation?" Mab's voice oozed impatience, "Why are you wasting our time with stories from your childhood that have nothing to do with anything?"

"Actually this has everything to do with the situation. The behavioral problems with our puppy were solved because she had no idea where the water, objects and loud noises were coming from. They were startling and inexplicable. She realized that certain actions seemed to prompt them to occur and when she behaved differently they didn't. In large measure our trepidation and bafflement in how to proceed is based on fear of the unknown."

"I didn't need to listen to all that psycho mumbo jumbo to know that!"

"I know Derek but sometimes it's helpful to follow a line of thought from its inception to ending." Lileas said smiling at Derek then speaking again to the group as a whole, "I'm suggesting that we activate the equipment using a remote control device. We can be hidden in case we actually contact somebody but then we'll know a bit more of what we're dealing with. If there are Beings out there and if they don't see us they may just think the machines are malfunctioning and may not feel it necessary to investigate as quickly or even at all. It may buy us some time to figure out whether we need to run or not." Lileas paused waiting for reactions.

"It certainly would increase our confidence if we felt we had some measure of control over the situation and the only way we can get that is by acquiring more information." Jinny smiled nodding towards her friend as Lileas handed the shell to Orla.

"That actually sounds like a good idea. But how will we pull it off?"

"Hmmm, if they don't know we exist, at least not until we're sure they won't do us harm, that would be a good thing." Hans mused stroking his beard, "But how to make a remote control system."

"I think we can adapt remote controls and/or create them from the electronics we've salvaged and maybe even from some of the stuff that's here in this room." Morna spoke quickly. "We will need a little time to work on this. You know I just had a thought. We could use some of the extra cords and by splicing them together perhaps incorporate older clunkier technology with their more advanced sort."

"What d'ya mean?"

"Well Derek I'm thinking that if we had some of the remote controls connected to the keyboards that affect the control panels we could exert control from the tunnel or anywhere else. That way the Beings couldn't see us and we would have more technological abilities than if we're just pressing buttons on a remote control device."

"What about us? Don't we get to help? What can I do?" Mab, Hans, Orla, Lileas and even Derek spoke simultaneously.

Jinny reached for the shell. "I think we should proceed with this idea. Morna, Mab and Hans would you three work on the remote control issues and would you Derek, supply them with any of the materials they might need. Lileas, you and I will go scout out the escape route and if you would provide us with nutrition and take care of the animals." This last aimed at Orla who nodded acquiescence.

A late afternoon start ensured Jinny and Lileas the security of spending another night safely within the protective confines of the Caverns, albeit in the mouth of the outermost Chamber. Orla had helped pack food and water and with sleeping bags dangling from the bottom of plump backpacks the two started the trek to the Surface, their departure almost unnoticed by the remaining five.

Soldering guns, some with convoluted tips, tweezers, lights, a plethora of micro instruments—all specially designed for this type of minutiae electronic work—were manipulated with such dexterity it seemed the tools were one with the Threan's extremities. Waving abstracted good-byes and good lucks, they'd barely paused in their work.

24.

"Well will you look at that." Stars twinkling against a wispy black backdrop decorated the skies above, while silhouetted in the light of the nearly full moon a landscape of snapped trees, their bent trunks supported by the upper reaches of branches and leaves extended as far as Jinny could see. As though quelled by a giant's hand these twenty to thirty foot trees, all felled five feet above ground level, appeared as if paying homage to a deity, or displaying the results of a monstrous game of dominoes. Shapes of leaves, rocks, sticks, boards and what seemed to be a brick chimney sitting on the Surface as if swept from its previous housing situation and resting before its next assignment, loomed within the eerie assemblage.

"The crowns of all those trees are facing the same direction, must have been some wind that blew them down like that. And where's the water?" Lileas asked looking around as if expecting it to make an appearance. "Weren't the waves lapping just over there?"

Shaking her head in puzzlement, "Yeah, I think so but it's pretty dark right now." The moon had retired behind another cloud. "Maybe our sense of proportion is off having spent so much time down below." Jinny started walking toward where the water had been, "Wow, you'll never believe, oh." Laughing because she hadn't realized Lileas was right behind her, "the water's receded a lot." She continued pointing at the water gently tapping in wavelet rhythm at the shoreline several hundred yards away. "It's almost back to what appears to have been the beach line here."

"I guess so, it's kind of hard to tell exactly where that might have been but we know those trees wouldn't have grown in sea water. Of course we don't know how far from the original water line they were. This is really creepy."

"Yes, it is." A glance passed between them and without comment they walked back to the mouth of the Cavern and began setting up camp. Dinner consisted of dried vegetable matter, and water. Exhausted from the hike up and the emotional toll taken they crawled into their bags right after dinner falling asleep in minutes. Neither one of them mentioned it at the time but in discussing it later they'd both hoped the other wouldn't bring up the issue of guarding the camp.

Neither reacted when a shadow fell over their figures, darkening their sleeping bags for only a brief moment before sliding off.

25.

Refreshed and curious they broke camp shortly after dawn. In the illumination of a brilliantly sunny, clear, blue sky day the full extent of the damage overwhelmed. There was indeed a chimney sitting just outside the cave entrance. Rubble of all sorts littered the ground, hanging from trees as though a new species of sphagnum moss. The odd thing about it, or at least, as Jinny related later, odd to them used as they were to litter being trash of the Threan engendered sort, was the nature of the rubble.

The area had been heavily populated with buildings of all sorts from skyscrapers to beach bungalows decorating the coastline. Looking around at the carnage Jinny felt and Lileas concurred that it was as though they'd been transported to a different region of the Planet. Save for the chimney and a board here and there no evidence of Threans or their civilization remained. The pristine shores that had greeted settlers arriving in the post discovery, exploration era were far different from what Jinny and Lileas viewed coming up from the Cavern. Sophisticated buildings and infrastructure seemed to have vanished into thin air, leaving behind detritus of a vegetative rather than industrial nature.

It had been decided that the two explorers should, provided conditions were conducive, head inland and north. Having seen the damage and the withdrawing waters the two opted for a northerly, coastal route. Receding waters had either taken the big stuff with them, or there hadn't been that much on these beaches to begin with. Broken shells, tree limbs, small pieces of what might have been docks or boats at one time and most notable in uniqueness a barnacle encrusted net sprawled on wet sand its peaceful undersea retirement disturbed were less overwhelming hindrances than the tangled woods.

"I don't really want to but do you think we should head inland at some point, after all we are trying to find a hiding place." Lileas asked after several miles.

"I think we should continue along the coastline for now, at least a few more miles. I'm not sure we could make any kind of time if we were all trying to get through the woods. I'm also thinking that if we need to hide our passage that near the water we can, if needed, walk in it. As long as the edge of the forest stays pretty close we can always duck behind, or underneath something. I was hoping to find some sort of building that we might be able to use but it's like we've traveled into the *Twilight Zone,* where are all the buildings?"

"I don't get it either. Even if they'd all been destroyed somehow or other wouldn't you think there would be evidence, wrecks, concrete, cement, bricks, wood, shingles, plumbing, a bathtub, a sink, *something* lying around? There are no roads, nothing." Lileas's pitch increased with every word.

"Let's not get carried away and make ourselves crazy. Just concentrate on our objective for the moment, an escape route." Before there had been devastation but at least the buildings, albeit in pieces, remained after the cataclysm passed, now it was as though everything that had been perpetrated by Threan ingenuity had been gulped up. Until they found out something definitive it seemed wiser to force the questions out of their heads—as much as was possible—and concentrate on that which they could be proactive about. Continuing on their northerly trajectory for the better part of an uneventful morning they decided to head inland after eating lunch. Remnants of the grandeur that must once have been the forest remained as detritus carpeting the ground on which they trod. Ruptures of green gashed in boughs and trunks gave testament to the freshness of the damage.

Then, reaching the edge of the forest they both . . . skin prickling, neck hairs extending as would the fur on a dog's shoulders, stomach's clenching, blood rushing to adrenals . . . stared silently at the void before them. Extending into infinity a broad expanse of brown soil met blue sky on three horizons. Standing on the fourth, the line of bowing trees behind them, both searched for any sign of grass, bushes or trees, buildings, parking lots, cars, any sign of life, to no avail.

"What happened?" Jinny managed to gasp out.

"I don't know and it's getting scarier and scarier. How can we deal with forces if we don't know what's going on? Let's head back to the Cavern. We're not going to find anything that offers protection up here."

"Let's go." Jinny not pausing to see if Lileas was following turned and headed back in the southeasterly direction towards the Cavern.

Shadows continued apace before sliding off as clouds took over temporarily masking the sun's rays.

PART II

THE CARETAKERS

PRELUDE TO AN ADVENTURE

"It will be most invigorating to be in the Threan physique again; I so enjoyed my previous experiences *comme ça*." He smoothed his shirt into consciously arranged casualness while turning to watch the next swirl of colors transform configuration. "Losing nothing of our mental acumen and acquired knowledge while still being able to interact fully with another species particularly those occurring on a different plane and dimension is a privilege, *n'est pas?*"

"Yes it is." Echoed the two configurations forming in the space lock one of whom continued speaking. "We must take a moment to align our energies so our Threan chakras will be properly situated for both the transfer and the period of Upheaval. And even you, since you will be appearing in a Threan form, will be in need of aligning."

The swirl of colors still not melded into a recognizable—by Threan standards—form proceeded to reconstruct until bounded by an opaque perimeter.

"Ah good . . . now first we will join in a guided meditation followed by hands on treatments to help us remain centered and attuned to the Galactic Life Force Energies." The speaker raised his hands over the bowed heads of his companions eliciting an immediate relaxation of their Threa forms. The focused Energy, drawn first through his head chakra then passing through the heart chakra before emitting from his palms into his companions Threan configurations, next traveled to those areas—within those configurations—needing it the most. As highly vibrational Beings in their natural forms centering was helpful from time to time but when manifesting as alien forms it was imperative.

Infrequently masked by clouds of particles wafting by, stars winked through the portholes scatted about the space lock as the foursome meditated. Connecting with their inner selves and energies within the physical configurations they would inhabit for the duration of the project.

While all at their level of vibration were connected with the Universal Galactic Energies the speaker possessed integral qualities exemplifying the harmonious mindset of total melding. In-depth study of the Life Force Energies coursing throughout the Galaxies was one of his most treasured pursuits.

"We wish to thank all the Galactic entities that were with us for this healing and clearing." He intoned signifying the closing of the session. All raised their heads, remaining seated, bodies wreathed in golden white auras exemplifying calm and centeredness. All chakras—the energy centers located in seven regions throughout each configuration—aligned and functioning well.

"I will miss not seeing you in person every day," said one of the forms to another on his left, "but we will be in speaking contact."

"Yes, I will look forward to those exchanges. I will also miss the personalized daily interchanges but my engineering skills can be put to more efficient use down there on the Planet than instructionally from here."

The four looked out a porthole towards an opening indicated by a sudden muting of the space fabric's pigmentation.

"It looks as though mechanics for the transferal are almost in place."

The figure last to change nodded at the other three, "Safe journey and successful mission to you all. I will make sure and appear as a Threan when I send intergalactic messages so as to not cause panic, should any of the evacuees happen to see me."

Three nodding heads precipitated the opening of a section of the space port onto a tunnel livened by a glowing amber light. *Sans* baggage the three walked through, disappearing from sight.

As the opening sealed behind the group, the remaining figure mulled the circumstances and events leading up to the necessity for a bit of galactic tuning that had precipitated this moment.

Euroswydd had been the driving force and originator of the Threa project. So prevalent was the feeling of exasperation with the situation that complete removal had been a popular solution bandied about by many members of the Council. Enough was enough they'd opined, the Threanoids had had their chance; they were irrevocably beyond redemption. Why waste any more time and energy on them when such expenditures would certainly be more productive elsewhere?

At the Determining Conference, the Supreme Council Members had cited the detrimental effects being perpetrated on the Galaxy and the repercussions continually experienced throughout the connected Universes resulting from the Threans blatant disregard for the natural rhythms of existence. As with every other issue of similar magnitude the nine Universal Voting Entities would have the final voting say as to what would be done to rectify the situation following the Supreme Council Members presentation of researched information and personal evaluation.

An advocate for Euroswydd's plan, Supreme Council Member Reiki Clowne, who'd enjoyed a particularly memorable lifetime on Threa as companion to the African drummer and Spiritualist Abab Ijnutalo, felt that his mentor's credo, "rhythm is the soul of life. The whole Universe revolves in rhythm. Everything and every action revolves in rhythm" succinctly put the situation into perspective. And while agreeing that a discordant planet equated with a loss of healthy rhythm that when magnified throughout its Universe eventually engendered discord of Galactic proportions he wasn't an advocate for the perpetration of the discord that would ensue following complete annihilation.

He'd not been alone in his conviction. While many members of the Council had argued that eventually the shock waves from the

Threans continued inability to learn from their mistakes would have far greater detrimental effects than those created by an induced planetary explosion, just as many had argued the opposite. Supreme Council members Oscáre Tarjáy and Mort, speaking for all the members of similar mindset, maintained that such a solution, while facilitating the removal of the problematic planet, contained loopholes of inestimable proportions whose resolution would require an expenditure of far greater magnitude than Euroswydd's proposal. Euroswydd's plan advocating healing and recovery, offered a middle of the road solution.

"Sending it all into space would be comparable to the haphazard filling of the Threan landfills and other atrocities that were part of the initial problem. The poisons' grip needs to be loosened, then processed into harmless particles." As a member of the Supreme Council Euroswydd had pleaded his case to the Universal Voting Entities, "Actually they would become so much more than harmless particles. They'd be vital building blocks, able to be utilized by either the Planet herself in the rebuilding process or by the returning terrestrial and aquatic life, when that time comes. The planet Threa is a living, functioning Being just as all the planets in the Universes are. As a living functioning entity who has been under siege and ill for some time it behooves us to give her a chance to recover her health. In so doing we would be saving a unique situation and helping reestablish homeostasis in the Galaxies found within the Universes rather than exacerbating the problem."

Many of the Elders on the Council carried with them fond memories of time spent on planet Threa. For centuries utilized as a classroom for mental, emotional and physical growth most had passed at least one lifetime there acquiring the knowledge necessary to facilitate their development. Some had even found it a spiritual place. The Beings that achieved the stature of membership on the Supreme Council—that of Elder—had spent many lifetimes on various planets in many galaxies throughout the Universes. Casyo's—their home planet—principles affirmed that no short trip or mere video viewing can replace the in-depth insight afforded by hands on experience. Ultimately, perhaps in deference to those memories, perhaps in deference to their principles of avoiding the perpetration of harmful actions, perhaps in combination, the Universal Voting Entities acquiesced to Euroswydd giving him the go ahead for the project they dubbed Euroswydd's Caverns.

Alive the model,
Reveals alike,
To both friend and foe,
It's enough,
It should be enough,
Yet never is it so.

7

SHENANIGANS

26.

Saturating the Caverns, mellifluous melodies of flute and drum filtered through the Tropical Rainforest Environment's entrance. Mort and Oscáre's duties having called them elsewhere, Reiki Clowne drummed for the life in the Greenhouse with recordings instead of the preferred live musical accompaniments.

Self proclaimed proficient and publicly declared inspired, Mort of bones and legend would, as the mood struck him, arrive at a gig with any of his many instruments. While his talents extended to all stringed and winded instruments the twelve stringed guitar from which he coaxed ethereal melodies with a decidedly Hispanic pulse was his favorite. Oscáre's musical aptitudes mirrored Reiki Clowne's in the percussion aspect and oftentimes the tinkles, clashes and thumps coming from the kitchen were his expressions of the rhythms playing in his head.

The plant life growing within this Environment provided home and food for a multitude of birds, insects, fungi, bacteria, nematodes, protozoa, actinomycetes and earthworms, all of which contributed their vital ingredients to the overall balance of the region. Reiki Clowne not only offered musical energy but additionally in his capacity of Reiki Master/Teacher acted as a conduit for the Galactic Life Force Energies to go where needed within the enclosure.

Drops of water gently pattered the organic umbrella above his head, bathing plants, contributing ionized particles and liquid. The dense canopy snarled high above his head, so thick it was impossible to tell which limb grew from which trunk, resonated the moss green of new leaf growth, a rare zig zag of brown bark peeking through.

Evidenced here, there and everywhere, even if only as briefly glimpsed head tilts, avian navigators glided through the upper entanglements weaving moving distinctions of color and melody through the green, complementing stationary flowers, vibrant color in shades of red, blue, orange, yellow and magenta.

Whether by wing, paw or slither there was always somebody moving about amongst the fruit, vegetables and herbs plentifully available to fuel such activities. Inability to fully utilize the abundance of crops had prompted Euroswydd's colleagues to open a new storage cavern in order to accommodate the surplus. Oscáre spent much of his time processing the food so it would last until needed, should such an eventuality ever come to pass.

27.

Reiki Clowne smiled as the jungle scene before him lost definition and his minds eye filled with scenes harkening back to their first days in the Caverns.

It had been seven Threan days since their moving into the Undersea Caverns and the three had been getting used to functioning with an unaccustomed way of assimilating nutrition and the oftentimes quirky ways of getting things done.

"*Mon Dieu!* The soybean processor won't . . . process I mean. What will I do . . . ?" Oscáre glared at the processor holding both front hooves to his head. "How can I cook the meal *incroyable* without the machines that work?" There was no one better to have around in a crisis as long as it wasn't one involving culinary matters.

"Here let me see. Look you forgot to plug it in." Movement never seemed to cause Mort's carved bones to rub together, in spite of lacking muscles, tendons and cartilage.

"Plug it in? I've not had to do that before; I pressed the little button . . . here," hoof pointing to the on/off switch Oscáre looked accusingly at Mort as though he, Oscáre, were the brunt of a joke, "and it processed!"

"This morning we added the sleeping quarters to the main energy producers. We unplugged everything to make sure we didn't overload any circuits." Mort explained. "We must have forgotten to plug the soybean processor back in when we were done. I do apologize. You were off watching the seaweed aquaculture videos, learning when to harvest and how to sow seaweed gametes, when all this was going on."

"Well, then that's that. By the way what's for dinner?" Reiki Clowne looked cheerily from one to the other.

"If this machine," disdainful wave and tone of voice from Oscáre, "actually does what it is supposed to I will do the experimentation with the herbs, soybean pâte and the red and brown seaweeds." Enthusiasm getting the better of his mood he continued with, "I am having the fun *incroyable* with the learning of how to use the plant life that provides the wealth of taste as well as nutrition . . . . I do not understand the Threans," he said shaking his head, long ears moving back and forth emphasizing his point. "Why did they not use these medicinal and culinary offerings instead of inventing poisons to take their place? Now go, *vite, vite,* let me to myself to create the Oscáre Tarjáy dinner Extraordinaire!"

28.

The sun breaking through the clouds roused Reiki Clowne from his reverie. Stretching his legs woven from yellow, beige, orange, blue, tan, brown, red and cream yarn while wiggling lapis lazuli colored feet he slowed his drumming to a soft, gentle ending rhythm. Knitted, cream colored, mitten shaped hands tempered to relaxation on the drum head. His striped stocking cap, ending in a burst of multicolored yarn strands tied together then clipped to form a ball, added nearly twelve inches to the twenty-four inch length of his knitted head, body, and legs. No factory clone replicated for bulk sale in stores, his trunk, legs and arms were horizontal multi-colored stripes, his cream colored face, beaming his every-present smile, round eyes and red, wooly, circular nose framed by the wide brownish red yarn comprising his hair sticking down from the fold of his stocking cap were unique among those of his ilk. Adorning his chest, just visible through his shirt, were two balls similar to the one dangling from his cap.

Feeling that the concept of time, at least the Threan interpretation, offered more constraints that it released he didn't wear a watch. Recollections of his life among Threans succumbing to overwhelming feelings of anxiety and stress at the prospect of being "late", not being able to complete a job by the appointed "time", being the victim of shoddy workmanship, then having to make up for that which, of course, took up even more "time" thus feeding into the inescapable cycle of stress and anxiety . . . AAAGGGHHHHH put his wool in knots.

"I wonder what part of the Threan cycle of twenty-four it is." he mused to himself looking around.

Golden shafts of sunlight displayed themselves as rods of color, edges softened by pearlescent bits of moisture. Those raindrops that had managed to slide between the canopy's leaves now found themselves suspended between sky and soil, clutched by and contributing to the heavy, humid atmosphere. A macaw beaming blue and gold landed on the ground just within Reiki Clowne's line of vision.

"Shouldn't you be helping Mort with the air quality programming? I seem to remember hearing a conversation about that last night." The gleam in the bird's ice blue eyes sharpened. "And before you ask me how I know, let me remind you that even we little chirpers have curiosity. I like to sit within the tree's hammock of leaves and remember what it was like before we came here. It's right next to the air vent and I can often hear your conversations."

Laughing, Reiki Clowne extracted his drum from its playing position between his supporting legs and put it aside.

"Yes, I'm sure he's wondering what's keeping me; I'd better get going." Rising his stocking cap bobbing, "Did you enjoy today's concert? I got lost in the music, and I'm not sure I have this drum tuned properly . . . it always takes a few tuning sessions to get it sounding just right after I rehead a drum."

"Wonderful as always. The missus particularly liked that part when you went a little crazy on that drum of yours. What's it called again, a djembe?" The bird cocked his head, looking at Reiki Clowne with his left eye.

"Yes, which translated from the African dialect means healing drum."

"Well, the drumming makes the kids flap their wings and hop from leg to leg a lot. That keeps them quieter at night." The bird winked at Reiki Clowne. "This way we get to have some alone time together. You know what a good mother she is. So much as a peep out of one of them and she stops everything to go check."

"Yes, yes." Reiki Clowne stopped in the Tropical Rainforest Environment's entranceway, the diaphanous membrane billowing around his body. "Please tell Amanda I wish her a restful day and I hope you both fly over to visit next time. Namaste my friend." Hands folded before his chest he bowed from the waist before straightening and proceeding down the passageway, little yarn balls jiggling with the cadence of his steps, the movement visible beneath the muslin fabric of his tan colored shirt.

29.

Upon entering the Engineering Chamber he was greeted with, "Ah, there you are. Could you grab that light pole and point it down here? I can't quite see this connection. Something's not quite right but I need to see, yes, that's it." Reiki Clowne held the light below Mort's cranium illuminating a conglomeration of wires, computer boards and soldered connections. "The latest Upheavals have managed to disconnect some of these. We'll have to get them reconnected, shut the system down for a moment or two then reactivate it."

"Oscáre isn't going to be pleased losing power like that. You know he's been in the kitchen all morning preparing supplements for the terrestrial animals. He's very exacting about how those ingredients are mixed and heated." Reiki Clowne's voice exuded unease. "Shouldn't we make sure he's finished before turning everything off?"

"When it's ready to be done, we'll check with him and if he's still working we'll find out when the best time will be. Shut down won't be more than 30 to 45 seconds. I don't want any life forms to suffer." Mort unfolded from his head first position down the hole containing the master electronic functions controlling the quality of gases needed by the life forms within the Caverns.

The air systems operated in a simple, constantly renewable fashion. Used air, in other words that depleted of oxygen and rich in carbon dioxide, flowed into the Tropical Rainforest quadrant as well as other highly vegetative areas for cleansing. Occurring during the darkest moments of the twenty-four hour cycle this replenishment procedure facilitated through vegetative photosynthetic processes converted carbon dioxide into oxygen. Replenished air moved from the restorative zones' to places of need just as it wafted in, a little at a time guaranteeing a steady, plentiful supply of needed oxygenated air while contributing rather than hindering the life cycles in all the Environments.

Threans, when they'd stayed on their proper level in the chain of life had—as does everything—provided necessary ingredients to the overall healthful checks and balances of the system. Now that they were no longer an influence, for good or bad—amusing not having taken the Threanoid presence into account when setting up the Complex—the recovery process had progressed more rapidly than projected. Ironic to consider or better yet remember that at one time Threans not only lived in harmony with Threa and her cycles but that they were a necessary part of the chain of existence! Not even Euroswydd had thought of that. Ah well . . . nothing the Caretakers couldn't make up for now. After all they were there to, among other things, make sure that any such glitches didn't threaten the successful completion of the project. Upkeep and troubleshooting . . . that was their job description. Of course being a simple system based on logic and common sense it was a rare occasion that major upkeep became necessary.

30.

An acute horizontal movement of the Chamber's floor threw Mort and Reiki Clowne to their knees.

"I'm glad that in this physical manifestation these old bones of mine aren't capable of breaking," Mort commented rising spryly to his feet, "I guess we should check out the stabilizers before doing anything else. It would certainly be a waste of time to have to do this twice."

"I hope everything's OK. That was pretty severe. I thought we couldn't suffer the effects of such Threanquakes where we're located and with the stabilizers on." Reiki Clowne rising from blue knitted knees spoke while simultaneously looking all around as if expecting something to momentarily land on his head.

"I'm wondering if those little shakes we felt yesterday didn't undo some of the connectors that operate the stabilizing mechanisms." Phalanges, metacarpals and carpals met Reiki Clowne's shoulder as Mort slapped his friend on the back. "Let's open this," He said leaning over to peel back the cover of vinyl like material—referred to as Lynivar after its creator Edmund Dexter Lyniva—revealing another hole in which more electronic and computer equipment functioned, "and see what we find."

While the operative principles, durability, longevity, protection and guidance, were the same as the old heavy metal manhole covers so prevalent on Threa, the material utilized by the Beings in

Euroswydd's Caverns also offered ease of maneuverability. Threan metal covers had been used to delineate portals to something as small as a water or gas meter to granting entrance into something as large as a sewer, subway or other system. Traditionally notations of various sorts identifying the particular cover were stamped into the surface of the metal. In keeping with that tradition each dot of Lynivar treading across the Chamber's floor displayed identifying notations. Below the coverings, the essence of the electronic system maintaining Euroswydd's Caverns resonated, each Lynivarian dot representing the access point to a unique set of components with specific duties and separated one from the other within a system of catacombs.

Mort's voice wafted up from his downward position, bony calves, ankles and feet protruding skywards, or ceiling wards as might be more properly described.

"It's a mess down here, I wonder if something got in. We really planned for any contingency." His voice softened and intensified as his head moved about, "I can't imagine that Threa's movements are causing this type of damage to the connectors."

"Didn't they set everything up so that no damaging elements could infiltrate our Complex? I mean I know they did . . . how could someone or something even get in much less do damage?" Reiki Clowne puzzled as he helped Mort extract himself from the hole.

"I'm not really sure. All we know is that damage has been done and we need to fix it before more systems are compromised. She's been more violent than ever these last couple of days and I can only imagine that it will get worse. We need to get those stabilizers working." Mort looked around the floor at the other Lynivar coverings scratching his head and crinkling his forehead, habits he'd retained from puzzling times during his Threan existence, "We shouldn't be this affected by the turbulence."

"Ah yes, my two friends are talking instead of doing. How will you ever get this done before I serve the wonderful meal I am preparing?" Oscáre looking down his well endowed muzzle, mustachio trembling, endeavored to appear stern and annoyed. "What have you found *mon amies*? That was quite the jolt of a few minutes ago. I landed on *mon derriere* in a most undignified manner."

Reiki Clowne looked at his friend with a smile. It's true, he thought to himself, to those not familiar with Oscáre Tarjáy, whose most treasured Threan existence had encompassed being the favorite toy of an only child whose affluent parents enjoyed the finer things in life, spoke several languages fluently and insisted their child do so also, he might initially come across as acting like something of a snob. He did speak the Northern Temperate dialect—considered the Universal language by Threans—with a bit of an accent, sometimes inserting words from his favorite French dialect and preferred a flamboyant style of dress, but underneath the outer trappings, Reiki Clowne mused to himself, his friend was a charmingly loyal, conscientious, and empathic Being. And how he did enjoy Oscáre's culinary marvels!

The culinary arts—that of other planets as well as the style prevalent on his home planet of Casyo—being one of Oscáre Tarjáy 's most treasured pursuits it had fallen to him to provide for the nutritional needs of the Cavern's inhabitants. He did this using offerings from the plants, both aquatic and terrestrial, as well as products of the living. From goat's milk he made yogurt, cheese and butter. Easily digestible and less complex in molecular structure than cow's milk, goat's milk and its resulting products increased the efficiency of assimilation ratio. Nuts, berries, grains, fruits, herbs and seaweeds fulfilled the rest of the nutritional requirements. Always coming up with a new concoction from the wealth of foodstuffs being produced within the Chambers he transcribed the results of his long hours of experimentation with recipes into a cookbook of sorts containing tidbits on cultivation and storage as well as philosophical meanderings. The texts would be included in the record of the group's time on Threa. Inclusion in the comprehensive library systems of the Galaxy would make sure any and all Universal inhabitants could avail themselves of the delicacies for millennium to come

His seven inch donkey body enveloped in the flowing comfort of an intense maroon and creamy ivory shirt reminiscent of the Salvador Dali style complemented beige muslin trousers—inseam four inches—which flowed with every step above hooves bedded down in a pair of plush garnet slipper shoes. Oscáre's long ears hung down on either side of a face from which glowed warm, brown eyes framed with the same creamy white as his large muzzle. His black bristling mane extended from forehead to below the neck of his shirt and matched the color of the waxed neat little mustachio adorning his muzzle. While donkeys can be many colors that which Oscáre chose to exhibit wasn't quite the usual. He preferred a coppery brown with tones of almost blond accentuated throughout his well brushed coat.

Reiki Clowne's smile deepened, comforted by the eccentricities so integral to Oscáre's personality. Sweeping a knitted hand towards Mort who was in the process of walking away from them, Reiki Clowne explained, "He's been sticking his bones down various housings checking out the electronic connections. In many cases they've been compromised." And seeing Mort peeling back another Lynivar cover he exclaimed, "And there he goes down another!"

31.

"*Mon dieu*. How and by whom or what is this problem being perpetrated?" Oscáre questioned as he and Reiki Clowne walked over to the hole Mort had disappeared into.

Thigh bones, hip bones connected to spinal vertebrae, rib cage and head bones came up into view. "I'm not exactly sure. It looks as though something caused the soldering of the computer parts on the mother and other boards to be compromised. It's as though they've been worn off or never existed. And it's not all of them, just enough to cause a problem without precipitating a complete system meltdown."

"Hum." Both Reiki Clowne and Oscáre watched as the figurative wheels cranked away within Mort's head. After a few minutes Oscáre asked, "Can you fix the problems?"

"Yes, I can." Mort said, "But I'm just not sure if the same problem won't recur again if we don't ascertain the cause."

"Is it possible that the culprits come from the ranks of the adolescent creatures living in the Caverns? Perhaps they are bored with containment or they have too much of the unstructured time to fill?" Oscáre looked at both of them with a gleam in his eyes, "Surely you both remember what it was like at that age? *Certainment toute les animals etes les* Threanoids 'feel their grains', or is it their 'oats' from time to time."

"I believe they 'feel their oats'. That's a good idea, whatever made you think of it?" Mort said.

"I hope that's what happened." Reiki Clowne proclaimed drawing in a deep breath before exhaling vigorously, as if relinquishing negativity, "I'd much rather think it a teenager's prank than something infiltrating our defenses."

"I saw two of the young chimpanzees in here yesterday and I will lay the wager that they had something to do with these problems. They looked quite guilty when I asked them why they were in here and couldn't leave fast enough when I gave them the permission to go back to their Environment."

While Reiki Clowne and Oscáre discussed the possibility of the saboteurs being from the pubescent chimp population, Mort continued peeling back covers and checking out the soundness of the connections housed within. Finally walking towards them he said, "First I want to get these connectors realigned and hooked up. Then I will need to turn off the entire complex for a few seconds before turning it back on." Both Mort and Reiki Clowne's head swiveled giving their full attention to Oscáre who burst out laughing.

"And you are both *tres* afraid that Oscáre will have the temper attack because of it, *oui*?"

"You know sometimes I think you enjoy messing with us." Mort said hands resting on pelvic bones, "You put on this front of being such a tyrant but at heart you're nothing but a kindly pussycat."

"I am a donkey *mon ami* not a *le petite chat*. And just as you are a bag of bones and you a knitted clown I am a stuffed donkey. At least in this dimension's manifestation. Of course we must do whatever we can to keep our charges happy, safe and living well. That is our task of the moment. So we will go ahead with the pursuit of the successful repairs. Please let me know when you plan to turn everything off and I will make a complex wide announcement and then *vive l'arrete*!"

"Maybe that will scare our suspects enough to keep them from more shenanigans in the future. I wonder if we can get them to admit to it. What do you think Mort?" queried Reiki Clowne.

"Couldn't hurt, I'm going to get busy on this." And so saying he picked up his tool case and went over to an opened cavity.

"I will return to the kitchen and continue with my work there. What a mess *incroyable* when that Cavern quake occurred." Lanky ears moving in tandem with his shaking head, his tut tutting faded as he moved in short, clipped strides along the passageway leading to the kitchen.

Walking over to the opening his friend had gone down Reiki Clowne peered in. Little puffs of smoke sprang from Mort's pipe pulsing rhythmically upward in quick succession. Knowing the cadence of the puffs mimicked Mort's level of concentration on a task, rather than interrupt by asking how he could help Reiki Clowne silently focused Galactic Energy downward towards his friend.

32.

"I have talked to the suspects' parents and they are with us on the method of teaching the young chimpanzees a lesson they will not soon forget." Oscáre informed Reiki Clowne upon reentering the Chamber several hours later. "We will keep the turning off of everything a secret from them and see what their reactions are. Their parents will make sure they think the turning off of the atmospheric controls is caused by some malfeasants and will act terrified." A smile wreathed his muzzle. "We do not wish to harm them in any way, but it will be much fun to hear about their squirming, *n'est pas*?"

Mort came up from the last hole and replacing the Lynivar said, "I would love to see whoever did this damage squirm. It requires a tremendous amount of patience and time to repair this type of sophisticated electronic machinery. No wonder the manufacturers installed them as a unit safely housed within their protector carriers. I'm sure they were confident they wouldn't need to be worked on with any frequency!" Dusting off his bones he refilled, then relit his pipe.

"Is it the time to shut everything down? I'm anxious to make sure *toute* is in proper working order before our meeting with Euroswydd. It is better to report the problem solved than the problem still in need of the solution."

"It's interesting how satisfying a good pull on the pipe can be. It brings peace and calm to my bones." Mort remarked to no one in particular before turning to Oscáre. "I'm ready to turn everything off. Shall we say in fifteen minutes? Will that be enough time for the chimp parents to get their kids set up?"

"Yes, that will be fine. Reiki Clowne would you send the dulcet signal to everyone else who will be affected that in fifteen minutes we will be undergoing thirty-five seconds of complete shut down? *Oui*? *Merci*. I will go to the chimps' parents and have them prepare for the lesson learning." Chuckling Oscáre disappeared down the tunnel leading to the jungle areas while Reiki Clowne flicked the switches that sent the pre-arranged series of bell notes ringing across the air waves.

Oscáre joined them several minutes before shut down commenced and the three took their seats before the consoles, ready to view the screens and make sure that all was well when the power came back on. Each Environmental section had several monitor screens facilitating comprehensive range of vision. They were not on all the time and great care was taken to not invade privacy. There had been no complaints.

"And now." Mort's fingertip touched the Master switch, effectively shutting the system down. Eyes glued to the big red seconds ticking off the time. At thirty-five seconds the red numbers stopped their climb and the hum missing those few seconds reestablished. Lights began glowing again the screens revealing functioning Environments.

The only screen showing any kind of notable behavior was trained to the chimp section of the jungle Environment. The three Caretakers burst out laughing. Both chimp adolescents were huddled together eyes tightly closed the very picture of the terror struck. Babbling almost incoherently, "We didn't mean to do anything bad. We were just fooling around, we won't ever do anything like that again." Both sets of parents looked quite severe although one of the mothers, her shoulders shaking, disappeared into the brush for a moment.

"Never do what again?" one of the fathers asked.

"We were in the Networking Chamber and maybe, just maybe we pulled some of the connectors off. Shouldn't we show them what we did so they can fix it and we won't be without life support systems again?" Clearly terrified and eager to reverse the situation post haste their words came out a spewed garble.

"I don't think there's any *maybe* about it. You two are in real trouble." Turning from the scene Oscáre, Reiki Clowne and Mort looked at each other in amusement.

"I do not think they will fiddle with the machinery again." Oscáre said.

"No, I don't think so either." Reiki Clowne chuckled, "A good lesson learned with no cataclysmic results."

"And I have more fodder for my storytelling." Mort said pulling long breathes from his pipe.

"Yes, I will try not to give away the ending when we hear you tell it to a group of impressionable youngsters! For right now however it's nearly time for our meeting with Euroswydd. Do either of you have any idea why he scheduled this special meeting?"

Mort and Oscáre glanced at each other, shrugging shoulders and shaking their heads.

Melodious murmurings
At times give way to
Dissident stutterings
Signal the issuance of
Burping stumbles
Awaiting smoothing
With competent assurance

8

GLITCH IN THE SYSTEM

33.

"How is it possible for the living Being to survive on the surface of this planet or anywhere near it? *C'est un feat impossible n'est pas*? What is it that makes you think living Beings and not the mechanical malfunction is providing the aberrant readings?" The meeting of the four Caretakers just begun Oscáre lounged on his streamlined version of a recliner. Its wooden frame, feather filled cushions and simple design the antithesis of the bulkier, pumped up versions held in such high esteem by Threan males.

Simplicity defined its sophistication. Changing position based on its occupant's weight adjustment negated the need for buttons and levers complete with inherent predilections towards malfunctioning. As with learning the idiosyncrasies of operating his kitchen Oscáre had had to adjust and compensate for Threan gravity's influence when manipulating his favorite chair. Sudden unaccustomed shifts in position causing him to be jettisoned, folded and once or twice to not change position at all had been cause for much hilarity before he finally achieved the necessary subtlety of movement. Experiencing personal acclimating issues with their seating arrangements Mort and Reiki Clowne were advised, "that the trick is the slow, easy shifting of the weight . . . and the keeping of the body in as relaxed a state as possible."

Leaning forward ever so slightly to place head to hoof in the classic Rodin position of contemplation he frowned at Euroswydd's electronic visual image, "Are all the equipments working properly? Maybe there is the glitch in the system. We have been undergoing the chimp caused glitches here." And as Euroswydd's eyebrows rose, "Everything has been repaired and punishment meted out. Two of the adolescent chimps were, how you say, 'sowing the wild oats', and tampered with the connectors keeping the stabilizer stabilizing. The severe tremors Threa has been creating made more connectors to be disconnected."

"The two chimpanzee culprits are, at this very moment and using very small toothbrushes, cleaning the outlet conduits used to exchange seawater." Reiki Clowne referred to a job that when done with the large scrub brushes designed specifically for the task took a matter of minutes to complete. "They are encased in the latest SCUBA gear and I think grateful at not having single handedly caused the death of the entire population of these Caverns. This job seems to be acting as a form of catharsis for them."

"And hopefully as deterrent of future such escapades. So everybody knew what you three were doing?" Filled in on the details Euroswydd hee hawed laughter the upper lip of his muzzle stretching up and out. "When I think of the things I did at their age . . . and I even got away with some of it, but it was devastating when I got caught and everybody knew."

"Yes, we had to tell everyone. They needed to know what had happened to cause the problems so they wouldn't be concerned about the possibilities of future malfunctions due to faulty equipment." Mort said, "We also needed them to go along with frightening the duo."

"Wonderful work you three . . . I will relay this all to the Elders."

"Couldn't the signals be caused by everything that's going on up there? The way She's been throwing herself about I wouldn't be surprised if something came loose."

"Sure it's very possible." First nodding at Reiki Clowne Euroswydd's image pivoted, acknowledging all three, "The signals seem to be coming from that subsurface Satellite Cavern complex we'd established within the ocean shelf off the coast of the Northern Temperate Continent."

"I remember that one. Wasn't it the last to be closed down?" Mort busily stuffed his pipe, his bony fingers well suited for packing the dried leaves down into his pipe's bowl.

Euroswydd nodded his head, "Yes it was. I've checked and double checked and it's impossible to tell exactly what's happened from here on Casyo. I even got the Aces to come and use their specialized discernment equipment . . . ."

"The Aces actually came and assisted?" Oscáre interrupted. "What caused them to change their minds? What happened to this project being the 'colossal waste of everybody's time'?"

"The caliber of the transplanted Threans now living on satellite planets has been instrumental in winning them over. The breaking of the stereotyping as it pertains to all Threan behavior and the work you're doing here has gone a long way towards winning accolades from those originally dooming this project to failure. The Aces are sure that the monitors in the Caverns have been activated but aren't able to electronically connect with them to figure out how or why." Looking at Oscáre, Euroswydd smiled playfully, "I guess you could say that there *is* a glitch in the system." Now smiling himself Oscáre bowed towards the screen.

"Well then what makes you think Threans activated the system?" abstractedly Reiki Clowne polished his glasses.

"Instinct, my gut tells me so."

"My word, how much time have you been spending with these people? I've never heard you speak so crudely before." Straightening his vertebrae, Mort's eye sockets focused keenly on Euroswydd's image.

"You know how much I love learning local colloquialisms, historical facts and speech patterns. The Threanoids are incredibly diverse and unique. The waves of change brought about by the Threan inhabitants of this Planet fascinate me. It's like no other in the Galaxy. Of course that's one of my reasons for wanting to allow Her to save it." Euroswydd paused, lowering his head in thought, "I feel there are Threans on the Surface . . . that it's not merely a mechanical malfunction."

"Her actions in this region of the Planet have been particularly tumultuous of late. It seems rather coincidental that the signal and the increased severity happened simultaneously. As both Reiki Clowne and Oscáre have suggested, and I'm not discounting your err . . . *gut* . . . couldn't this simply be something falling on the controls activating them?"

"Theoretically anything's possible but given how I feel I think we should proceed on the grounds that there may be survivors." Euroswydd replied.

"What procedures can we go ahead with?" Reiki Clowne held his knitted hands, larger portion together, thumbs akimbo. "We're here strictly as observers and caretakers. We've given our word not to interfere with Her desires!"

"Absolutely, we can't interfere no matter how much we might wish to. We gave our solemn oath and even our technology would be bested by the violence going on up there." Mort's bones vibrated sincerity.

"Ah *oui*, to interfere would be abominable but what if there are the living Beings tampering with the equipment in the Satellite Caverns?" Oscáre said, "We are here to make sure everything goes smoothly, are we not?"

The three Caretakers looked at each other then Euroswydd as he spoke, "It seems that the next step is to figure out a way of finding out exactly what is going on in those Caverns. If Threans are responsible they have remarkable survival skills. Which leads to my next question—why were they left on the Surface if they were the 'right kind'?"

The process of deciding who would go and who would stay had been arduous. A slow, laborious, carefully monitored operation—initially involving screening every Threan life form on the Planet—the gradual weeding out of those not deemed worthy of removal had culminated in a final list of appointees for transplantation.

"Because this situation is so fraught with issues I would like all of us to think about it for a day and if it's OK with you three, meet at this same time tomorrow to discuss possible scenarios. If not handled just right we could open a possible Pandora's Box." Euroswydd looked from one to the other.

"I think we are all in agreement with that, *n'est pas*?" Oscáre spoke as Mort and Reiki Clowne nodded acquiescence.

"Very well, until tomorrow," a sly grin spread across Euroswydd's muzzle, "same Bat Time same Bat Channel." The screen went blank.

34.

"What could he have meant by that?" Mort looked at his two companions.

"I believe there was what they labeled a Superhero on Threa named Batman. I've watched clips from the original television series and that sounds like a phrase used on the show. He is 'messing' with us; you remember his sense of humor." Reiki Clowne explained.

Oscáre nodded, "Ah well, I'm off to do the meditation. It always helps me come to the insightful conclusions."

"A Superhero . . . these Threans had a lot of Deities didn't they?" Mort commented to Reiki Clowne as they followed Oscáre into the passageway.

"They certainly seemed to worship Superheroes. Although to the best of my knowledge they didn't have any churches erected in their honor the way they did for some of their other dignitaries. Be well." Reiki Clowne waved his knitted hand as Mort stopped before the entryway to the terrestrial Environment mimicking the area he'd lived in when enjoying the incarnation that had prompted him to take the appearance and mannerisms of a skeleton from the Day of The Dead celebration for this mission.

Fifteen inches tall and carved from wood, his eye sockets were deep pools of black outlined with muted red. Slashes of black paint adorning his head, chest, pelvis, arms and legs edged and defined the skeletal features. Brushes of pinkish red here and there added external visual warmth to that emanating from his inner soul. Soaking in the landscape he remembered the conversation he'd had with Oscáre and Reiki Clowne as each had related why they'd chosen the forms and mannerisms they presently manifested. They'd been discussing the Threan preoccupation with protecting material possessions and use of the "Alarm System".

"You lived on Threa in the 20th and 21st centuries you must have been familiar with them. And what a disruptive, unhealthy, awful noise they did make." Grimacing Reiki Clowne had held knitted hands to the sides of his head as if physically bombarded with the auditory torture.

"No, during that time period I lived in a region of the world that didn't have such 'advancements'. The mentality of these people didn't encompass hording, sharing being necessary for survival. By the worldwide standards of the day the region of the Planet that I lived with the Gonzales family was considered 'third world' and very primitive."

"And this is the life that you loved so much that you picked this wooden frame representative of bone to memorialize it."

Mort had nodded acquiesce towards Reiki Clowne before continuing, "I lived lives in different guises on many Planets before assimilating the lessons necessary to graduate from Karmic Cycling and be inducted into the ranks of the Elders. While the life I lived as the son of this family proved to be the most economically challenging and my shortest, it was the most soul satisfying. Before and after succumbing to the knife—I died defending my home from marauding infidels—the love, security, and compassion exuding from my family and fellow villagers was unlike any I'd experienced before. That life was my last on this Planet and I sometimes feel as though it was given to me as a gift . . . kind of a graduation present for having achieved understanding." Smiling Mort had leaned further back into his stuffed chair. "And it's where I became enamored with the wondrous delights and practical value of storytelling. There were no digitalized entertainment units so socialization and exchanging stories were the most prevalent form of entertainment. It facilitated relaxation, lesson learning and the handing down of their historical legacies from generation to generation." Pausing, he drew a breath through his pipe.

"Every year on November 2nd, *Dia de los Muertos*—Day of the Dead—my family visited my gravesite. Unlike the other Threan families I'd lived with, these people viewed death as a continuation of life, embracing rather than fearing it. To them, life was the dream and only in death could they truly awaken. The entire village gathered in the cemetery, each family attending to their own gravesites—decorating them with marigolds and candles—before participating in a day of fun and celebration. Everyone brought picnics enjoying the company of their departed while eating their favorite foods. The prevailing sentiment was joy and my family celebrated my having achieved the ultimate. Some might even have been envious I'd had such a short life. These people honor their dead instead of trying to avoid the reality of death by relegating their loved one's remains to somber, mournful remembrance the ilk of which I've experienced in so many other cultures."

"I understand *mon ami* why you have picked this physical manifestation. I wish I had had the opportunity to experience this Day when I was on Threa." Oscáre had commented as Reiki Clowne cleared his throat to speak.

"I too have had such an exceptional life experience on this Planet. My little girl was the daughter of a family from Southern Extrematia who'd emigrated to the Northern Temperate Continent and remained for close to forty years." Reiki Clowne had reminisced. "They were successful in their quest for material possessions—a result not possible in their home country—but had spent the years eagerly awaiting the time when they felt it safe to retire and return home to their native land. My child wishing to remain in the area she viewed as her home did not return with her parents. She formed a lifelong emotional bond with me which, surprisingly, didn't fade as the shackles of maturity clanked shut. The stifling aura's extending from the majority of Threanoids was enough to puncture even my most resilient outer layers but my little girl—I always think of her in those fond parental terms even though she was 95 Threan years when she passed—was one of the exceptions. She didn't fall prey to the generally accepted standards of existence. Never relegated to 'storage' as so many toys were I was always out where the action was—usually her living room. I learned a great deal about perception and perspective just as did you in your most memorable lifetime; I applaud your choice of Threan forms." Reiki Clowne had bowed his head towards Mort.

Turning from the Environment Mort drew deeply on his ever-present pipe sending the sweet smelling smoke wafting through the air as he resumed walking to his bedchamber.

35.

Oscáre Tarjáy raised his hoof saluting the insignia of a thistle carved into the arc above his bedchamber's entrance. Inscribed beside it the five Reiki principles offered guidance. Just for today I will not worry, just for today I will not be angry, just for today I will give thanks for my many blessings, just for today I will do my work honestly, and just for today I will be kind to every living thing.

Inside a feather bed mattress covered with a light cotton blanket headed by several feather pillows, each skirted with a sham of lilacs cascading on a light blue background, topped a bed frame snuggled in an alcove.

Oscáre's brief interlude in the kitchen to make sure all was in order and to put the dinner's custard in the Chiller—or refrigerator depending upon terminology familiarity—had caused Reiki Clowne, who shared the room with his partner, to arrive first. Sitting on one of the chairs fashioned from wood and cloth, resembling in design Oscáre's chair in the Monitor Chamber, he was playing his drum when Oscáre entered. Settling into another chair, this one a rainbow of colors, Oscáre joined in with a drum fashioned also from a hollow tree but featuring a horizontal opening—rather than topped with goatskin—which when struck with a specialized wooden stick released deep resonating notes. They often formed just such a relaxing duet before retiring to bed, meditation or initiating an important conversation.

After several minutes of playing Oscáre, putting his drum aside, leaned back against the lavender upper pillow of his chair. "I believe I will meditate a little before resting. It always helps to clear the mind for the proper thinking."

"Yes, I'm anxious to do the best in this situation as well. Guidance often comes to me while I sleep. When I wake up the answers are present in my conscious mind ready for access." Reiki

Clowne answered climbing under the top moss green cover. A deep sigh signaled his entrance into the tranquil realm preceding sleep.

Oscáre's hooves relaxed into his lap as he went deeper and deeper into a meditative state. An hour passed before he too climbed under the cover.

Mort passing the open entrance on his way to his own quarters, smiled as he looked in. His domicile didn't contain the type of accoutrements found in Oscáre and Reiki Clowne's, their taste exemplifying the flowery genteel drapes, soft colors, art works from different galaxies, eclectic look. His collection of musical instruments drums, flutes and stringed instruments from various interplanetary cultures placed with artistic as well as accessibility considerations in mind adorned as well.

In deference to the life he held so dear on Threa, Mort had decorated his room in a more austere manner. Saddle blankets with geometric designs, colorful ponchos and artwork portraying dusty villages, farming and celebrations enhanced floor and walls. His bed a hammock hung against the far wall—a sheet dangled from one of the hooks embedded in the rock—sported colors of brown, white and beige. Each side festooned with lacy decoration, geometric designs woven into the cotton masterpiece, it was an art form in its own right. A small chiminea, candles and a packed bookcase surrounded a leather well padded easy chair. Mort headed to the one divergence from the austerity of his favorite past life.

36.

As the Caretakers rested and contemplated, two very weary adolescent chimps trudged the tunnels. Their homeward course wending past many of the Environments, among them the sections devoted to desert dwellers. Within the general desert Environment quadrants mimicking the conditions unique to regions such as the Narahas, Ibog and Thaed Valley zones flourished. Temperatures, ratio of daylight hours to nighttime, desiccation levels, elevation above or below sea level—all atmospheric and terrestrial conditions duplicated as they'd once existed on the Surface—provided home for indigenous desert plant and animal life. All the general Environments were similarly delineated by zonal characteristics and with operating principles based on recycling existing resources maintaining the divergent climatic environs housed within Euroswydd's Caverns required little effort.

While the water and air, even at the great depth that Euroswydd's Caverns had been built, had been easily acquired and recycled from existing sources, light production had been a more challenging proposition.

The resulting two modes of light production operating within the Cavern system while in one sense contrived, still took advantage of Threa's natural processes. Incandescent lighting principles were used to form the self-luminescent suns and stars providing the specific light, heat and ambience particular to each Environment. The energy for this production coming from the heat emitted from naturally occurring chemical reactions within the hypothermal vents located below Euroswydd's Caverns.

Bioluminescent bacteria serviced those areas simply needing light to facilitate visual acuity. These bacteria, living within the thin transparent walls of their host—sedentary creatures who once permanently attached to a substrate extract food in the form of waste particles floating in the air around it—gave off a cool form of illumination. This is not to say that the color didn't give one a feeling of warmth, simply that the chemical reaction occurring didn't require the same energy expenditure or release as incandescent illumination.

Used as they now were to all the varied wonders visible through the protective entryways, the two chimps didn't take in the fresh blanket of snow covering the Snayalamihs, walking obliviously by the jagged peaks sparkling white powdery puff balls in the moonlight.

Eventually passing through the membrane separating their home Environment from the connecting tunnel they headed directly to their sleeping quarters. Soon only the nocturnal Beings and Shadows pursued an active agenda.

Microcosms develop
With each passing concept
A solution rises to an issue
Meeting resolution in perseverance

9

HOW BEST TO GO ABOUT IT

37.

Mort murmured his morning greetings to the four corners of the Planet—North, South, East and West before bowing to the Central Core of all Being within Threa. Then, lifting his head he expanded his scope beyond the Planet's circumference greeting the extremities of the Universe before continuing his rising rituals with some yoga—though carved wood in appearance his bones were viable tissue needing limbering along with his mind—then neatened his quarters before leaving for the kitchen. Passing Reiki Clowne and Oscáre's room he poked his head in to see how their morning ablutions were progressing.

"Ah, Mort do come in. We are just finished with the morning meditations and the greetings. As soon as we make the bed we will be ready to go to the kitchen where I will prepare the break to our fast." Sweeping Mort into a chair Oscáre turned, lifting his cooking shirt from its overnight storage peg and glancing at Reiki Clowne, busy pulling the coverlet over the bed.

"Have you arrived at any conclusions regarding the problem Euroswydd told us about yesterday?" Oscáre asked Mort as passing the Subtropical then Tropical Environments the three Caretakers glanced through the clear portal membranes.

"Look at that will you." Reiki Clowne nodded towards a family of panthers, the little ones tumbling head over tail under the ministrations of their mother's rough pink tongue.

Laughing Mort said, "It's nice to see so many of the animals that were on the brink of extinction doing so well here."

"*Oui, absolument.*"

Once in the kitchen they each set about their breakfast making tasks.

"I think we need to find out more about what's causing this blip." Mort said, belatedly responding to Oscáre's question.

"Yes." Reiki Clowne looked briefly at Mort before returning his attention to the coffee grinder, "Yes, I too agree that we need to ascertain the reason behind the aberrant message being received by Euroswydd."

"*Oui, oui mais je suis absolument* sure that we must not make ourselves known in the process." Oscáre took the procedure of providing nutrition in a tasteful and healthful way seriously, putting his whole mind and body into the task. If the toast wasn't perfect he would become quite perturbed. Reiki Clowne and Mort always amused at their friend's preoccupation with providing the perfectly executed meal usually performed their pre-breakfast tasks as unobtrusively as possible. Once everything was on the table and the three were eating he reliably returned to his usual vivacious, interactive self. "Perhaps we can *fini le conversation* at the breakfast table so that I don't do the irreparable damage to these omelets?"

Smiling at each other Mort and Reiki Clowne bent silently to their tasks, Reiki Clowne's stocking cap bobbing with his head movements.

Adept at juggling the slicing, dicing, mixing, pouring, flipping and subsequent serving all while toasting bread to golden perfection and crisping soy bacon on his six burner professional grade stove, Oscáre's immediate attention was riveted on his special omelet pans whose design enabled him to serve all three omelets in unison. The distinctive scents of oregano, sage, thyme and coriander mixed with the smoked goat cheese melting into the beaten eggs becoming omelets wafted enticingly around the kitchen.

Soon they were dining at the table carved from sandstone complete with indentations securing cups, saucers, plates, bowls, silverware and glasses should a particularly severe quake manifest. Designed to interface with the native rock, chairs of limestone comfortably supported each Caretaker's unique body configuration.

Pulling out his tobacco pouch, the reddish brown leather worn to a comforting suppleness, Mort prepared his after meal pipe. The mixture, a self-created recipe of herbs, included comfrey, bone knit, pau d'arco and parsley, relaxed, wasn't addictive and provided necessary vitamins and minerals to keep his bones in good shape. Smoking his pipe was as necessary to Mort's existence in his present capacity as eating a nutritious meal. Oscáre made sure that his ever-present "tobacco" mixture was properly and freshly prepared.

"So . . . we are in agreement . . . the cause of the readings that Euroswydd has been receiving needs our attention. How do we go about it? We certainly can't leave this Complex until the Upheavals are completed and we can't access the Station without breaking our word regarding noninvolvement." Smoked plumed from his pipe.

"Is there no way we can look through a monitor at the Chamber to see exactly what is going on there? I know we promised noninvolvement but how is merely looking breaking that vow?" Reiki Clowne displayed determination in his knitted body language. "We can't ignore the possibility that there are energy Beings there. Whether they are good ones or bad we are responsible for the welfare of those housed within this Complex. If somehow there are Beings at the other Complex and they figure a way of finding out that we are here, all the lifeforms we are safeguarding may be in peril. We also gave our word that we would keep them viable until Threa cleanses herself. It's our responsibility to find out what is going on up in that Satellite Station. Another possibility, albeit it a very dim one, is that Beings from another Planet are infiltrating Threa. Remember when we had to deal with the Krell on our Planet? There's always the chance that radicals such as they could be problematic."

"Ah yes my dear partner, you are as usual *absolument* correct," Oscáre glanced soft eyed at Reiki Clowne. "We will clean up after our breakfast meal then go to our meeting with Euroswydd."

"All we have to do is find a way." Rising Mort put his pipe away before clearing the table. Reiki Clowne rinsed plates and Oscáre placed them in the dishwater. The geothermal vents beneath the Complex provided them the hot water needed to wash the dishes and the steam to power the dishwater from cycle to cycle. Mort's cold process soaps cleaned everything from dishes to clothes to their own bodies. Loofa plants grew in the Terrestrial Environment and for gentler cleaning sponges were procured by the sea life and given to the Caretakers on an as needed basis. Grey water resulting from the dishwashing cycles, siphoned off into a holding tank placed above the Complex, allowed for the addition of water to any system needing it simply by letting gravity have its way. Coming into the Caverns then seeping through the layers beneath allowed for filtration and cleansing before the cycle began anew.

Using hair donated by the Threan animals, linens, towels, clothes and other fabrics had been woven and fashioned by the inhabitants of Casyo. None of it had been shaved, stripped, scalped or otherwise "stolen" as the animals felt it had been in previous times. No trees were destroyed for paper goods, the electronic equipment came from recycling the space detritus floating about.

38.

Several hours later all three were seated in the Monitor Chamber. Although some cultures might have dubbed this particular room the "Command Center" it should be noted that "command" wasn't a concept nor a word used among the Casyoan Beings. An individual or group might provide encouragement or information regarding a project by virtue of expertise, but it was by no means similar to the competition or way of being "better" than another that the Threans put such stock in. Euroswydd, Mort, Reiki Clowne and Oscáre were on equal footing, each with their own tasks to perform, respectful of each others talents, thoughts and processes. Recognition of one another's idiosyncrasies enhanced the experience rather than offering leverage for abuse.

Euroswydd's grey, spectacled face appeared on the screen exactly twenty-four hours after initially sharing the discovery of aberrant readings coming from the Planet's Surface.

"Hi ya'll! Very good, same Bat Time same Bat Channel." Chuckling and shaking his head, "Why did those Threan's occupying the southeastern regions of the Northern Temperate Continent refer to each other as large sailing vessels? Anyway I'm glad you could all be here." Euroswydd's muzzle nodded to each of them.
"I really do miss your physical proximities. Digital transmissions aren't the same."

"No they're not. We miss you too." Reiki Clowne spoke for them all. "Have you come up with any thoughts in relation to our conversation of yesterday? We three agree that it's necessary to find out what is going on at that Satellite Station while preserving the sanctity of our agreement with Mother Threa."

"Good, I concur. Any suggestions on how to do that?"

"First let's figure out exactly what we need to accomplish." Mort spoke up first.

"*Vraiment*, we must set up the parameters for what we hope to accomplish leaving the room for the change." Oscáre chimed in.
"There are many unknowns."

"I will type out our conclusions." Reiki Clowne said adjusting the glasses balancing on his nose. The frames, golden in color and spun from silk, were light as a feather. He loved typing in his slow, precise way on his old Underwood typewriter. There was, he maintained to skeptics, such exquisite symmetry and balanced process in the undertaking. The distinctive aroma of the ink, clanking keys, ringing bell and whoosh of the carriage returning brought life to the recording process in a way no digitalized advancement could. Bowing to others sense of time constraints Reiki Clowne saved the treat for meetings with his three friends, none of whom minded a leisurely pace.

"Thank you. So Oscáre what scenario do you think we should follow?" Euroswydd asked.

"First we need to establish the link with the Satellite Station contained in the offshore Caverns. We need to do so for the purposes of ascertaining whether the signal beacon there has been activated due to the Threan intervention—or some other living Beings—or the natural phenomenon. We need to do this in a way that will not interfere with the chores of Mother Threa and the Cleansings and in such a way that if there are the Threan life forms within that facility they do not become aware of our existence. We need to be able to get the signal into the facility and to establish the link between it and do so in the way that arouses no suspicions," Oscáre nodded towards Euroswydd's image, "since it is not possible to do this from Casyo."

"There's no way of getting a signal through the turmoil without interfering and possibly making our presence or that of our Planet known. And before you ask," Euroswydd nodded smiling at Mort, "because of the current Upheavals and our oath to not interfere with Threa in any way we can't bend space or in this instance water to form our version of what the Threans would call tunnels, bridges or what have you to expedite passage on their terrestrial superhighways or interstates shortening what would otherwise be an overwhelming travel distance." He paused shaking his head, "Of course our higher vibrational levels and knowledge of different spatial dimensions allows us to make use of the intergalactic 'interstate' when traveling through Space. The Threan scientists had hypothesized a 'bending' of space to form 'wormholes' allowing for expedited travel, but they barely cracked the tip of the conceptual iceberg. If we tried to use the principles of acceleration and/or deceleration of time in dimensions that are beyond their ability to consciously perceive or understand it could be tantamount to opening a Pandora's Box."

"This is a very delicate situation isn't it?" Reiki Clowne taking a moment from his typing commented, "It's too bad we can't send a sea life form out with a periscope and ask them to peer into the Cavern then tell us what they see."

The friends looked at each other, eyebrows raising, smiles gradually relaxing their faces.

"Interesting concept, maybe we can do something like that. Instead of creating a vortex access point shortening the travel distance we can cover the entire physical mileage with an electronic link to the cavern and set up a digital 'periscope' able to view but not be seen." Excitedly Euroswydd looked at Mort. Actually they were all now looking at Mort.

"I suppose you think that I'm going to be able to come up with a way of doing this eh?" In spite of the wry words Mort was grinning.

"I will need a little time to come up with something workable. It's extremely dangerous to be out in the shallow areas at this time, plus who knows what's going on in the Satellite area, the whole thing may have collapsed. We must be able to facilitate an electronic or some other sort of hook up without creating peril for any emissaries we might send out or in the Satellite if there are indeed any living Beings there."

"OK, but please come up with something as quickly as possible. I'm not comfortable with this particular unknown. It's mandatory that any threads, no matter how tenuous, possibly leading to our existence and that of the Caverns be severed." Euroswydd's words were clipped. "Anonymity and the safety of our charges must be maintained."

"I will go to my quarters and leave the three of you to finish this meeting. I'll gather you all together again when I've got finalized plans." And so saying Mort left the Monitor Chamber.

"Is there anything else you wish to discuss?" Oscáre asked.

A sheepish look came over Euroswydd's face. "Would you do me a big favor?"

"What is it?" Their voices blending harmoniously.

"Would you get your instruments and play? I miss our weekly circles. I've got my djun djun right over there," His face disappeared from the screen then reappeared, an approximately three foot by two foot hollow wooden cylinder, each end of which was covered with a piece of goatskin—all the drumheads had been donated by goats participating in a program similar to the Threanoids post death organ donation program—pulled tight by rope which extending end to end was attached to the metal hoops holding the paper thin skins in place, hanging from his neck.

"We'll be right back with our instruments." Reiki Clowne and Oscáre went to their room and returned with a djembe and Oscáre's favorite drum. The three friends played for about half and hour before closing the transmission.

39.

From Mort's Diary

I need to come up with a way of using the capacity of water to carry a signal to the Satellite Station. Cell phone towers, satellite dishes, any wave length conveyor of that sort is long out of commission and even if any were still functioning there's a chance that our signal would be picked up by someone we'd rather didn't know of our existence. So it's got to be sent through the water perhaps using water as the conduit. But how will I get it to the Cavern without it being detected? I wonder if there's any possibility of sending it through the ocean floor. Maybe the substrata can be used as a medium to send the signal but then what kind of signal? I'm going to have to do some research on this. I will go to the library and access information.

According to what I've found in the archives all Threan water seems to be an excellent conductor of electricity. Their news transmissions are filled with numerous accountings of Threan electrocutions resulting from stepping in water with an electric source attached! The more minerals in the water the higher the ability to conduct which means Threan sea water is an excellent conductor of electrons and electricity. If a hookup from the Complex to the Satellite Station can be created using a mini video cam carried and placed within the Satellite Station we might be able to access the needed information. Although I'm reluctant to ask any Beings to go into an area of danger, doing so may be the only way.

How then to make sure that if there is anyone there, they don't catch on to what's happening? Maybe we could ask the geothermal worms to help. If they went as a relay team, each group going a specified distance before handing the mini cam off to the next team and so on until they reach the Satellite Station, it just might work. If that turns out to be doable then maybe we can achieve a connection. They could act as spies, sending signals back to the Complex, letting the team know what's going on. They could be the "periscopes". Even if they were seen there's little chance they'd be viewed with suspicion. Best case scenario they'd be ignored, worse case the living Beings might be curious about them. The worms would have to be trained or what am I thinking . . . they've survived millions of years on this Planet, much longer than any of the life forms we are trying to keep alive. They can tell us a thing or two about survival and getting things done.

I know they can certainly survive conditions considered harsh by some but I wonder how that translates to conditions that might be seen as harsh to them. Equipped as they are for life at the bottom of the ocean within the specific conditions of the hypothermal vents mightn't the conditions found nearer the Surface overwhelm them? There's only one way to find out, they will have to be questioned.

I am going to propose that we talk to the Worms and other Beings that subsist on the crowns of the Mother below this sea's Surface. Those geothermal vents are the energy source propelling many of our various systems and they are prevalent in this area, one of the many reasons this area was picked by Euroswydd to house this huge Complex. The continued survival of these Beings—once sophisticated exploration began—is directly attributable to the Threans inability or unwillingness to accept or even consider that there could be sentient Beings existing under conditions that don't follow the already discovered and prescribed set of functioning notions. Instead they spent billions searching the galaxies for conditions mimicking their own.

Perhaps these deep sea Beings, familiar as they are with the naturally occurring idiosyncrasies of their own Planet may have suggestions on how we might successfully complete this project.

40.

When Mort entered the kitchen Oscáre was nearing the end of a siege of slicing, dicing and chopping. With two quick twists rejuvenating his drooping moustachio to its usual flair, Oscáre sighed deeply, "I have always admired those that ate the vegetarian diet, but I never fully realized the work that is required to do so. All this slicing and dicing and so little of it can be done ahead of time! Oh *non, non* . . . to do so would mean the bruising and browning of the fruits and vegetables not to mention the losing of the tasteful constituents! When I work with the herbs I can dry the leaf or distill the oil, incorporate them into the foods or cubes to store them. Soaked in the olive oil, vinegars or honey they are always ready for the culinary tasks. I am not surprised that the women dwelling in developed countries were thrilled with the TV frozen dinner. Not to have to labor so every day. Ah *c'est ci bonne*!"

Reiki Clowne sitting on a stool shucking peas looked at Mort and smiling shook his head, "He's been mumbling like this for over an hour now, but when I offer to do some of it for him he said I won't get it, *'comme ça'*."

"Ah," waving his hoof, "you will always be there to help me . . . just your presence has helped me in this kitchen." And looking at his friend, "I am aware of the Energy you have sent my way, *mon cher*. Let me have what you've done so far. The rest can be *fini demain*. Tonight we have the stir-fry, all this chopping and it will only take *une* moment to cook. *Voila*!" Placing the shucked green peas into a bowl he triumphantly waved at the dozen or so bowls containing various seaweed—green, red and brown—peas, carrots, fava beans, slices of young eggplant, garlic, onion, raisins, tomatoes, daikon radish, and olives in various shades of black, green and purple.

"Let me help." Mort didn't wait for acquiesce having learned in situations like this to act, rather than pause for a reply. Oscáre when faced with a faite accomplice had no recourse but to gracefully—for he was a gentleman donkey after all—accept, enjoy and say *Merci*! As he took his chosen responsibilities seriously if offered a choice he reliably refused, unwilling to burden others.

"You drive yourself way too hard. Have a bit of thistle and relax your hooves a bit. I will soak the textured soy protein strips and ready them with seasonings for the cooking of the stir fry." And drawing in a deep breath, "I have always loved the smell of cilantro and you're also using dill and serranoes," a deep sigh, "I do so enjoy your flair with taste sensations." Chattering away Mort placed about a cup of light tan dried out pieces of textured soy protein in a bowl, added filtered water from the tap—the fresh water stored in a tank that had been processed from sea water—then pinches from the spice and herb mixtures that Oscáre, on less intense days, had blended from the herbs grown in various Environments and dried in the desert Environments.

"One great advantage of living in a Complex with every Environment from grossly humid to dessicatingly dry is that we can take advantage of each depending on what task needs accomplishing." Mort looked sideways at Oscáre. After all the kitchen was Oscáre's domain and he could be a bit possessive of it. Smiling and sitting on a stool he was leaning muzzle to hoof on one of the tables.

"Have you finished with the ramblings my friend? I am most appreciative of your help." His smile lessened a bit as he continued, "I am concerned also about what may be happening on the Surface. I do not want anything to threaten the safety of Threa or the lives in this Complex. If there are the Threans in the Satellite station and they are representative of the baser types so prevalent in the past their destructive capabilities would have to be, how you say it, squelched. I do not like the violence, and if the planet Threa has been unable to take care of them, how will we? I admit my worries have caused me to be short tempered with the tasks that I usually find the solace in."

Reiki Clowne placed a knitted hand on his friend's back offering comfort and focusing Galactic Life Force Energy.

"Ah, so that's what's wrong. Once we know what the situation is we will be better equipped to come up with a solution of some kind." Mort pulled out the wok and placed it on one of the unlit burners. "For right now I think we should hold off on the actual cooking. We have a meeting with Euroswydd in thirty minutes."

"*Trente* minutes? Have I become so engrossed that I've forgotten the planned meeting?" Oscáre looked quite perturbed.

"No, I called Euroswydd and set up the meeting. I hope you don't mind my not consulting you both first, but I want to tell my thoughts to all of you at once. Then I will know whether to continue and make arrangements or to think this over again. I need everyone's input to complete the plan." A grin spread across his face, "I have the basic skeleton of an idea. We'll all need to do something to get this underway and I think it imperative that we get going as quickly as possible." And nodding towards Oscáre, "as you say we don't know what's up there and it needs to be addressed post haste."

The tip of his knitted stocking cap vibrating Reiki Clowne interjected, "Shouldn't we do the daily check of functions to make sure everything is going OK before the meeting? We usually do it at the time we will be meeting with Euroswydd."

"*Oui, c'est vraie.* Good thinking *mon ami*, let us go and take care of that now.' Looking at Mort, "Just leave everything as it is. After the meeting I will cook the stir fry and we will dine most sumptuously."

41.

"Congratulations, I knew you would be able to come up with a practical plan." Euroswydd looked pleased upon hearing Mort's suggestions. Then looking at Reiki Clowne and Oscáre, "What can you tell me about the inhabitants of the vents?"

"These are communities of boiling temperatures and pressures 160 times greater than that which was experienced by the Surface dwelling Threans. The natives include six-foot long tubeworms, eyeless ghost shrimp, shellfish—giant clams, mussels and scallops—as well as various bacteria. Chemosynthesis which is, as you know, the harnessing of energy from the breakdown of hydrogen sulfide, is facilitated by the bacteria. These bacteria are eaten by or live symbiotically with other organisms. We know for instance that the giant tubeworms are an example of this type of symbiosis. The chemosynthetic bacteria provide the worms with a constant source of food and in return receive shelter. Threan scientists were incomplete in their research. Among other things they stated that many of the hydrothermal communities were uninhabited. This was a deliberate artifice perpetrated by the members of these communities to keep Threans from returning and causing irreparable damage." Reiki Clowne paused, waving his knitted hand towards Oscáre.

"The Extremophiles, as the scientists who discovered them insisted on calling them, might have used the same term in describing the Threans. The 'chemical soup'—a Threan term—they inhabit, viewed as home and the perfect environment for them made the photosynthetic, dependant on solar radiation method of the energy providing, seem *tres* primitive and impossible to dwell in. Fortunately the scientists were lacking the acumen to fully realize the ramifications, much less the extent of their discoveries. They saw a scattered few organisms and thought that was all there was. The Extremophile communities and social interactions are extremely sophisticated and advanced. None of their citizenry needed to be brought under the protective wings of our project, in fact some are even actively participating in helping Threa destroy the toxins pervading her system. If any sea Beings could manage to get across the waters and infiltrate the Satellite Station I think they stand the best chance for success without casualties. They would be the perfect group to approach and ask for the help in ascertaining what is going on in the Satellite Caverns."

"Excellent, as it turns out there are many more vent fields than we'd originally thought scattered across all the ocean floors on this Planet. And of course all the life there is much more cognizant of what's going on around them and able to communicate and interact than any Threan could imagine. I'll bet they'd be quite capable of getting to the Satellite Cavern without mishap. All those old natural storage areas sucked dry of oil were rarely the isolated chambers Threans imagined them to be. The Extremophiles should be able to thread their way through those catacombs without getting caught, noticed or damaged. This just might work!" Euroswydd seemed as though a kid in a candy shop his delight so palpably transmitting over the light years that his visage appeared real rather than an electronically transmitted manifestation. "Is everyone in agreement?"

Reiki Clowne and Oscáre nodded at Euroswydd while patting Mort on the back.

"Thank you" Mort included them all in his look then nodding towards Reiki Clowne, "While I work on the specifics of the mini video cam I was hoping that you would talk to the vent creatures or Extremophiles, whichever or whatever they prefer to be called."

"Actually they all have names and prefer to be addressed by them." Reiki Clowne quipped. "But as a group they rather like the idea of being known as Extremophiles. I will establish contact with them tomorrow. They've probably gone in for the night and I don't want to start off by disturbing them to ask for such a favor."

"Thank you. You've spent more time getting to know the Beings we are responsible for and interacting with them than me. I've been more involved with the engineering aspects. I don't want to perpetrate a diplomatic *faux pas* through ignorance and there isn't time for me to properly learn their ways in the next few hours."

"No of course not, and it's really my pleasure to do the interspecies interactions. I'll be happy to go talk with them, will you come with me?" Reiki Clowne looked quizzically at Oscáre, "You have had many interactions with them yourself haven't you?"

"*Oui*, the herbs, the heat, the energy production. We have discussed much. They are delightful and much can be learned from their way of life. I have not previously had the opportunity to talk to Beings that live in such an Environment. It is similar but different from that found on Upsala. Similar in that there is the breakdown of the hydrogen sulfide to provide for the energy needs but on Upsala the harshness of the temperature exhibited as coldness instead of the extreme heat and the entire Planet was set up that way, not a segment of it."

"So that means you'll go with me?" Reiki Clowne asked, as Oscáre paused in his soliloquy.

"*Bien sur mon ami* I will most eagerly accompany you."

A time to teach
As a time to rehearse
The dance of embodiment
Transmuted
By the perceptual enigma

10

OCEANIC CURRICULUM

42.

"Finding out what's going on in the Satellite Caverns is necessary but I don't want to lose any lives in the process. No heroics or grandstanding of any kind, just a good solid plan and careful execution. This must be stressed when talking to them."

"*Mai oui mon ami.* I will be *absolument* sure to carefully explain what we are hoping to accomplish, the dangers as we think they might exist and that we really don't have the definitive answers about any of this." Oscáre patiently reiterated to Euroswydd.

"As usual you've hit the nail on the head. Yes, we know very little except that we need to know more."

"Would you like to participate? I know you prefer learning cultural customs through personal observed interactions rather than second hand reports." Mort questioned Euroswydd, a speculative gleam lighting his eye sockets, "I should be able to connect the translators to the auditory boxes that'll be used to communicate with during the meeting enabling you to see and hear everything as it happens."

"If it's not too much trouble." Then after a nod from Mort, "Thank you."

"I'll connect the translator auditory speakers from the individual Ensembles to the main control panel here. I'll also try to set up audio so that you can verbally join in but know it's going to take some creative manipulating to accomplish that before the meeting." Initially clad with the far away look stereotypical of one not fully participating in the conversation Mort's face affirmed full disconnection by the end of his verbalization.

"When I speak with the Extremophiles I will suggest that although this is an emergency and we need to move expeditiously an afternoon rather than morning meeting time would be preferable." Reiki Clowne proposed.

"I'll be on standby until this situation is resolved so if you need me just point and click." Euroswydd said a grin widening his grey muzzle.

"You just have to use the sayings, *n'est pas?*" chuckled Oscáre flicking lint from his shirt sleeve. "Good night my dear friend."

"I know how you prefer mental rather than physical workouts—I have no wish to disappoint and I strive to make sure you don't forget about me while you're engaged in your tasks. Goodnight and *a bientôt!*" The screen visually linking Euroswydd with his companions darkened.

43.

Keeping watch within the zone in question, her mind's eye reveling in a world of sunny blue skies, puffs of white clouds swirled into familiar shapes, a pristine sandy beach, azure sea water and tanned beach goers frolicking in an oceanfront haven, Orla's eyes reflected rather than registered the interactions between the four Aliens. A curving boundary—craggy, light brown cliffs rising to green, and darker brown forested crests—delineated the beach area. Edging between the silken splashes platinum rocks supported black cormorants, grey and white seagulls, terns, sandpipers and white rumped storm petrels.

Languishing in her beach chair Orla's partner refused the invitation to go swimming so Orla entered the soft, warm, salty water on her own. Thigh deep she stretched her arms towards the rippling surface curving into the shallow dive that would carry her to deeper waters.

Senses acclimating from the shocking chill of sudden submersion she reopened her eyes; waking with a jolt. Panic transported her visual focus to the now figureless screen whose darkness soothed Orla into relieved relaxation. Humming softly to herself she thought of vacations by the seashore, vaguely wondering where such a notion had come from and why it seemed so realistic. Her turn at watch soon over Orla reported no sightings to her replacement before retiring to her cubbyhole.

44.

"Are you ready to raise the Extremophiles on the radio *mon ami*?" Oscáre posed the question as Reiki Clowne finished his morning ablutions.

"Yes, but first we should take a few minutes to observe the Oceanic Classroom, it's right on our way and we did promise Abbie."

"*Absolument*, I had forgotten. *Mai oui*, we will observe the class then talk with our marine neighbors." Linking arms they left their sleeping quarters.

"Everybody quiet down please, the bell has rung." Positioning into layered floating tiers of diverse aquatic species the immature assemblage gradually offered attention in silence.

"Thank you, now are there any questions about yesterday's lesson?" The white iridescent head still, only her golden eyes surveyed those signaling with lowered lids their intention to escape embarrassing verbal scrutiny, those physically watching her and those beholding sights not of the Chamber, lost in daydreaming, the centuries old escape of the classroom bound adolescent.

"Garth," changing an erupting smile into a look of severity as Garth's head jerked around riveting his full attention to her, a mild look of panic on his youthful bluefish face, "describe for me the Zones of the Citnalta Ocean please."

"Well, not just the Citnalta but all the oceans have been viewed in terms of layers for centuries. The Epilagic and Mesopelagic receive enough light to accommodate photosynthesis and display lessening pressure the closer to the surface of the Epilagic Zone one gets. This zone denotes the area of the sea that begins with the Surface and extends downward 200 meters."

"And how many feet is that," the sailfish had already picked her target but pretended to scan the room, "Percival?"

"That's uh . . . " Percival's right fin waved in the water as if doing calculations, "why that would be 656 feet."

"Very good," and turning back to Garth, "you may continue."

"Oh," Garth's gills fluttered, the exclamation in tandem with a returned rigidity of stance. Once more his mouth and gills opened hugely then shut before he continued, "The Mesopelagic Zone begins at the 201 meter mark and drops to 1000meters or 3,281 feet. Also known as the Twilight Zone the amount of light filtering down is minimal. The Bathypelagic Zone extends from 1001 meters to 4000 meters or 13,124 feet. The only light visible at these depths is produced by bioluminescent Beings."

"Very informative and thank you . . . in spite of your apparent lack of attentiveness you do seem to have learned something. Perhaps you were ogling the Bathypelagic Zone with the intent of memorizing its parameters?"

"Yes, m'am, I mean no m'am, I mean . . ." Garth stopped speaking staring helplessly at his Teacher, "I'm listening really I am."

Turning from her now heedful student her eyes swept over raised fins settling on a tautog floating on the periphery of the gathering. "Bert, can you expand on the information that Garth and Percival have shared with us so far?"

"Yes." Bert answered.

"Would you be so kind as to do so then? And don't be a smart aleck about it."

Smirking and looking around as if to see who might be admiring him Bert deadpanned, "There's the Abyssopelagic, 4001 meters to 6000 meters or 19,686 feet; then the Hadalpelagic, 6001 meters to 10,000 meters down to the deepest depths of the ocean which is believed to be around 32,810 feet. We're all inside Euroswydd's Caverns and having to endure this class because our bodies couldn't survive being outside. We'd turn into squozen, frozen blobs of gel."

"Yes, and we're lucky to be here. This Cavern housing us mimics the conditions—tidal changes, storms, and fresh water run-off—we're most comfortable with." Delilah, a young flounder spoke up from the lowest tier. "Nobody was forced in here; we were all given the choice of whether to come or stay and I for one am very glad we came." Her dark eyes glared up at Bert, "We should be grateful not arrogant."

"OK . . . well then, thank you both. Now who wants to tell us what they remember from last week's lesson on the climates that prevailed at one time on the Surface of this Planet?" Spearing through the water the tapered bony extension of the teacher's upper jaw guided all eyes to Hannah, a brilliantly yellow, pinkish lavender, fluorescent lime green, beige and blue parrotfish.

"Very basically the climatic regions of Threa can be delineated into five categories. Of course within those categories there are subdivisions and sub-climates. The five main categories are as follows: tropical moist—all months having average temperatures above 18 degrees Celsius or 64.4 degrees Fahrenheit; dry climates—

those experiencing a wide range of temperatures and far less than optimal amounts of precipitation, moist mid-latitude climates with mild winters, moist mid-latitude climates with cold winters and finally polar climates—frigid winters complimented by cold summers—the temperature never rising above 10 degrees Celsius or 50 degrees Fahrenheit." Hannah stopped, looking expectantly at her Teacher.

"Very good Hannah. Now what might you add to that Jamie?"

The young dog shark swam a brief, tight circle before answering. "Well, ma'am environmentally speaking there are obvious similarities in climatic regions as they existed on the Planet's Surface but each had evolved as a separate unit with its unique aquatic, vegetative and animal life. So while life from one continent could exist, actually flourish on another, infiltration often led to dire consequences."

"And why was that?"

"Because infiltrators disrupted the established system of checks and balances keeping living Beings from proliferating to the point of overwhelming each other. It wasn't possible to retain integrity and mix life that had never interacted before. Such accidental occurrences on Threa had resulted in conditions detrimental to survival. Seeds and animals transferred from one continent to another created havoc resulting in imbalanced, diseased living conditions and often the death of specific life. Given the unwelcome possibilities and with the idea of simplifying environmental control issues as well as conserving energy, each climactic region that existed on the Planet's Surface is housed in a single Cavern but within that Cavern delineations keep unwelcome interactions from occurring." Jamie swam in several tight circles to recoup the oxygen not absorbed during his speech before continuing, "Every microclimate and species of flora and fauna is represented throughout its native region and safely ensconced within this Complex. As I understand it they are comparable to—although on a much grander scale—exhibits once found on the Surface at the more sophisticated and humane Botanical Gardens and/or Zoos."

"Very good Jamie and now to continue." Pausing to make sure of everybody's keen mindfulness, "While the task of creating and stocking this Complex would have been impossible for the Threans to undertake, the Elders of Casyo had tackled numerous projects of such magnitude. It seems there were many other planets whose 'advanced' forms of life ultimately posed a threat to the continuation of their lives as well as the life of the Planet they inhabited. Different methods were employed with different case scenarios. Sometimes a space station was built to house evacuees until they could be returned to a cleansed planet, other times populations were transferred to a new planet. Of course, following a period of rigorous education. The decision in the case of Threa to make use of the natural system of caverns located at the bottom of the ocean was based on practicality—less actual construction and availability. If the Environments were housed in Outer Space the individual segments housing the individual Environments would not only have to be built and programmed in but they wouldn't have been able to take advantage of the naturally occurring environmental elements."

An octopus in the front top tier raised a tentacle.

"Yes Ian?"

"Didn't their mothers teach them how to take care of themselves?"

"Whose mothers?" She asked cocking her head to the left.

"The mothers of the Threans. My Mum always tells me to watch, learn and do just what she and Dad do. That being respectful of sentientness is crucial. Didn't their parent's care enough about them to take the time to teach them the difference between right and wrong?"

"I'm not really sure Ian. I think some tried but there just weren't enough to turn the tide of the general mindset. I like to think they lost their minds instead of thinking the insanity was purposeful. Imagine . . . not just allowing but actually condoning the destruction of that which supplies you with the means to live." Nodding at the assemblage she continued, "The creators of this Complex used every bit of space down here to advantage. The entire unit encompasses not only acres extending along the ocean floor in a linear fashion but horizontally descending into Threa's depths as well as rising above. This massive high rise, if you will, comprises the three dimensional geographic area of the Northern Temperate Continent." Sighing she motioned for Bert to speak.

"What's the point in our knowing all this? Isn't it good enough that we're safe and sound and will probably get to go back to the Surface eventually?"

"No it's most definitely not good enough. Not understanding and caring is what brought about the devastation that has us all living at the bottom of the ocean. 'Knowledge is power' as the old saying goes and used wisely can ease a great many ills. And there goes the bell ending today's class." Bell chimes muffled their way through the watery classroom. "I look forward to seeing you all and continuing this discussion the day after tomorrow."

She waited several minutes for the splashing, water swaying bedlam to subside before, in a now empty Chamber, turning to the monitor.

"Thank you for taking on this task Abbie. We know they can be trying but it is important to reach as many of them as possible."

"Believe me, Reiki Clowne I know. The Bert's of the world do perturb me but by the same token I know that no matter the species there will always be more Bert's to try our patience. It's the others that make it all worthwhile and actually quite a lot of fun. Now if it's alright with you I'm going to go home and relax a bit."

"*Bien sure.* Again thank you for what you're doing and for allowing us to observe. I am most impressed." Reiki Clowne bowed with Oscáre's words.

With a dexterous flick of her tail she soared out of the Chamber into a connecting watery passageway.

45.

"Look Oscáre, they've already gathered—do you think they knew we wished to speak with them? I wonder if they have clairvoyant powers." Reiki Clowne waved knitted hands towards the group of four Extremophiles hovering on wafts of steam rising from the vent located just off the port side of the glass portal. All four faced the glass emanating expectancy. "You know I'd neglected to take into account the size of these Beings, do you think they'll be able to get through the tunnels and into the Satellite Complex without raising a fuss?"

The Conversing Chamber's seaward side—a clear glass portal similar in design to the bay window's of ancient times—bulged from the Chamber's interior, the 'window seat' housing the controls enabling communications between terrestrial and oceanic Beings. A non-invasive series of knocks signaled whoever the Caretakers wished to converse with and if inconvenient for those being called the equivalent of an electronic mailbox recorded and then delivered any message left.

"We will never know unless we speak with them *mon ami*, I tend to think *oui*, but we can spend the time conjecturing or we can find out." Oscáre replied, left leg crossing the right as he leaned back in his chair.

"True enough. Are you ready to open the com and begin?"

"I am most eager to."

Reiki Clowne flicked two switches on the control panel as the Extremophiles bowed ceremoniously. "Greetings our friends and neighbors. We received word that you wished to converse with us. I am Deere," and with a sweep of his tubeworm head he presented the crab Heulwen, Cu Roi the blind shrimp, and Scully the scallop. Each conveyed respectful greetings, bowing heads and gracefully waving claws while Scully moved his blue eyes in a downward motion before returning them to relaxed conversational position.

"We wish you good tidings and thank you for being here. We hope it was not inconvenient in any way." Reiki Clowne continued, knitted hands held together at chest level.

"Not at all inconvenient. While we have spent millennium avoiding those not of our depths," Cu Roi's pinchers waved in emphasis. "We have always been desirous of learning how others live. Particularly those living in what to us seems such a harsh environment. We welcome relations with you."

"Thank you, we are honored by your trust in us." Reiki Clowne and Oscáre both bowed. "We have a mystery that we need to solve and are hoping to discuss it with you and ask for your help in solving it."

"Yes."

"You seem to already know what we intend to propose." Oscáre said realigning his shirt.

"We have a bit of an idea, yes, but would like to be able to discuss it with you at the meeting you wish to set up. Euroswydd will be there will he not?" Deere spoke eagerly, "We are most interested in meeting with him. We haven't had a chance to exchange thoughts since he last visited this cavernous complex—right before the examinations of the Threans began."

"He is most eager to exchange thoughts with you as well. Would what Threans refer to as 'early afternoon', say about 1300 be good for you? Our clock will let you know what time it is if that is suitable for you."

"Thank you Reiki Clowne but your timepiece is unnecessary. We will sense what time it is and meet with you then. We will send couriers to show you the way." Heulwen spoke without visibly consulting his companions. The four bowed towards Reiki Clowne and Oscáre confirming, "Til 1300," before gracefully undulated away towards their underwater city.

Engineered by the gastrointestinal machinations of Mother Threa the dwellers of this metropolis lived in cathedral splendor. Over millennium what was termed by the Threan's as spreading ridges had formed from the eruption of hot lava spewing into cold sea water forming hot springs. These spreading ridges forced Threa's older crust to spread as new took its place. One of the most extensive and ancient of Extremophile communities, this particular city had originated of one million year old serpentinized periodotites and gabbros, rocks from the deepest layers of the oceanic crust. Both active and inactive hypothermal vents existed and over time there had been numerous engineering revisions. Some of the vents were 180 feet (55 meters) tall chimneys, some of metallic minerals, others of carbonates (CO3 typical of the rock limestone). The chimneys contained multiple spires up to 30 feet (9 meters) wide at their apexes and delicate, feathery minerals on their tops and flanks. Unknown to the few Threan scientists who studied these phenomenon the Cities—as the Extremophiles referred to them—had the materials provided by Threa, but the designing and embellishing had been engineered by the Extremophiles themselves.

Threan scientists spent much time trying to figure out why there were such differences in physical design from cluster to cluster—as the scientists referred to them—even when formed from similar materials. While those Extremophiles living in areas of carbonate deposits created the most ornate structures and those in areas of harder deposits the more austere, all expressed their individual whimsical fancies, oftentimes stretching the parameters of the available materials as do artists of any culture.

"Euroswydd will be pleased." Oscáre rubbed his front hooves together. "I too would like to become better acquainted with these Extremophiles. Their physical forms alone are most notable. Deere must stretch at least six feet *n'est pas* and those eyes, so black and bulging from the head. They emphasized the body almost specter like in coloration."

"Yes, transparent and yet not. In the light from the bioluminescence all the Extremophiles seemed to be greyly ephemeral even while appearing solid. And each mimics the form of their Surface cousin. It's interesting the differences brought about by the presence or absence of photosynthesis."

"*Oui mon ami*, at least on this Planet I presume you can say that the crab is the crab is the crab, and the shrimp the shrimp no matter where they live but in addition to the lack of pigment the difference in size between surface and bottom sea dwellers is intriguing."

"Yes, the size of these Beings of the depths far exceeds their Surface cousins. I'll bet Cu Roi weighs at least a pound, Heulwen was at least two feet in diameter and Scully's shell looked to measure a foot from stem to stern. Beings such as they tend to eat less, live slower more relaxed lives and as a result grow more slowly. In reaching largess we can only assume that they've accomplished venerable old ages." Reiki Clowne looked speculatively out the portal.

"So I am to assume that it will be the younger, smaller Extremophiles that will be the runners for this mission, provided they agree to participate." Oscáre speculated, muzzle on hoof.

"I would imagine so, but even at that those of smaller size could have quite a lot of experience."

"*Vraiment.* Well shall we go relay our news to Euroswydd and Mort and prepare for the next step?"

"Yes," Turning from the portal Reiki Clowne hooked his knitted hand with Oscáre's hoof for the walk to the Monitor Chamber.

What to one appears
Outwardly and
To all intents and purposes
As a pile of strewn rubble
Transports another to
Realms of
Awe and respect

11

CATHEDRAL SPLENDOR

46.

"You will let Mort know so he can have everything ready, won't you?"

"Let Mort know what?" Mort walked into the Monitor Chamber festooned with wires and tools resembling the screwdrivers, shears, tweezers and hammers of ancient times but remodeled to accommodate the needs of a digitalized society. Light bulbs the size of green peas hung from cords draped over his left shoulder.

"What must you remember to tell me?" He repeated, plunking his tools down on a table, eye sockets regarding first one then the other.

"The meeting with the Extremophiles will be at 1300 this afternoon. Will that give you enough time to set up for Euroswydd's image transferal to the meeting site?" Reiki Clowne asked.

"Yes, that's plenty of time and you will be able to verbalize. We can even give it a trial run if you wish." Although looking at Euroswydd he continued fiddling with the electronic assemblage in his hands.

"I wish we could but I will be in meetings with the Councils until noon your time. Maybe between then and one?" hope edged out resignation as Euroswydd gazed at Mort's equipment.

"That should work—I'll see you then." Setting his glasses in place Mort returned his full attention to his task at hand. "Come on, come on you can fit . . . ah good . . . now . . . ." A unique self implemented design, when increased visual acuity became necessary he disconnected the nose rest holding the right frame and lens to the left, positioned the spectacles in place on the bridge of his nose then reconnected into a single unit. When not in use the eyeglasses hung, chest level, from a cord circling his neck.

"It's amazing those bony fingers can work with such small circuitry; I don't think I could manipulate such in this physical manifestation and I would think that being a skeleton carved from wood would pose difficulties but he doesn't seem to have any problems." Reiki Clowne commented to Oscáre as they headed to their respective morning activities. "What are you doing this morning Oscáre? I am going to drum for the Temperate zones today. I've not been there for several days. Have you had a chance to check up on them at all?"

"*Non*, but I have checked their readouts in the Monitor Chamber and no one has raised the alarms or tried to communicate at all. They are the easiest of groups. Although none of them really pose too many of the difficulties. It's mostly the adolescents that have created the issues worth addressing and I suppose that is par for the course whatever life form one happens to be." His tone taking on a rather speculative resonance, "I must say though that the patience of these parents in dealing with their repeatedly recalcitrant offspring is most admirable. The chemically induced attachment parents of the single or double births develop for their offspring seems the most necessary component in survival of the species. I can well imagine there would otherwise be many little ones left to fend for themselves." Reiki Clowne listened, nodding occasionally as they walked down the tunnel.

Stopping at the entrance to the dry Neanarretidem type regions Oscáre continued, "Well enough of the expounding for one morning I am going to go in here. I need some grapes and the lavender to make the preserves. There are times when I so very much miss the Neanarretidem regions where my child and I used to spend the vacation time. The soft ocean breezes, the blue sea and airs and the so perfect warmth and comfortable temperatures. We often went to the beach, it was just the moments walk from the house, and followed the white ribbon of sand abutting the water until we came to the cliffs. Sometimes we climbed them, often we swam. Ah the scents of the place—and the wines from those grapes." Oscáre's expression personified wistful longing.

"Yes, I to miss the areas where the seas meet the terrestrial manifestations of Mother Threa as well. My little girl and I used to spend most every day down by the water." Shaking his head, "We are certainly passing time this morning being opinionated and nostalgic—I will continue on to the temperate cold winter zones and see you later." Throwing a kiss to Oscáre Reiki Clowne began humming, his knitted feet and hips moving in sync. Waving after his gyrating form Oscáre turned to the entry way pressing a button before entering through the momentary lapse in the membrane's impregnability.

Moving through the fields of blooming lavender nostalgic thoughts danced around the periphery of Oscáre's mind. Gently sweeping a *Hidcote* here and an *Augustifolia* blossom there until the aromas from the aroused flowers combined with the sea spray brought a contented, relaxed smile to Oscáre's muzzle. His body swaying in synchronized motion to the snip of clippers he placed the sprigs of harvested lavender stems and flowers into the crop basket. Humming a distinctly French tune he, after filling the basket and setting it on the path, moved on to the acres of grapevines just beyond the herb gardens.

"*Bonjour monsieur, Ça va*?" Oscáre looked up to find a crow, sitting on one of the wooden supports for the wires offering growth area for the grapevines, eyeballing him, "Those grapes are quite tasty this year. *Vous etes tres bonne* with the clippers I must say."

"Ah, you refer to our technique of pruning this past fall?"

"*Oui monsieur.* I have to admit when you three showed up with so many tiny scissors and showed us how to use them I was skeptical but it turned out to be fun and *ou lala* the harvest this year. *C'est magnifique*! We and all the bird species here have been eating our fill and there is still much on the vines. I am glad you are taking some for yourself. I do not want them to go to waste." Indeed the rather rotund birds were doing more walking than flying.

Smiling Oscáre motioned to his basket replete with grapes. "I am going to take all that you aren't able to eat and make the preserves. Nothing will go to waste. How is everything going here? We have been preoccupied of late and I'm sorry none of us has come by to visit in several days; I hope this has not upset you."

"*Non mon ami*, we're all fine. This is the best time of year, particularly now that Threans aren't in the picture. All we can eat buffets within easy beak reach and very little competition for housing. Most species have had their lot of little ones for the season and are taking a bit of a breather. The weather has been perfect and," reaching around with his beak to move some back feathers about before continuing, "we are rather enjoying life. So different than before, our fledglings don't fully believe the stories we tell. They've never had a day of real distress in their lives. Of course they do deal with some predation but that's just the natural way of things and it's nothing like before! It's hard for them to comprehend life as it used to exist for us, all the dangers we had to be constantly on the lookout for. We pray they can remain blissfully innocent and unable to fathom the depths of anxieties that used to be part of everyday life. I know eventually we will return to the lands up above," he paused for breath, "but hopefully things will be different than before. All the animal species here have found volunteer storytellers. These will be the historians and they will make sure that accurate renditions are passed down from generation to generation so that we don't lose the skills and lessons learned from days gone by. You just never know when they'll come in handy."

"Ah *quelle bonne idée*. Yes, until we've undergone the severe deprivation of some sort or other the mind and emotions aren't able to fully comprehend when someone describes such circumstances. Please extend my, Reiki Clowne's and Mort's good wishes to all here. We will come soon to visit further, maybe you would like some preserves?"

"*Oui*, that would be wonderful and express our delight at hearing that all is well outside of here to Mort and Reiki Clowne. We look forward to your next visit. *A tout a leur*."

"*A bientôt*." Oscáre put the now full basket of grapes on the cart and proceeded back to the basket of lavender. Capable of holding six large sized baskets the cart consisted of a frame reminiscent of a unicycle with not one but three wheels placed as if on a tricycle—providing a bit of a ledge in the back of the cart allowing for the placement of a seventh smaller basket or package—and an extended navigational handle. The area for the baskets encompassed the frame work above the first and largest wheel. Hooks, three rows of them were fitted onto the frame and the baskets, fitted with loops, handily attached then hung securely in place facilitating easy overall manipulation and travel. Weighing only ounces the cart made from iron clad bamboo exhibited durability, strength and maneuverability. The bamboo, grown in the temperate zones of what used to be known as the Farflung Eastern Continent, had intrigued Mort inspiring him to design and build the cart. There were now several in the various climactic zones ready and waiting to transport objects from one location to another.

47.

Mort had also incorporated the bamboo's versatility to provide storage in the kitchen. Much the same way late 20th century Threans utilized particle boards with little holes throughout to hang hooks and objects from them as well as hooks dangling from ceilings and horizontally from attachments on walls, he used the grapevines and bamboo to fashion elegant, utilitarian and environmental noninvasive means of storing plates, cups, glasses and cooking implements of all kinds. Strategically placed frames hung from the rock ceilings their hooks dangling pots, pans and other stovetop cooking items within easy reach. Others held upended glasses ready for filling.

Each wall's decoration included its own framework of grapevine to which he'd attached hooks and there resided the cups and other kitchen items capable of being hung. Plates were contained, each in its own section, within the framework sitting on one of the tables. Each plate having its own cubbyhole minimized chipping and facilitated drying. Bowls separated by size and use sat in areas all their own.

Oscáre kept various implements and containers specifically for herbal use. The kitchen space itself was one of the larger of the cave areas used by the caretaking trio for living space. Nearly 300 square feet, it contained not only a caste iron stove with dual ovens and a steam table, but a large Chiller, a sink area for general use as well as a separate sink area for herbal pursuits, and an alcove set up for dining.

Each sink area contained two sinks and high rise faucet spouts. The stalwart butcher block, strategically near the stove, held Oscáre's knife collection the handles standing at attention along its backside just as Royal guards hold their bayoneted rifles outside Palace doors. Just as each Royal Rifle was kept in tip top shape so to were his knives.

The cave walls being of rock precluded lots of attachments so frames had been set up to accommodate everything from the aforementioned necessities to the cupboards. Reaching from floor to ceiling these contained all manner of stored items from dried herbs, herbal tinctures, honeys, vinegars, balms, grains, to preserved veggies and fruits and the list could continue on *ad infinitum.*

Into this kitchen Oscáre wheeled his latest harvest of lavender and grapes. It had not taken him long to fill the rest of the cart's baskets, harvesting being the foreplay to cooking's delights. There was something soul satisfying about interacting with the process, being outside with growing living vibrational Beings. Even Threan scientists, he mused to himself, at least the physicists that believed in "string theory" knew how integrally vibrations applied to life. While there were Threans who couldn't or wouldn't believe in possibilities beyond their visual ability to concretely see, there had been those in both the scientific and spiritual realms, who acknowledged and had a glimmering of the reality of perceptions and vibrations. They realized they were only exposing themselves to the tip of the viability iceberg and while not able to visually prove the existence of a world beyond they fully recognized its possibilities and the reality that they didn't know the full extent of those possibilities.

Oscáre often likened the visualizing conundrum to the example of the flat two dimensional object not being able to "see" in three dimensions and therefore refusing to accept that such a thing could exist. The flat two dimensional Being needed to let go of preconceived notions instilled by those unable to see beyond the obvious and allow for the possibility of something "unprovable" except by numerical equations or a particularly enlightened individual.

Sighing Oscáre realized there wouldn't be time to do more than give the grapes a quick rinse and the lavender would have to be happy sitting a while longer in its basket. It was nearly twelve and time for the equipment testing that Mort wanted to do with the unit.

48.

Mort poked his head in just as Oscáre finished putting grapes on their drying racks, "Ready to come see if this will work? Reiki Clowne is already in the Monitor Chamber in his Ensemble. Euroswydd's on screen, he looks tired; his meeting must have been really tedious."

"He hates the rhetoric and what he views as waste of time. Even for such a people as ours we get long winded and follow circuitous paths." Oscáre intoned as they walked to the Monitor Chamber together. "He sees clearly to the crux of an issue and grows impatient with the embellishments some insist upon clouding and confusing it with." Entering the Chamber and seeing Reiki Clowne his tone lightened, personifying amusement as he delicately raised a hoof to hide a sudden smile, "*Bonjour mon ami, common Ça va?* You look most technical in that get up."

Reiki Clowne gave him the thumbs up. Encased in his Ensemble, a bright orange jumpsuit complete with boots and facemask, its black frame securing the incrementally bulging translucent membrane, his entire knitted body was covered from head to toe. Custom made the Ensembles comfortably encased each wearer's unique body configuration.

"OK Reiki Clowne, if you would go down the corridor to one of the storage rooms and stay in there—oh wait you need this." Mort handed him a small microphone. "Just plug it into your facemask in one of the ports you'd otherwise use for a video camera. It should come on when you turn your com on and automatically send and receive signals. I will give you a second one to take with you when you go to the meeting. You will also be carrying a specialized screen that you can hook up to so that the Extremophiles can see and hear Euroswydd and you can do the same." This last was addressed to Euroswydd.

"You've been busy this day. Well done." Euroswydd smiled. "You really love working with this kind of technology don't you?"

"Yes, it's one of my favorite ways to spend time. It's a little like doing a diorama except I use diodes, wires and such like instead of figures, buildings and items that clearly represent miniaturized versions of the living world."

"He is in the position," Oscáre said returning from escorting Reiki Clowne. "He has attached the device and turned everyone on as if he were under the water with the Extremophiles."

"Good, thank you – well let's see how this is going to work." Mort took a deep breath and pushed a series of buttons, apparently following a prescribed sequence as he counted off to himself, "Red left, green right, over to yellow down to red and again."

Oscáre and Euroswydd exchanged amused glances. To the uninitiated those enamored with the inner workings of electronics seemed compelled to add unnecessary complications for their own amusement. Why not just press one button?

"Hi Oscáre, hi Euroswydd and Mort can you read me?" Reiki Clowne's voice boomed over the com.

"Reading you loud and clear, any distortions there?"

"No, but wait just a minute while I turn the volume down a bit, you just about blew my eardrum out." Sounds of fumbling and some electronic scratches followed by, "OK now say something please."

"How's this?" Euroswydd responding to Mort's signal replied to test both the volume and whether he could be heard from his screen.

"Perfect. Can I come back now?"

"Yes, we'll get some nourishment before our meeting." Mort said glancing towards Oscáre.

"I'm sure that I can whip up the *vite* meal. We will see you in about forty-five minutes." The last bit addressed to Euroswydd.

"Right oh, see ya later Gators." Euroswydd's screen went blank.

"He does love to use colloquialisms doesn't he?" Reiki Clowne reentered the room facemask and headgear in knitted hand.

"*Oui* he does." Heading for the kitchen Oscáre announced, "Lunch will be served in ten minutes, please do not be late or you will miss the opportunity to enjoy the Tarjáy culinary treat." And he disappeared down the hall.

Without replying Reiki Clowne quickly divested himself of the rest of the Ensemble and joined Mort in the short trek to lunch.

49.

"We would be more than willing to assist you in any way we possibly can to figure out what is going on in the Satellite Cavern." CuRoi said, as several members of the audience waved their feelers in gentle agreement. The meeting begun at 1300 had presented several surprises for Euroswydd's team. Exiting through the porthole into the depths of the sea they'd been met by several young shrimp who, though clearly blind, accurately escorted them to the meeting site, which could only be described as a coliseum. Columns of limestone carved and delicately structured rose from the sea's floor. Minerals pulsed blooms of efflorescent color, iridian in the bioluminescent illumination. Individual seating—formed cavities in the limestone with mollusk backrest—was located on an area that was clearly a stage. Fanned out and upward the populace of the vent city had assembled on terraced limestone bleachers surrounding the stage on three sides. Columnar expansions of kelp—red, green and brown—swaying ever so slightly with the prevailing current flow, protected the backstage area from prying eyes. Escorted to their onstage seats

Reiki Clowne and Oscáre rose again within minutes as Deere, Heulwen, Scully and CuRoi arrived.

"Greetings to new friends and to you my compatriots." A great cheer rose from the audience, water swayed, claws waved and snapped, feelers moved with the rhythm of the surrounding waters. It took a couple of minutes for everybody to settle down then a few more for the water currents to ease off. This happened surprisingly quickly for any more used to the turbulence of Surface currents. At this depth the water seemed to move in a slower, more thoughtfully sedate manner. Smiling Deere asked for the meeting to come to order and for Reiki Clowne, Oscáre or Euroswydd to begin.

"So you see our predicament. We have been unable to ascertain what's going on in this Satellite Cavern and it's imperative that we do so." Euroswydd spoke from his screen set up on a chair. "If you are able to help us with our plan we would be most grateful."

Not a sound had emitted from the audience the entire length of Euroswydd's dissertation. The blue eyes of the scallops, the faces of the sightless shrimp, the crabs, the tubeworms and other natives of this realm all riveted to this emissary from another galaxy.

CuRoi's sweeping glance included them all, "We can go as far as the underbelly of the caves. There are many connections directly below the crust of Threa as well as just above within the protection of the Ocean's waters. Our only insurmountable problem lies within the cave itself. We are unable to be away from our vents' nutrition for any great length of time not to mention dealing with the pressure and temperature differences and we cannot be out of the water for long or we will be in great pain."

"We've actually thought of that and Mort is in the process of designing a video cam capable of being sent up a shaft that may be able to view what's happening in the Satellite Cavern and send the signal back to us here. It will need to be transported to the site then activated. Now that we know more specifics of your bodies' capacities Mort will be able to design just what we need for the project." Reiki Clowne bowed his upper body to the Extremophiles. "Providing that is a suitable scenario for you."

First glancing at the other three Extremophiles that seemed to make up some sort of Representative Council then up at the crowds Scully brought her blue eyes back to the stage and they all nodded confirmation.

Heulwen rose on his claws and waving to include all the population in the statement of acquiescence he offered, "We would be honored to join with your group in this venture. We look forward to a possible unification in the future between Beings of different Environments and appearances rather than a continuation of the furtive lifestyle imposed upon us. We will be ready to embark at any time after tomorrow morning. This will give us time to map and plan what route would be the best, as well as decide who will be the chosen swimmers. Does this offer enough time to design and build the necessary equipment?"

"Yes, Mort should be able to get everything ready tonight. We should execute a trial run tomorrow to familiarize the runners and ourselves with the parameters of the cam then all will be ready to begin." Reiki Clowne turned to look at his friend as Oscáre began to speak.

"I would hasten to add, *mon ami* that we are also very honored that you are extending your trust to us. We will not let you down." Oscáre rising from his seat seemingly made eye contact with each individual while verbalizing to the entire gathering.

"Our best wishes and we will be in contact tomorrow morning." With that Euroswydd's screen darkened. The audience of Extremophiles rose, floated, crawled, scurried and squirted out of the Coliseum. Reiki Clowne, Oscáre and Euroswydd's screen were escorted back to the Caverns.

"I will be in the kitchen making the preserves with the grapes and the lavenders." Oscáre informed them once they'd returned the Ensembles to their storage compartments and filled Mort in on the meeting with the Extremophiles.

"I will go take care of the systems check. Is there any task we can take care of for you so that you can concentrate on doing the video cam set up?" Reiki Clowne asked Mort.

"No, I don't think so but thanks. In anticipation of needing extra time I took care of many duties while you were at the meeting. Of course if you find something amiss when you do the systems check I may need one or both of you to help me." Mort answered in an abstracted voice, already busy drawing schematics on a pad. "That looks like it'll work, hhhmmm."

50.

From Mort's diary

I've adapted a miniature video cam and placed it on the end of a snake. Not a living snake but an apparatus similar to that once used by plumbers to unclog drains and other passageways rendered useless due to large masses plugging them up. The video cam is approximately 1mm by 2mm and quite versatile. It will be able to record as well as send digitalized signals across the waters of the ocean to our receptor screens. I've tested it using a large tank filled with sea water and I think I've got everything calibrated and working within acceptable parameters. There is even clarity in the verbal signals, something I was apprehensive about. They are much harder to have travel across time and space—or water—and after arriving at their destination have all the sound molecules reform into a clear, intelligible vocalization than other types of sound emissions. The "snake" is approximately 1/2 mm in diameter and the video cam is embedded in a bulbous protrusion securely surrounding it as would a cocoon. The apparatus will be wound up and placed in a special carrying case for transport across the ocean and when the Extremophiles can go no further they can unfurl it and send it the rest of the way through the tunnel system into the Satellite Cavern.

Well, I have done all that I can, the equipment is set up, tested, packed and ready to go and my bones are weary. I think I'll go to the kitchen to see how the preserve making went and have a bite to eat before going to bed.

Rejuvenated by Oscáre's seaweed tart—seaweeds and herbs in a creamy cheese sauce oozing from delicate pastry, my mouth begins watering just remembering this delicacy—I've been looking at the schematics of the Complex done when the system was installed. Euroswydd had held them up to the screen from his position on Casyo and we'd photographed and made copies from the image. It appears a body of sea water has formed from rivulets seeping into the Satellite Cavern system and pooled within twenty feet of the Satellite Room. It wouldn't be visible from the inside of the cave since it's trickling slowly in from the tunnels filling a cavity below the floor level of the Satellite System. It's dark enough there for the Extremophiles to be able to get as close as possible without compromising themselves. They won't be able to stay there very long, since neither temperature nor pressure will be as pronounced as they prefer but by rising slowly to such a lesser pressure and higher temperature and not spending too much time there—just enough time to set up, make sure it's working and then descend back to their preferred depth—it should work quite well. Provided no extenuating circumstances interfere the Extremophiles should have an easier time than we'd originally thought.

I'd really like to be able to establish a rapport with these Beings. They seem quite sophisticated, friendly and looking at the Coliseum and the setup of the stage area, as though they have a well developed cultural personality. To be able to share how they've expressed their artistic bents under the sea using the materials, forms, sounds and life experiences so different from any other group we've encountered would be fascinating. However, now hardly seems the right time or place to bring up such interests. They've had bad experiences with other Beings—most notably those living on their very own Planet—I don't want to do anything that might create a mistrustful atmosphere. After all the others came out of curiosity and fascination but instead of gleaning the information in an ethical manner they removed their subjects of interest from their environment, poked, prodded, dissected and otherwise tortured them. Casyons like to exchange words and concepts rather than bludgeoning the focal points of our interest. Perhaps after the successful completion of this project we can do a little exchanging of philosophies, and cultures.

Called forth to serve
They await mission completion
Pieces in the puzzle
Being placed this way
Then that

12

AN INDEPTH CLARITY

51.

"Good-luck and may whichever Spiritual Energies you look to for support be with all of you on this mission." Euroswydd spoke solemnly to the soon to be departing couriers as Reiki Clowne, Mort, and Oscáre joined the friends and family of the Extremophiles gathered around the point of departure. The com system had worked flawlessly during the instructional period and now in its carrying case was strapped to the back of a sturdy looking shrimp. He and his other young companions, a tubeworm and a scallop rested on a piece of limestone waiting the arrival of their first escort.

The initial part of the journey would see them taking an overland route following the ridges formed by centuries of hydrothermal activity. Hundreds of miles would pass before it would become necessary to drop below the crust and begin navigating the catacombs that spread in all directions. Prior to their demise in the Upheavals the roadways riddling the Surface world placed as they were to—ostensibly—expedite traffic flow with their sophisticated entrances and exists, multiple lanes of traffic flowing in all directions at once, were primitive in comparison to the comprehensive interconnected webbing of the thoroughfares below the crust of the Planet.

The team would resurface—figuratively speaking of course since they would still be below the surface of the ocean—for the final several hundred yard leg of the journey to facilitate their entry into the catacombs that would lead them directly to the Satellite Cavern. Once there they would get as close as they could before employing the snake device that would get the video cam in position allowing the visual and auditory connection to be established.

The Seekers—as they had been dubbed—would be aided along the way by Beings of the Deep, most particularly a species of giant squid. Ephemeral Beings almost translucent in the water they could grow to lengths of twenty-five feet or more. Known among sea dwellers for their adeptness at carrying objects all the while maintaining speeds of twenty-five miles an hour—wisps of tentacles deceptive in their innocuous appearance trailing behind streamlined ghostly bodies, gossamer wings undulating trills as capes flowing in the breeze of the ocean's current—these creatures had survived for millennium, never "discovered" by Threankind. While preferring depths of 11,000 feet (3,380 meters) they could rise to the Surface without suffering bodily harm.

By the time all was ready for the inception of the journey word had spread across the ocean currents that the Seekers would be traveling through and why. It was considered extremely doubtful that any creature, no matter where its position on the deductive reasoning and/or food chain would bother them. Compromising Threa's efforts to return to health would put their lives at risk.

As if the bearers carrying the Cipmylo torch these three Extremophiles and their companions would be greeted, protected and nurtured as they made their way across the ocean bottom. The younger members of each species expressed strong desires to see them, no matter the time of the passage of twenty-four, and many already anticipated recounting their experiences and how those narrations would be passed down through the generations.

First bowing to all present then thanking Euroswydd for his good wishes the three Seekers curled comfortably within the protective embrace of the squid's tentacles, and amidst much waving and shouting glided off on the first leg of their odyssey. Reminiscent of the lavish sendoffs stereotypically seen on Threa during the times of the big cruise ships this was an event of frivolity, laced with optimism and confidence. As the final glow disappeared into the blackness several miles away the second of several squid ready and waiting to pick up the Seekers and continue them on their journey eagerly awaited his turn in the relay.

"May all the positive energies of the Universe be with you on your journey to the Satellite Cavern," Reiki Clowne said, hands outstretched open palms facing the departing Seekers. Agreement with that sentiment murmured through the gathered Beings.

"Shall we head back to the Caverns?" Mort asked, "I'm anxious to get to the Monitor Chamber."

"Ah, *mai oui mon ami*, are you coming as well?"

"Coming," Reiki Clowne responded, "See you later Euroswydd."

"Good job well done, yes until later then."

The trio took their leave of the Extremophiles as both groups returned to their respective living areas. After Ensemble removal Mort headed for the Monitor Chamber, Reiki Clowne to the Observation Chamber used to view the sea world beyond Euroswydd's Caverns and Oscáre to the kitchen but not before a quick stop at the aquaculture station to pick up some fresh new seaweed.

52.

The aquaculture station chamber's walls embraced pools of seawater specially designed to hold the racks necessary for growing macroalgae. Fresh sea water from beyond the Cavern's interior swept in and out as would a tide, providing nutrient flow and keeping the water in the pools from becoming stale. Having wholeheartedly embraced the aquaculture process Oscáre did, from time to time, add nutrients from his specially designed brews.

From the Diary of Chef Oscáre Tarjáy

I will cook up the sautéed embellished rice tonight. We have not had that in a while and I will look for the fresh Nori. Also the Chocolate Irish moss pudding for dessert. I include my recipes as they are my very own.

Nori is the red algae previously supplied by the aquaculturalists of the coastal Napaj province of Farflung. It is quite interesting how they went about the process of growing the algae. First they planted either bamboo or brushwood—hibi—to increase the substratum for the nori. In the fall the hibi were placed in rocky areas where the *Nori (Porphyra)* spores liked to settle and once growth had begun they were transferred to sandy areas for growth to continue during the winter. Refinement of the original natural process occurred as knowledge of the life cycle increased. This led to the artificial seeding of ropes which greatly increased production.

And now the recipes.

<u>Fried Rice with Nori and Dulse</u>

1.5 tsp sesame oil

1.5 cup chopped Vidalia onion

¾ cup shredded carrots

1.25 cup roasted Nori

½ cup chopped celery

2 cups favorite rice—cooked

4 to 5 tbsp water

2 tbsp juice and pulp from freshly grated ginger—always a good addition for the immune system, the taste buds and the possibly stressed out stomach.

½ cup roasted sesame seeds

4 tbsp Braggs

dulse to taste

To begin the preparation procedure place the oil in the pan and sauté the onions first until translucent then add the carrots and nori, allowing several cooking minutes to pass before adding all but the sesame seeds and dulse. Stir continuously allowing everything to reach the desired consistency before serving. Top off with a sprinkling of the roasted sesame seeds and dulse.

Chocolate Irish Moss Pudding (Blancmange)

½ cup fresh Irish moss or if necessary ¼ cup dried

1 quart milk (soy, cow, goat—whatever is available)

1.25 tsp vanilla

sea salt to taste

After having thoroughly washed the Irish Moss—if using fresh—soak in cold water—ten minutes for fresh, thirty minutes for dried. Place in a cheesecloth square and bring up the ends to form a bag. Bring the milk to a simmer and suspend the bag in the milk. Continue to simmer the mixture for thirty minutes. Press against the bag with a broad spoon to help release the gelling agent. Remove the bag and add vanilla, salt and flavor—in this case chocolate. Pour into a bowl or mold that has been dipped in cool water. Chill until set then serve.

I attempt to provide variety using the materials available to me without doing anything unethical. The seaweeds that I use are grown on the aquaculture racks set up for this express purpose. Since we are saving each species in their own environmentally controlled units we do not harvest from there.

Surprising how few of the Threans realized the bounty that could have been theirs. Instead they walked along the seashores complaining about the seaweeds that clung to the shells and the rocks they collected. Ripping it from its substrate then discarding allowed one of the most nutritionally valuable elements occurring around them to go unused.

Most seaweeds are grouped by color, green seaweeds belonging to the division *Chlorophyta,* the red division *Rhodophyta* and the brown *Phaeophyta.* Seaweeds or kelp are considered to be large algae that grow in saltwater or marine environments and although plants, they lack true stems, roots and leaves. They do possess the leaflike blade, a stipe that is stemlike and a holdfast that resembles a root as well as containing an amazing array of necessary vitamins, minerals, and other nutrients. Although the Threans recognized seaweeds' properties and put them to good use as fertilizer direct consumption didn't appeal to many cultures.

While Farflung natives took full advantage of the overwhelmingly positive all encompassing properties of seaweeds for millennium it just goes to give credence to that old saying, 'there's an exception to every rule'. I must admit that my background in the cuisine *Francaise* did not include the use of these wonderful plants. I am fortunate to be enjoying the learning and experimentation process while participating in Euroswydd's project.

Only recently did I learn of the high protein content of most algae. One does not have to acquire protein from the demise of sentient beings, it can be found in the vegetable world and in other ways than the consumption of beans which seem to cause some Threans extreme gastric distress. This is not to say that I am necessarily a proponent of a strictly vegetarian diet, although in this particular existence I am eating as such. We are in the process of saving these lives so that once they are able to be transferred back to the Surface the species will continue to exist.

It should be remembered that within each of these Environments the checks and the balances, some of which include the death for food and other uses of living creatures, are being maintained as they naturally unfold. These occurrences are neither cruel nor vicious as the Threans chose to describe them but just the way of things. Neither good, bad or indifferent, just designed to operate in the fashion that works best to maintain a healthy balance, minus the negatively interfering hand of Threans.

Ah . . . again I am a donkey on the soapbox. Enough of this, I must get to the preparations for tonight's dinner. First I will stop in the Temperate Zone Cavern and collect some of the stinging nettle—it's a good thing my hooves aren't susceptible to its stinging powers—and dandelion greens for the salad. Perhaps there will be the ripe yellow pear tomatoes as well!

Carefully closing the Aquaculture Station's outer protection Oscáre went off to the Temperate Zone with a bag of seaweed slapping wetly against his thigh. Upon exiting that Zone now with a bag of stinging nettles and dandelion greens held in his hoof he whistled his way to the kitchen where a startled Mort pulled his head from the Chiller displaying a somewhat guilty expression.

"I was just looking for a little snack to tide me over until dinner time. You know, kind of like a tea time treat?"

"You *mon ami* look like the little boy caught in the cookie jar. You may have whatever you wish. Provided it's not something I intend to use in the preparation of the dinner."

"How am I to know what you'll need for dinner or not?" Mort looked at Oscáre his countenance expressing exasperation.

"Leftovers are usually the safe thing to try. If I am serving the lunch I will look to see what is in the Chiller but not generally plan the way I do for the dinner. Help yourself."

"You've been recording your thoughts." Mort now munching a burger of textured soy protein, veggies and herbs, motioned to the journal now sitting on the table.

"Yes, I got caught up in it in the aquaculture chamber. I will have to transfer it all to disc. How is the burger?" Oscáre asked pulling the seaweed from its carrying bag.

"Wonderful, I'd better get back to the Monitor Chamber; so far they've changed squid carriers three times and have passed through several densely populated areas. In each Region they've been cheered as they went through. It's quite awe inspiring to hear about." He disappeared out the entryway. Oscáre singing French words to himself concentrated on the food preparation.

53.

Relaxing in his chair four days into the Seekers voyage, Reiki Clowne watched the sea Dwellers living in the waters surrounding the Complex go about their routines. When so sitting he always pictured the people traveling on space ships, the kind he'd seen on the many SciFi programs his little girl had loved to watch. Resplendent beyond those starships' viewing ports passed a wondrous collage of stars, novas, and clusters inspiring wonder and imagination. He experienced the same awe, wonder and sense of privilege soaking in this aquatic panorama.

Beings of many hues passed by and while not brilliantly colored they weren't merely the monochromatic milky grey hypothesized by Threan scientists. A coelacanth, whose ancestors were given credit for being the "fish" deciding to try terrestrial existence, swam by. Coelacanths had tried reestablishing colonies in shallower waters but following "discovery"—the 20th century media had had a field day with the resurfacing of a species long believed extinct—and a precipitous decline in population, had been compelled to return to the depths.

Many sea creatures similar in shape and demeanor to their Surface cousins drifted about. A chambered nautilus, sixgill shark, sperm whale, and a variety of squid including vampire, giant and gossamer winged, viper fish, hagfish, deep sea angler fish, gulper and eels, hatchetfish, fangtooth, tubeworms and isopods of all sizes, oarfish, dragonfish as well as lobsters, shrimp and other mollusks that resembled but weren't part of the Extremophile contingent. These lobsters, shrimp and mollusks while able to withstand the high pressure preferred the colder temperatures found away from the hypothermal vents. Ethereal jellyfish visible as diaphanous veils pulsed through the water, their movement identical to a scarf soaring on thermals.

Reiki Clowne always took note that these sea Beings didn't radiate the constant levels of stress found in Surface dwellers. Living with his little girl he'd been appalled at the emotional turmoil constantly emanating from the waters near their house.

Sparkles of light flickered on and off, swung to and fro. Intricate weavings of bioluminescent emanations indicative of prey/predator interactions. Using their photophores for divergent purposes one hopes to confuse and protect while the other suggestively entices. Light is just as important if not more so to these creatures of the dark, cold depths, Reiki Clowne continued musing to himself. Within reach of the sun's rays light is taken for granted but down here the Beings must provide their own light and a way of creating energy to achieve that goal. And in these dark depths where there is very little by way of hiding places, how one reacts to each Being's way of manifesting that light could mean the difference between life and death.

For everything gained some amount of energy must be expended, no matter who or what is involved. Interesting, I must remember to write that in my journal. There needs to be desire, fuel, a reaction then a result, hopefully a positive one. Reiki Clowne's reverie and philosophical musings took him to the point of almost napping before the great slide of two sperm whales heading downward past the window roused him to visual observation once again.

"*C'est tres jolie n'est pas?*" Oscáre's voice came from behind. Sitting he arranged his beige slacks so the pleats fell just so, "One can't help but feel the awe for such creatures, so large, so graceful, so adaptable to the differing conditions."

"Yes that they are. All these Beings are. Look at how many millennium they managed to evade the crusading scientists always on their thirsty quest for knowledge. I would be extraordinarily hypocritical if I didn't say I understood that thirst but at what price? There are ways of observing and learning that don't involve brutality."

"*Oui, mon ami je suit* in agreement. But for now look at the wonders that are these Beings. They have developed ways of using the darkness, temperatures and pressures of the depths to their advantage. Just look at the beauty and enjoy. Hopefully when all is restored there will not be the necessity to go through a project such as this one again. At least not on this Planet. *Et voila, regarde ca.*" A show of flickering lights ended in something akin to fireworks.

Euroswydd's Caverns encompassed a vast area stretching from the Abyssopelagic Zone into the Hadalpelagic. The Observation Chamber, within which Reiki Clowne and Oscáre now sat, placed as it was to encompass a three quarter mile or 1,390 meters span afforded those Beings unable or unwilling to rise too far out of their comfort zone as well as those unhappy with venturing too far down the opportunity to interact with the Caretakers and each other. For those leery of being perceived as either predator or prey it was also considered a neutral zone.

"Do you think the chemical composition of the oceans will alter enough to change the composition of the mollusks' shells?"

"Ah Reiki you are always looking for the answers before it is possible to see them. We will have to wait until such an eventuality may arise."

"I guess you're right. It will be interesting to see if the bicarbonates and calcium that the freshwater systems have been gifting the sea waters with over millennium will continue to be provided in enough abundance to allow for the continuation of the mollusks and other sea dwellers that utilize them to make their skeletons and shells. Of course if the proper alkalinity or acidity depending on your perspective isn't able to be maintained it won't matter. Although it's the saltiness of the water that tends to stand out so in the mind as the most obvious chemical difference between the sea and the fresh waters, in reality the differences are due to many of the minerals needed by the sea dwellers occurring in greater abundance in the fresh water. The proportions being controlled by the surface qualities the fresh water runs through and what's added from rains and other forms of runoff. Once incorporated into the seas the constituents are utilized by the Beings of the seas to house—as in the case of crabs for example—and keep their skeletons and shell systems strong. The explanation for color gradations within the clam species, for instance, can be traced back to the concentration of the elements that they draw from their surrounding watery habitat to form their hard outer shell."

"Ah incredible, the sensible system. I did not realize you were such a study of the interactions between the fresh and salt waters of this Planet."

"I've found it to be interesting. The ways these sea dwellers have adapted to the encroachments put on them by the scientists and pollutions of the terrestrial inhabitants has inspired my great admiration for their adaptability."

"So, it's not just the Extremophiles that you are referring to? I am most interested in learning their history and if they started out living in the Environment where they now find themselves or if they moved to it out of need."

"I must admit I rather took the Beings that do exist at these intense pressures and temperatures rather for granted. Not that I didn't think them fascinating but having been exposed to the many different interplanetary species that we've come to know it didn't surprise me that Beings would consider what some bipedal Surface species deem extreme or unpalatable living circumstances home. I've come to realize through watching them from this Observation Chamber and occasionally striking up a conversation with some that tales of their history show many of them to be the survivors of ancestors from the photosynthetic regions of the Surface. Persecution forced them to flee and find new homes."

"How did they become the Beings of today? Did they have the means to survive down here or did that develop with time? When did they start this migration?"

"Some aquatics, for example the Coelacanths, had descended before the Threans became such an all pervasive threat to the delicate balance of nature, and there were many species already dwelling in the depths. But from the conversations I've had it seems a particularly intense downward migration began around the time of the Threan Industrial Revolution. With the advent of the Industrial, the Digital then the Great Expansion Revolutions Threans developed and exploited the capacity of negligence to impact their Environment and the Beings therein in catastrophic ways. In addition scientists, in the interest of gaining more knowledge, caused massive harm and chaos to all the Beings of the oceans. Fortunately the marine inhabitants could and did retreat to areas that were difficult for the Threans to gain access to and Outer-Space beckoned and became the popular 'Final Frontier' thus seizing the governing bodies interest and financial support. Of course even within those aquatic 'safe-zone' regions the toxins dumped into the atmosphere and oceans had to be dealt with. These Threans who decried such events as the Holocaust, other atrocities of genocide not to mention the starving of millions based on religious dogma and other subjective criteria had no ethical qualms with regard to causing widespread pain and anguish amongst the sea dwellers."

"Ah *oui*, the hypocrisy of the Threans. A major character flaw. I do not comprehend why they could not simply try to talk with the Beings in their own Environment. They had the large capacity for invention, couldn't they have come up with the means of communication that would have answered their questions and not posed such a threat?"

"You'd think so. And the irony of all this is that the sea dwellers were just as curious about the terrestrial Beings as they about them. They would have been quite amenable to such an endeavor, perhaps even contributing to the means by which they could exchange information." Turning to Oscáre, "Look at these beautiful, sentient Beings—it's so hard to understand how any other sentient Being could be so cruel or presumptuous and torture them so for the sake of some knowledge."

Shaking his head Oscáre looked quite perturbed, "Such attitudes were the main reasons why there was such reluctance to save any of the Threans. Remember how hard Euroswydd had to work to persuade the Universal Voting Entities that it would be the fatal error to not save the few enlightened Beings left?"

"Yes I do, it's just that now these sea dwellers are becoming friends and as such the atrocities hit even closer to home."

Moving over to sit next to Reiki Clowne, Oscáre put his front legs around his partner's shoulders, "You have always been so caring of others. Sometimes I think too much so for your own good. You take on their pain in the way that weighs you down *mon ami*. Perhaps a little of the Life force energy or the drumming to relieve some of the negative energy in your system right now?" Oscáre gently stroked Reiki Clowne's brow.

"Maybe in a minute Oscáre," Reiki Clowne leaned his head against Oscáre's, "just now I want to watch the scene outside this window and sit with you. Events have been so intense of late, we really haven't had time to be together in a relaxed state."

"*Tres bein,* I too would like some time for each other." Oscáre and Reiki Clowne relaxed into each other's embrace soothed by the deep sea world before them. Black anonymity giving way to illumination revealed the continually stewing of life, whirling particles of sand, scales, diatoms and other nearly microscopic sea dwellers. Two purple vampire squid their bodies the size of a pen, their blue eyes equivalent to those of large canines, stopped before the two figures waving their tentacles in greeting before continuing into the silky black beyond. A six foot long, light bluish pink gulper eel with her oversized jaw, capable of swallowing prey larger than her before sending it into her slender snake's body slithered by mouthing a few words of greeting. The silvery hatchetfish rolled their tubular eyes in greeting then stopped.

54.

"Is everything all right?" They asked in unison bluish bioluminescence emanating rows along their belly, "Nothing has happened to the Seekers has it?"

"Everything's fine." Answered Reiki Clowne, "So far so good, we're just taking a minute to rest."

"Ah good," a couple of oarfish, red dorsal fins glowing in the light, joined the conversation. "We will be glad to row around and pass the good news." And off they went, maneuvering their flat, elongated, blue/black streaked bodies as if rowing. The hatchetfish respectfully bowed and with a flick of their fins swam off in their wake.

"You have made friends with these sea dwellers, eh my little Reiki Clowne." Oscáre observed.

"Yes, you'd be surprised at the insightful, philosophical, intriguing conversations we've had. They knew all about the issue with the Satellite Cave and the Extremophiles had kept them up to speed with the means by which we're trying to solve the dilemma. It seems that there are many systems of communication occurring down here and while there are certainly predator, prey relationships mostly it's seen as a means to an end rather than fraught with malicious intent. The weaker or those whose end of existence on this plane is nearing provide sustenance for those expected to remain a bit longer. There is no lack of compassion and they have managed by and large to come up with ways of living in harmony rather than dis."

"Very impressive. Have they given the permission for us to document your findings and pass them on to Euroswydd? Or haven't you had the opportunity to ask them yet?" Oscáre smiled at his friend. Reiki Clowne often went about his business in a quiet, peaceful fashion before presenting *a fait acomplie.*

"I've talked to them about that. They've agreed to share their history and tales with us and I have assured them that they will be added to our library of history and will never be used to try and take advantage of them. They're eager to continue sharing and we of course will share with them." Also smiling, Reiki Clowne looked less wan than a few minutes before.

"This Planet is turning out to be much more interesting than even we'd thought possible. *Etes bien.*" The two continued observing the sea world outside, its inhabitants seemingly suspended in the semicircle of bioluminescent light provided by the photophores suspended outside the observation window for several more minutes before rising and knitted arm entwined in velour front leg made their way back to the Monitor Chamber.

"Ah there you two are, where have you been? I was just about to start calling you." Mort's facial bones looked flushed. "They've arrived at the point of entry into the catacombs beneath Threa's surface. Look." His extended finger quivered with excitement towards the monitor.

"*C'est bonne, n'est pas*? Why do you look so flushed *mon ami*?" both Oscáre and Reiki Clowne looked with concern at their companion.

"I'm excited; I haven't been involved so closely in such an integral, dangerous mission in what seems like centuries. And the video cam is working. I created that little cam. Do you know how long it's been since I had the opportunity to really be inventive for such a worthwhile purpose? This is positively exhilarating." Mort fairly danced around the room, grinning from ear to ear.

"Look there they are." Reiki Clowne had caught the fever. The three Extremophiles waved at the cam before turning it off in anticipation of entering the Catacombs.

"We now wait for them to navigate the Catacombs *n'est pas?*" Oscáre looked at Mort who clearly still delighted with the way things were going said, "Yes, but I don't think it'll be too long."

"Sounds great." Reiki Clowne interjected still watching the now empty screen.

"Do the Extremophiles have the special suit which affords them the ability to rise to the Surface without being damaged by the decrease in pressure or do they possess the natural ability to do so?" Oscáre asked.

"I believe they have a bladder system, which they can fill up or empty out depending on what they need to do." Reiki Clowne smiling looked sideways at his companion.

"A bladder system . . . this doesn't have anything to do with the urination *mon ami*?"

"No, a bladder is anything that contains a liquid or air. Those animal skin wine sacks you're so fond of could be quite accurately called bladders." Mort intervened chuckling.

"Somehow the idea of calling such a vessel a bladder does not appeal to *moi*. That seems to me a most unappetizing association. I prefer my wine to be separated from the urine." Oscáre looked at Mort his eyes atwinkle, "But I do comprehend your point in this matter. The Extremophiles have further displayed their physical sophistication. They are quite the efficient, intelligent well adapted beings."

"And I would add adventurous and stalwart." Reiki Clowne said.

"Yes, I would agree." Oscáre nodded his head towards his partner. "Let us go occupy ourselves with the tasks we must perform to make sure that this station runs at the tip top efficiency. We will send the Extremophiles our most positive energies and wait until they signal us that they are in position."

"They've reached the Complex . . . they're near the Surface and they're OK. Their bladder systems seem to have done the job. They've not breached the inner sanctums of the Satellite Station yet but they're in the cavity below and it does hold salt water." Mort barely contained his excitement. "They've turned on the video cam and look they're waving at us." The three Extremophiles were waving their various appendages at the screen looking quite pleased with themselves.

"Can we talk to them? Can they see us?" Oscáre took his eyes from the screen just long enough to glance at Mort.

"They can see us but it's probably not a good idea to have verbal communications just in case it's picked up by whomever or whatever might be in the Satellite Station." Mort replied eye sockets glued to the screen.

"Isn't there a chance they might pick up this transmission?" Putting on his glasses Reiki Clowne bent ever so slightly towards the screen

"There's always a chance of anything happening but I think they are more likely to be concentrating on picking up sound transmissions than visual. Since it's not necessary to see in order to hear they could cover a broader area that way."

"What are they doing now?" Oscáre had not taken his eyes off the Extremophiles now pointing at the screen and waving even more vigorously.

"That's the signal that they're going to turn off the video cam and start setting it up. We should keep monitoring the screen here so we don't miss the first pictures when they come through." Mort flushed cheekbones darkened in hue. "I'm not sure how long this will take but it could be as soon as a few minutes."

"Then we'd better contact Euroswydd and tell him."

"I'm already here Reiki Clowne. I've been keeping an eye on things and just happened to check a few minutes ago, you've all been glued to the screen. I'm delighted with the Extremophiles, what an adaptive and ingenious group, and what a sense of humor. Did you catch the scallop? She just opened her shell and did the scallop version of what Threans used to call 'mooning'." Euroswydd smiled, his head bobbing up and down as he brayed with humorous delight. The other three twirled to face the now black screen.

PART III

TO THE CAVERNS

Each cell contributing
To a recognizable embodiment
Seeks its version
Of enlightenment

13

PORT OF CALL

55.

Relegating to history memories of stumbling through foster care with no one or where to call his own he floated along the bedrock walkway emboldened with how the confident must feel. His Being, supplanted with an antithetical force no longer reflected the sense of deprivation hitherto influencing his sense of self.

Not one of his Threan companions knew what it felt like to be a pariah. Even the word sounded foreign. Looking it up in the dictionary at age twelve when first used in reference to him he'd found the word described him to a T. He was an outcast, castaway or a reject. He'd just turned ten when his parents decided they didn't want him around. After the divorce neither wanted a reminder of their "failure" as the marriage had been described.

"Son, it has nothing to do with you, it's us. Your mother and I just don't love each other anymore. You don't like it when we're fighting do you?"

No he didn't like it when they fought but he liked living by himself even less. How else to describe what it felt like in that first household and all the foster care facilities thereafter. Even surrounded by people he was alone, singled out by his very ineptitude, something his teachers and fellow students took great pleasure in reminding him, whenever he actually was in class.

The ad had read, "Looking for stalwart boy to become a son. Must be at least 10 years of age and willing to work hard. Good country air, food and devout living conditions. Please respond at RSVP@goodsamaritan.gulp. Immediate opening." That he should be the lucky recipient of this position was the first thing his parents had agreed on in years. Within a week he was under the strict tutelage of the most holy Rev. Benedict. Within nine months he was ensconced in the foster care system, all three of the parental figures in his life—mother, father and Rev. Benedict—washing their hands of him. Gone were the days of warm, fuzzy, secure feelings taken for granted while safely under his parent's roof. Even during the worst of the fighting he'd never thought to question his sense of entitlement regarding their duties in supplying a stable home life. Life swirled, eddied and flowed but certain issues were set in stone, or so he'd been led to believe.

Youth engendered naiveté crushed he nevertheless yearned for the quiet peace of belonging, of being comforted by those who understand and cared. Animals always accepted him as he was why couldn't people? Animals didn't expect him to clean, work and do all those tiresome tasks adults did. Living as they pleased, animals ate when they wanted and didn't clean up after themselves, enjoying the pleasure of wandering over large territories, master of all they surveyed. They ate when they caught something, munched on vegetation, walking away from their messes leaving a little something for another member of the food chain to enjoy. A much more equitable way of doing things than he was forced to adhere to. Why should he be accountable for anything when he didn't get anything he wanted out of it?

"Remember son, you have to take care of yourself. Don't give anything away, always get your price and don't ever let them get one over on you. Ever!" his father's words of advice continually reverberated in his head. And by golly he wasn't going to let them get one over on him . . . ever. The new group of Beings that he'd met in the tunnels of the Satellite Caverns intrigued. Of course he wouldn't share them with any of his Threan friends, the Alien Beings didn't even have to say it once much less over and over again the way they kept doing. His fellow Threans would ruin the whole thing if they had so much as an inkling of the existence of these Aliens. He assumed them to be Aliens even though they looked nothing like the figures seen on the monitor. He'd never thought to ask. They'd been mistreated just as he, abandoned and homeless. They understood him in a way no one had ever done before. Able to see into his mind and his soul they still didn't condemn.

These Beings were beautiful swatches of colors able to convey their thoughts without the need for verbalization. Bonding with the first one he'd met, he'd instantly decided to switch allegiance. The emotional bond with his new friend—Derek named him Pariah—increased on a daily basis. No longer was there a need to navigate the tunnels of the Complex any faster than a treacle slow pace, bursts of energy expenditure leaving him feeling impotent and eerily empty. The vacuum of his discontent now filled he reveled in serene kinship.

The Aliens had originated on a Planet in an elliptical Galaxy in a far quadrant of the Universe unknown to Threankind at the time of the Upheavals. Pariah named the Planet for him but unfamiliar with the pattern of pronunciation the designation had gone from Derek's head almost upon hearing it. As punishment for imagined transgressions overbearing Beings on their Home world had stripped the Aliens of their shape shifting abilities, relegating them to the ignominious lifestyle they'd been forced to endure the several centuries since. Traveling from Planet to Planet had been their lot, each time eventually being forced to leave because of the Native's perception of imagined transgressions—Derek sympathized with his friends' predicament, his own kind perpetrated the same lack of understanding and ostracism—until reaching Threa which had been most promising until recently.

Of course persuading his Threan acquaintances to provide homes for the rest of his Alien's disembodied friends would take some doing, if it was even possible at all. He'd tried to convince his bonded friend of the implausibility of gentle persuasion. The other six

Threans weren't going to listen to him go on about how the Aliens had been mistreated, sent away from their home world and needed hosts to keep from dying. No, none of his Threan companions would be noble or charitable enough to go out of their way to help these Beings the way he was. A more forceful agenda was in order.

56.

The four Caretakers were discussing their recent experiences when the screen suddenly filled with Threan forms.

"There *are* Threans in the Satellite Complex. Oh *mon dieu*, how have they survived?"

"They look pretty scruffy to me. When do you think we'll get audio?" Euroswydd asked looking over the top rim of his glasses at the Threan figures.

"Should be any time now. The Extremophiles were going to get everything set up and establish visual before tackling audio. One step at a time." Mort peered at the screen, "By the look of their attire they haven't seen a clothing store in quite some time."

"Do you have that hooked up Hans?" the woman with wavy, mid-shoulder length auburn hair asked.

Smiling and nodding in her direction the man replied, "I'm working on this group of connections now. We need to be sure that we can operate these controls without being visible. How are you two doing?"

"Almost done fine tuning these remote controls. You know it's funny I really had problems with needles and thread and all that fine small work that I was supposed to want to do as a little girl." Orla said looking down at the inner workings of the uncovered remote control in her hand, "I'll tell you though this electronic stuff is even more minute and yet I seem to be able to do it with no problem. Funny huh."

"Necessity is the mother of all invention. You didn't want to be forced into sewing but this may save our lives. It will certainly help us figure out who has been on that." Hans said pointing to the blackened screen.

"Yeah, I guess so, there that's done." Orla closed the remote control's back panel with a triumphant snap. "Too bad there's really no way of testing these things out before we try them for real. I wonder how Jinny and Lileas are. I don't like that we don't have any way of communicating when we're out of each other's visual range. Perhaps that's something we should work on next. I mean we're going to be venturing farther afield at some point or other and we'll need some way of keeping in touch. I don't think Verizon Wireless is going to be 'hearing us now' anytime soon."

The Threans on the screen laughed and bent to their work.

57.

"There must be more than these three." Mort said.

"Yes and they seem to be trying to figure out a way of getting the controls to work in order to find out where they're connected to."

"I think my little Reiki Clowne, from what we have gathered from the lip reading, that they have seen us and are trying to figure out who and where we are. You notice they referred to 'them' on that screen." Oscáre nodded towards the image of the inactive screen visible behind one of the women's back.

"I'll bet we were visible at some point on that screen and they are trying to figure out who you are just as we are trying to figure out who they are." Euroswydd said, a solemn thoughtful expression on his face.

"So what do you think we should do for now?" Mort looked from one to the other.

"Let's observe their activities and listen to them talking. We should be able to figure out if they are the sort we would have evacuated before the Cleansings began or if we would have purposely left them on the Planet. I know we took the children that hadn't been corrupted yet. I wonder if these young adults weren't on the cusp or if they somehow eluded capture. Or if they were awful and we decided to leave them. We can't come to any sort of decisions until we know more about them." Looking at Mort, "As I understand it the Extremophiles will leave the video cam set up and the signal will continue to come to us?"

"That's the plan. We should be able to control it from here once they've completed set up. As long as the Threans don't find the monitor—an eye of microscopic size—and mess with it we can continue to see and hear everything going on in the Station. I'm sure they're working on the final adjustments as we speak."

"Wonderful." Intoned Euroswydd as attention returned to the Threan filled screen.

"If these Threans survived the Upheavals there could be others, couldn't there?" Reiki Clowne thought aloud.

"*Certainment* . . . but I can't imagine how these have survived. And what to do about it. If they had not found the Satellite Station we would not be knowledgeable regarding their presence and wouldn't be worried that they would discover our existence. Only the Beings in this," Oscáre waved his front hoof in a semi circle, "Euroswydd's Caverns are expected to have knowledge of us."

"True enough but since these Threans have broached our bulwarks, we're faced with a situation that must be resolved one way or the other."

"I suppose one way is to help them and the other is to not?" Mort offered, refueling his pipe.

"On the one hand they mustn't do damage to any of our equipment and on the other they can't be aware of our existence if the sanctity of our agreement with Threa is to be preserved. Since they have found the Satellite Station and displaying rather advanced technological capabilities seem determined to get our machinery up and running we're walking a very thin situational tightrope." Euroswydd continued with a shake of his head, "They're clearly inventive enough to survive, and cognizant enough to be able to figure out the mechanics of the machinery in the Station. Therefore they may be able to affect for good or evil our project and/or the ability of Threa to cleanse and return to a healthier rhythm. One of the great issues of the pre-Catastrophic era was the use of advanced technology. Increased sophistication and convolution on the part of the technology engendered a flourishing of avaricious, self-centered behavior on the part of the Threans. Nothing mattered except the accruement of more wealth to the detriment of their civilization and home world. It's our duty to do our best to keep the possible seeds of that destruction from being planted and germinating again. When she's done cleaning and we return the Environments to the Surface we plan on leaving and letting what develops develop on its own. Having destructive, knowledgeable Threans as part of the mix would be unacceptable."

"Hey it works." Hans's voice boomed over the com into the Monitor Chamber in Euroswydd's Caverns. Eight eyes stared intently at the screen.

"It speaks." Oscáre announced.

"Somehow they seem more real now." Mort answered.

"So Hans are you pleased with yourself?" The woman with the auburn hair asked the man.

"Yes Orla I think this is just about ready how about your end Morna?"

"Yup, all set." The woman with straight brown hair answered. "So I guess we wait for Jinny and Lileas to get back?"

"Yeah we don't want to do anything without a complete group agreement." Hans replied. "I wonder where Derek is."

The four in the Monitor Room of Euroswydd's Caverns looked at each other.

"I'm supposed to be supplying you with what you need and I got hungry so I made us all something to eat." Derek announced as the foursome viewed a rather barrel chested male appear within the framework of the screen. He carried a plate of sandwiches and a cylindrical blue cloth container, perhaps a foot tall with a circumference of six inches, by its twine handle. Placing the plate of sandwiches on a working table—the area set up to provide work space so as to not be working on the computer screens themselves—he swung the water bladder next to them. The bag dangling from his left wrist produced several glasses along with napkins.

"Thank you Derek." Hans began, stopping upon seeing Derek's raised hand.

"I know, you're wondering what I'm up to. After all I never do anything nice without some sort of an ulterior motive do I?" Derek stopped and looked at the semi-circle of companions, their expressions guarded. "Believe it or not I'm just trying to be good and help."

"OK, well then thank you for the food and will you join us in the meal? Ah here you are," Orla said as Mab came into the Chamber. "Derek's made us some lunch, let's eat."

"Are we going to try and contact them? Or just try and figure out who and where they are?" Derek chose a sandwich, filled a glass with water and sat down.

"The idea is to try and reestablish visual contact and see if we can continue to watch them without their being aware of it. If we had some sort of a translator establishing audio it would be helpful but I don't know how or if we'll be able to understand anything they might have to say. Just look at the trouble we're having with their writing." Hans said shaking his head in frustrated admiration.

"The more we find out about these Beings without their finding out about us the better equipped we will be to come up with a way of dealing with the situation. Knowledge is power or so my father always used to say." Mab spoke through munching on her sandwich, "This is really good—where did you learn to cook this well?" she said looking speculatively at Derek.

"I've always loved food and I used to experiment when I was a kid. I got tired of frozen TV dinners but then when I got older everyone made fun of me when I said I wanted to be a Chef so I stopped."

"Well start up again, this is great!"

"It's just egg salad with a few embellishments." Derek looked shy, secretive and pleased.

"If you can make egg salad taste this good imagine what you can do with other dishes." Morna reached for seconds.

In Euroswydd's Caverns the screen went blank before promptly reactivating.

58.

Mort holding up his bony hand pronounced, "That must mean they've connected the monitor to the controls that we will use. Let's give it a shot." Extending his fingers over the control directly in front of him he pressed a couple of colored lights and zoomed in on the man named Hans. Pressing another brought the angle back out and over to one of the corners of the Satellite Station's Electronics

Chamber. Moving a dimmer switch up the Monitor Chamber in Euroswydd's Caverns filled with the sound of the Satellite Station and with a quick downward swipe shut them off completely.

"Congratulations it seems to work wonderfully." Oscáre said clapping Mort's shoulder blades.

"Yes, my friend congratulations, you have done well." Euroswydd looked proudly at Mort. "How long before the Extremophiles return, do you know?"

"I would assume at least a Threan week, maybe longer. They won't rush as they did to get there."

"Please let me know when they do return, I want to thank them personally. Now about these Threans—I suggest we watch them for a while, this is recording everything is it not?"

"Yes it is."

"Great, I'll be back in a bit." Euroswydd's screen went dark.

"I'll take the first shift if you like." Reiki Clowne volunteered looking at the screen with avid interest.

"And I the second. I wonder where the Threans named Jinny and Lileas are." Oscáre wondered rising from his chair.

"And what are we going to do about their apparently sophisticated attempts to figure out how to use our electronics!" Mort asked as he and Oscáre left the Chamber.

Most images pass . . .
From view, from memory,
From meaning . . .
Those that remain
Transform
Uplifting the recipient
To different realms

14

PHILOSOPHICAL REPERCUSSIONS

59.

"What in blue blazes is going on here?" Eyes' black thunderclouds of frustration, fists clenched knots by her side Lileas stood in the entryway of the Chamber. "We've been busting our butts on the Surface, facing all sorts of dangers and you people decide to take a holiday?" Her words blazed a fiery trail through the sudden silence.

"Oh grab a sandwich and shut up. We've managed to get everything done. The remote controls are in place and we were just waiting for you two to get back to decide what the next step should be. Here." Mab thrust the sandwich plate towards Lileas before addressing Jinny, "What did you run into anyway . . . she's acting like you nearly died up there."

"It's pretty bleak, but no we didn't seem to be in any immediate danger. You wouldn't believe what it's like now. Remember all those old movies showing what happened after nuclear bombs were detonated? All the destruction and leveling of the world around the people in the towns and cities? That's what the Surface reminds me of, only there are no cities or towns, not even rubble to speak of. Massive areas look as though they've been razed—they're completely bare. Where there is forest, the trees are bent to the ground. The waters must have risen even higher after we entered the cave for the first time and decided to come down here. They've receded now but you can tell how far they encroached from the line of seaweed and other oceanic detritus with barnacles and shells all over them."

"This sandwich is delicious . . . who made it?" Lileas broke into Jinny's recounting. Four fingers aimed at Derek.

Glancing first at each other Jinny and Lileas simultaneously focused on the group sitting before them.

"OK, what's been going on while we were gone? You're all sitting here enjoying sandwiches made by Derek of all people," a harrumph from Derek, "laughing, joking and saying everything's taken care of." Jinny spoke for both of them.

"We're not exactly sure . . . we did get everything done and I guess we felt like rewarding ourselves a little. It's very peaceful down here. No storms, noise, overbearing rules and regulations, plenty of food and there really haven't been any threats of any kind. Whatever Beings built this stuff," Morna waving her hands at the surrounding array of machinery, "they don't seem to be monitoring it at all."

"Maybe it's an abandoned station."

“Anything’s possible; when are we going to activate things and see what’s what?” Lileas asked.

“First I don’t know about you but I’m wiped. Being on the Surface wasn’t exactly a walk in the park. How about tomorrow morning first thing?” Seeping in, painful exhaustion was replacing the stress induced muscular rigidity from Jinny’s stint of constant vigilance.

“You both must be exhausted,” then prompted by a nod from Lileas, Hans continued, “until tomorrow.” Turning to the other four, “Who’s up for a game of poker? Strictly for chips of course.” Mab, Derek, Hans and Orla settled in to play as Morna joined Jinny and Lileas in retiring to their cubbyholes.

“It would appear as though the others have returned. They seem to have come back from the Surface of the Planet which they found in much disarray.” Oscáre told Mort, “You can’t see them now, but two Threans, both female, returned shortly after I took over the watching. They spoke most distressfully of the Surface conditions and how they have changed.”

“Where are the two now?” Mort looked intently at the screen showing four Threans, one of whom was sweeping a pile of plastic chips edged in various checked shades of color towards her. “What are those four doing?”

“The others have gone to rest and those four are playing something called poker. I believe it to be a card game in which bets are placed by the participants against the possible sequence of cards held by the individual players. I have been taking the notes to try and figure out which 'hand' is considered better or worse. I have to admit I am still confused, they talk of runs, houses, full houses, flushes and the bluffing. Ah, *mon dieu.*" Shaking his head Oscáre continued, "I have certainly participated in the games but nothing like this."

Laughing, "Ah yes poker. In the early 21st century it was all the craze. I also believe in the mid to late 19th century in what is termed as The Northern Temperate Continent's Western Regions. In those days players shot bullets at each other when the game didn't go well for them. I'm glad to see this group isn't so primitive. Losing doesn't seem to bother them. Look they're actually laughing and wishing each other a good night's sleep!" The four done with the last hand were indeed heading for their cubbyholes laughing and wishing each other well, Orla carrying a small canvas bag bulging fragmented edges of rounded discs.

"Perhaps these aren't destructive Threans. We will have to make more of the observations. I am now going to join my little Reiki Clowne and get the rest. I will see you in the morning *mon ami.*" Executing a half pirouette Oscáre waved before entering the tunnel.

"Sleep well Oscáre 'til tomorrow." Mort murmured to the lifeless monitor, questions circling in his mind. Certainly they needed to know whether the Threans were the good sort or the bad, but then what? If the Threans were successful in activating the electronics in the Satellite Cavern and found out about Extraterrestrial life what might they do with that knowledge? What could the Caretakers do that wouldn't be going against their agreement to merely house Beings until they could be returned to repopulate a healed Planet?

Surely if these Threans were OK an exception could be made? The major problem, of course, the possibility that the Threans would activate the computers using their remote control devices before Euroswydd's team had the chance to find out enough about their mindset and then what? Mort's thoughts quagmired in unknowns.

60.

"I'm not coming up with anything constructive on my own." Mort told Euroswydd at the following morning's meeting. "These issues can make you go in circles, one question leading to another and then eventually back to the beginning."

"Isn't there some way we can keep them from activating the equipment until we can gain a better understanding of their mindset?" Reiki Clowne interjected looking up from his typewriter. "Can we modify the video cam from here to send out a signal that might mess with their remote control devices long enough for us to get the information we need?"

"Mess, that is the technical term?" Oscáre's mustachio tips lifted becoming more eloquent as he smiled.

"Yes it is. And you know very well what I mean." Reiki Clowne bantered back, the rhythmic clunks of the lettered keys imprinting paper accentuated each word.

"Hmmmm, perhaps there is some way we can delay their use of the remote control devices by sending out a disruptor beam from the video cam. I'm sure they will adjust but if I can figure something out before they start doing their first 'tests' we may be able to buy some time." Puff intensity increased. "I believe we can send a pulse beam through the set which should confuse them a bit and keep the devices from working. It will give us the opportunity to see how they react. That should tell us something of their makeup."

"Actually this may provide us with quicker answers than anything else. Mort please do whatever you need to do to get that ready to roll. Reiki Clowne, Oscáre . . . how are things going with the rest of the Caverns. Have you heard from the Extremophiles yet?"

"Everything is fine in our Caverns and no we've not heard from the Extremophiles as yet. But you know the old adage, no news is good news. They'll be showing up soon." Reiki Clowne replied to Euroswydd's question.

"Good, I want to personally thank them for taking on this mission and get to know them better. They're truly unique both in the longevity and sophistication of their culture as well as the way they've managed to remain in harmony with their environment. It's a sterling example for other worlds to emulate."

"Ah *oui mon ami, c'est vrai*. They have managed to achieve what the Threans could not. Hee, hee I must admit to the bit of delight from seeing such a turn of events. Those thinking themselves to be so high and mighty being quietly usurped by those considered so lowly. Hopefully this Threan frailty will be dealt the final blow with the course of action being taken by this Planet."

"I agree. The Extremophile culture is to be savored and enjoyed much as one would a fine wine. Whereas their entire populace mellowed and improved with age only individual members of the

Threan race showed such aptitudes to fully escape the depravity of materialism and competition."

61.

Reliance on their own good deeds for fulfillment rather than depending solely on the momentary heady high resulting from the acquisition of material goods proved to be an esoteric principle embraced by few of Threa's natives Euroswydd mused, indulging in a bit of philosophical reminiscing. His most memorable and influencing lifetime spent on Threa had been as companion to a child who'd matured into one of those few and had been held in high esteem and a guiding force by others of similar mindset.

While many Threans had been interested in investigating and perhaps experimenting with such a path, in their minds survival precluded what they considered the pursuit of a luxury. Having to earn a living in order to pay the bills to keep a roof over their heads and food in their bellies fused fear with acquisition leaving little room for what they viewed as extraneous spiritual exploration.

Euroswydd had spent time at many a spiritual gathering in which the participants came into contact with advanced Beings from other galaxies. Probably the most influential factor in his desire to save Threa and select few of her Threanoids had come from his awareness of Threans capable of realizing a higher vibrational reality. There was in those select few the capacity to be released from the stiflingly slow vibrations held in abeyance by fear and subservience.

He'd read the following excerpt from his personal written reflections to the Supreme Council Members at the Determining Conference as part of his case for preservation of select Threans.

The white muzzle nuzzled the food, lips barely brushing as he gently took the shrub grass from her hands. It's a good thing donkeys like coarse grass she thought, there's certainly no money for hay or sweet grain. Entranced by the gentle demeanor of the injured animal she'd gotten in the habit of hand feeding him in hopes of keeping his spirits up. Donkeys are after all highly social animals and because of his injuries this one had been by himself for several days.

Except for that first night she'd not been able to move him other than rolling over and pulling him towards her to clean his resting area. He'd tried to help using his front legs but could only manage a semicircular movement pivoting around his unresponsive hindquarters. Thinking back on it she couldn't believe she'd managed to coax him the quarter mile from the road where he'd been injured to the lean-to shelter next to her house. He'd not protested when she draped his useless hindquarters over her cart helping to support and propel him—using only his front legs—to his present resting spot. He'd not yet been a recipient of the reflective tags that were now being put on donkeys so they wouldn't be hit at night, lying as they liked to on the warm roadways.

He'd heehawed softly as dipping her cupped hands into the water bucket she'd offer him a little sip before shoving the bucket close enough for him to plunge his mouth into. Displaying none of the typical reactions a wild animal enduring the ministrations of a Threan would be expected to, he'd never once shown any inclination to bite, kick, run or otherwise exhibit fear or fearful reaction. Umber eyes alert below his upright chocolate brown fuzzy ears glowed with cognition, empathy and gratitude for the help she offered. It was as if he knew she wasn't the cause of his dramatically changed life. She'd never experienced such a gentle, knowing Being.

No other of her village would have nursed a creature such as he. Viewed as material objects at best and nuisances at worst, plentiful as they were one more or less didn't matter. The prevailing tenet decreed that precious food and time be better spent in more lucrative pursuits than helping a donkey! Those not struggling to survive had the time to spend on such things as attaching reflective tags. In her village if an animal couldn't earn its living through work it must do so as food. Not being flesh eaters the members of her society didn't see the worth of a donkey not able to walk.

Eventually however, as often happens in such circumstances, his system slowed and one morning he didn't wake to greet her when she arrived with food. Sprawled on the lean-to's floor his still form emanated nothing but relaxed contentment and peace. Watching the young woman stroking the dead donkey as she'd so often done to offer comfort when he was alive I'd (Euroswydd) felt a strong pull to return to Threa in a form more conducive to close interactions than my present of spider. On no other planet I'd visited thus far had I witnessed the perceptive grasp of the truly significant and purity of soul interaction that those of us from Casyo perceive as routine.

The Being that had dwelled within the equine form perceived as worthless when measured against Threan calibrations in touch with the knowledge of the Universe! While the most sincere Threans studied and worked for years to attain just a degree of such enlightenment, this donkey understood by virtue of his existence. Additionally in going against the tenants of her village and caring for the injured donkey in the manner that she did not only showed the young Threan woman to be in possession of similar enlightenment but also the courage to act on it rather than give in to societal pressures.

Symbols are important images providing a solid manifestation and reminder of ideologies that might otherwise be lost in the welter of life struggles. Not intended as ideological icons to be utilized by those wishing to accrue power, Casyoans used the forms most likely to be seen comfortingly supportive by the individuals in need.

After the birth of her son I (Euroswydd) prompted her to sew a sawdust filled donkey whose form became mine. Wishing to imbue her son with the ideology she held so dear—that displaying gentle kindness and respect to all living things brings a return in kind—she often told the story of the special donkey she'd saved to the youngster.

Realizing that social interactions during his formative years might create confusing doubt in her son's mind regarding the validity of her ideals when old enough to respectfully care for a stuffed one she gifted me to the boy. Intended initially for use as a toy, then hopefully as he grew a symbolic reminder, I did indeed become a symbol of altruism and understanding of the generally, on Threa, unrecognized principles of the Universe as well as a source of comfort. I was my Threan's constant companion and source of inspiration throughout his life.

For my part I learned to observe without prejudice and apply the acquired information towards self improvement. Many Threans might be incensed to equate their behavior with that displayed by chickens, ducks, dogs, cats, horses or donkeys yet the characteristics are similar. Well truth be told identical. Not all display the same range of features but just as Threans feel there are finite shapes so to the finite behavioral characteristics displayed by bipedal Threans mirrored those of their fellow animal Beings.

Names such as Ihdnag, the Ailad Amall, Dr. Iusu, Asor Skrap, Enaj Lladoog and others were reverently and frequently referred to during this lifetime spent on Threa. Each of these people exemplified the consequences of simplicity and compassion steeped with plentiful doses of common sense realism combined with interaction between their souls and the naturally occurring unifying rhythms of the Planet. While a heightened sense of vibration defined and exalted these people in many cases earning them widespread respect there wasn't sufficient behavioral emulation and modification on the part of others.

The confusing issue—as seen by us Casyoans—is that while on the one hand speaking as if applauding this type of life style on the other, most Threans aspired to and duplicated the small minded, control based acquisition of power lifestyles as modeled by their 'great' leaders. No wonder their offspring were so confused. In many instances, including this, the phrase 'do as I say and not as I do' was uttered by Threans to their offspring supposedly by way of explaining and excusing their—the adults—confusing, contradictory actions. How can forming minds grasp anything but the concrete obvious? And so the cycle continued on.

We Casyoans cannot and would not be able to sustain our work were it not for the continued desire by all participants to continually acquire knowledge and reevaluate concepts. There are, of course, certain philosophical foundations upon which we broach no compromise. Our ethic of reciprocity espouses non-violent, non-tyrannical interactions between species and members within individual species. This doesn't refer to predator, prey interactions and indigenous healthy interactive cycles but bipedal—in this case Threanoid—contrived standards of measurement for 'acceptable' and 'unacceptable' and the contributing factors thereof. Understanding that differences can't be seen as fearful ostracize worthy characteristics but as opportunities for broadening and growth results from such an ethical principle. To end suffering not through domination and subservience to a supreme commander(s) but through non-violence and reintegration with healthful natural rhythms is also a principle broaching no compromise. While so many men and women existed on Threa throughout her millions of years of existence who exemplified these traits when push came to shove they were either relegated to the realms of the forgotten, or used as the craven images that religious zealots so decried—when not their own—to act as symbols which tyrannical Threans used creating a fearful populace eager to comply.

It's been our experience in the field that within societies whose members live on the slower end of the vibrational scale the more intricate a civilization, the more divisive 'class' delineation becomes resulting in an ever increasing gap between those that have more than enough and those that have nothing. So many Threans in their thrill of materialistic knowledge looked down their noses at those who in times past had feared and sacrificed to the 'gods' that surely must control the unknown, often devastating forces cascading around them. Mythological figures were Threan contrived representations of the crash of thunder, the zig zagging burn of lighting, sea monsters, the very water itself, crops, whatever existed that could either make or break their lives. Now that the mechanics of all these phenomenon were known apparently there was no reason to continue respecting the very machinations that supported life.

These functions are not TV's, toaster ovens or phones which once broken can be easily replaced with a comparable or improved product. Once overwhelming Threan philosophy embraced lack of respect and embodied fearful compliance to the deities of contrived wealth acquisition Threa and all life on her became candidates for extinction.

Change can seem shattering and foundation rocking but the measure of a Being is taken from their reactions to this inevitability. Humility—not self degradation and self loathing designed to engender pity and excuse—but the realization of individual fallibility coupled with the confidence to rectify situations without attempts at self aggrandizement has been the bulwark of societies that have stood the test of time. Threans convinced of their righteousness in seeking submission declined to interact instead continuing to bludgeon their Planet's Environments and themselves. The results speak for themselves.

I must admit to a particular fondness of Threa and her more enlightened inhabitants. I gained much wisdom during those lifetimes which eased assimilation of other concepts during other lives on other planets. Recognition of issues both positive and negative became clearer faster than would have occurred otherwise. All is energy; how we vibrate and balance momentum is up to our own individual selves—to use a very Threan descriptive term! The capacity to access the knowledge of the Universe depends on perception of balance.

62.

"Look there they are." Reiki Clowne's hands were limp on the typewriter keys, face turned towards the screen. Extruding from the outer tunnel Threans crowded the Control Chamber before, now equipped with remote controls, disappearing from view.

"I'm ready when you are." Hans's voice announced.

"Me too." Two other Threan voices simultaneously responded.

"Mort have you had a chance to get an interrupter beam in place? This would be a good time to use it. I think they're ready to try." Euroswydd asked Mort not taking his eyes from the screen.

"Just a few adjustments . . . all set. Let them fire away."

"How come this isn't working?" Orla's voice came from behind the pentagon of tables.

"It's as though the signals from the remote controls are being deflected." Hans's voice sprang from just outside the doorway. "I don't know why. We'll have to refigure and try again."

"And what's with that ball . . . it's glowing pink, orange and pale yellow swirls." A rising Lileas appeared from the other side of the pentagonal arrangement walking as if pulled towards the orb. The molasses slow amoeboid movements flashed off after several minutes.

"Well that was eerie." Jinny commented to the circle of six.

"Yeah, so far that thing's not done anything but sit there." Hans murmured, eyebrows drawn together. "I guess it's somehow tied in with the machinery but for the life of me I have no idea how. Let's get to work on refiguring these remote controls. Maybe if we can get them working we can find out what's going on with that ball."

OK's resounded. As time passed, although catching each other sneaking peeks at the orb no one noticed Derek's absence.

63.

The Caretakers watched with interest as the Threans sedately tried to figure out what had gone wrong. Spending the day running tests and making adjustments after eating their dinner meal the decision was made to once again try the machinery the following morning.

"I honestly can't figure out what happened, everything seems OK. It's as though some sort of energy wave or beam or something appeared and sent the signals emanating from the remote controls in random patterns." Mab scratched her head in puzzlement. "Hans and I have reconfigured each remote control allowing for refining the signals in case the same thing happens again. Hopefully that will take care of the problem.

"Any guesses as to what might have caused it?"

"No idea Jinny. We don't have equipment that can sense any of the waves or energy fields out there. For all I know it could be something emanating from the computers as a safety device or something from the rocks around us or something that this Planet is sending out that's causing the Upheavals to occur." Mab's shoulders and palm exposed hands rose in tandem as shaking her head her eyebrows arched.

"I wonder if it's something those figures are doing to keep us from finding out about them."

"As we keep saying Hans, pretty much anything is possible. We've got to keep on trying. If they do know we exist they haven't done anything to hurt us so maybe they don't want to. In any event we have to keep on plugging away until we get some answers one way or the other."

So, what can one divine,
from these first impressions.

15

BECOMING ACQUAINTED

64.

"They seem intimidated by us or at least by their lack of knowledge of what we are or what we could possibly do to them but they don't seem particularly antagonistic. That's encouraging." Euroswydd spoke slowly as was his way when thinking out loud. "Let's keep an eye on them throughout the day, but unless they display aberrant behavior I think we may have to let them make contact with us tomorrow and go from there. That may actually be safer than continuing to thwart their attempts. They may do some untoward damage to the equipment that could actually exacerbate the issue. Agreed?"

Reiki Clowne, Oscáre and Mort answered solemnly and in unison, "Agreed."

The next morning Euroswydd watching from his screen, the rest ensconced in their chairs stared at the screen awaiting the appearance of the Threans.

"We are agreed then, if they get through verbally or we can tell that they can see us we will respond." Mort, pipe clenched between teeth, sounded a trifle nervous.

"Yes, but we are going to be rather noncommittal regarding our whereabouts. I don't want to give anything away that we don't have to, or that they won't guess." Euroswydd reiterated.

"So, if they ask us anything beyond the fact that we are talking to them we are to evade the questions. How politically correct as the Threans used to portray it." Oscáre commented a grin wreathing his muzzle.

"Yes and we could take lessons from their techniques in spite of not condoning their actions. It's easier said than done; we need to extract all the information we possibly can from them while telling them almost nothing about ourselves. I wonder what emotions that will arouse in them . . . fear, frustration, unwillingness to cooperate . . . what if they figure out where we are?" Concern emanated from Reiki Clowne's knitted body.

"We can say that we are physical manifestations of life forms that their eyes are equipped to visualize and that we are from a different planet . . . I hardly think we can do anything else but tell them that truth. We must try and keep the Caverns and what's happening on Threa a secret." Euroswydd nodded his head at them all. "We will have to provide answers of some sort to their questions; I just don't want any volunteering of information they haven't asked for. And be as vague as you can in your replies, I know it's not easy but we have to try." Now smiling, "I don't think any one of us would have been successful politicians on this Planet."

"There they are." Mort pointed at the screen and all heads turned. The Threans were entering the Satellite Chamber whereupon with very little conversation each picked up a remote control device and hid from view.

"I forgot we wouldn't be able to judge their reactions using their body language; we will have to go completely on voice differentiations." Euroswydd commented excitement edging his voice.

"OK, Jinny are you ready?"

"Ready." One after another the members of the Threan contingent pronounced themselves ready.

"Then let's get this show on the road." Pointing her remote control towards the sensor precipitated a whirring as lights, gold, silver, green, red and blue began sparkling on the wall. Mab's reflection beamed from one of the screens.

"Well that's on; it's your turn Morna, point and shoot." One by one the machines declared themselves activated with a chorus of electronic humming and singing. Lights glowed, flashed then settled. One by one their dark glassy exteriors giving way to a countenance of neutral blue the monitors reflected other Threan images crouching in the Chamber.

"Wow, there they are." Wonder tinged with fear rippled through Lileas's voice. One of the screens sharpening from blue displayed the images of Euroswydd, Reiki Clowne, Mort and Oscáre Tarjáy staring intently at their screen.

"None of them are moving. You know we really shouldn't be talking if we're trying to pretend we aren't here. We're assuming because we've only been able to see them thus far that they don't have auditory capabilities." Orla's voice came from the far left corner.

"So what do we do? Just sit here and stare? They don't seem to be moving . . . oh . . . there goes one of them." Mort had turned his head to look at Reiki Clowne cocking what would have been an eyebrow if it had been covered with skin and hair.

"Greetings Threans," Euroswydd began, "My name is Euroswydd and these three are my companions. We have been watching you for several of your days now and wish to make your acquaintance." Reiki Clowne, Mort and Oscáre nodded in agreement, trying to keep their amused thoughts from showing on their faces. As if fish reeled in by anglers the Threans seemed drawn from their hiding spots, compelled to approach the screen. Knitted hand, skeletal arm and velour hoof raised in greeting, Euroswydd nodded his head.

"Might I suggest lowering your remote control devices and speaking with us. It would be best to avoid activating the other bits of electronics at this time. There could be reactions and repercussions the likes of which you might not want to experience. I am Mort." And so saying he bent his carved frame at his flexible hips and bowed.

"Who *are* you?" Jinny asked.

"We are observers and caretakers. We have been in existence for many more of your years than your brains can encompass. My name is Oscáre Tarjáy and this," a sweep of velour hoof, "is Reiki Clowne."

"Where are you from and why have you not done something to help us if you are so 'advanced'? As caretakers and such 'superior' Beings surely you abhor the violence that has been perpetrated against the living creatures of this Planet." Morna feet slightly apart, knees locked, arms folded across her chest glared at the screen.

"Unfortunately the destruction that has and continues to occur is not within our jurisdiction. The inhabitants of this Planet created the circumstances prompting these happenings. You do know that planets are life forms do you not? They are living, breathing, highly sophisticated, complicated life entities that have the enabling ability to support a wide diversity of life forms. Just as a mother suckles and cares for her young, providing food, shelter and nurturing education to help the young one live an equitable life so too do planets provide food, shelter and nurturing education—for those perceptive enough to pick up on the lessons being provided—to those living Beings residing on the planet's surface." Reiki Clowne paused for breath giving Hans the opening he'd been waiting for as he burst into speech.

"Why do you look like stuffed toys and a skeleton? These are body types we used to see on Threa all the time. I always thought that you Extraterrestrials would look really wacky or different. You know, silver heads too big for your bodies or large pointy ears, membranes all over."

"You sound a bit disappointed young man. We don't actually have bodies the way you perceive them. We have reached a vibrational level that makes us—with rare exception—invisible to your eyes. Therefore we take on the forms that bring us the most pleasurable memories from our times spent on Threa." Reiki Clowne waved his knitted hands at his companions. "Each of these manifestations represents a visit to your Planet by this individual."

"You were spying on us?" Lileas accused.

"*Absolument non*, as part of our personal growth and development we spend lifetimes on different planets in order to learn the lessons. We have found that nothing teaches better than the practical experience." Oscáre explained with a little bow towards the screen.

"Learn what? I don't really like the idea that you feel yourselves so superior that we lowly Beings are providing you with insights into how the dumb and dumber act." Orla's left arm crossing her chest supported the right arm whose hand cupped her chin.

"That's not what we are saying. Just as you Threans strive to learn and better yourselves throughout your lives, so too do our people. In order to better help those in need, when we can provide assistance, and in order for those who will eventually grow to reach the Higher Orders to do so, we have to do more than merely read and watch." Euroswydd explained. "Those of us in training for Higher Orders must actually experience what it feels like to be in the brains that perceive events and circumstances differently from ours. In order to do that we delve into the real thing. We find it a much more edifying experience than the virtual scenarios contrived by various cultures who would rather we didn't know them quite as well as we do."

"OK, so you haven't done anything to harm us and you aren't able to offer us aid so why then have you contacted us?" Jinny had been drinking in every detail on the screen.

"Well that's the rub of it. You found the Satellite Station; you're now operating some of the machinery there and you've seen us. We're no longer a secret, at least not as far as you Threans are concerned." Mort answered looking at his companions.

"You mean those UFO sightings reported over the last few hundred years was your group?"

"No that wasn't us. Wanting to disturb as little as possible we did not explore your Planet with the spaceships but rather sent our living Entities within the confines of the various figures and characters already present and comfortingly familiar to the Beings of your homeworld. There are allusions made to the toys that came to life in various of your folktales—for example the *Nutcracker, Pinocchio* and *Toy Story*—but those were always deemed to be the products of the fertile imaginations rather than stories told with their basis in truth." Oscáre explained, "Please understand that we are observers seeking to assuage our curiosity and to learn the lessons. Unlike most scientists of your Planet and actually those planets who chose to obtain knowledge through capture and observation within the confines such as a prison might exemplify we obtain our information by assimilating into the population of a functioning society. We think this a much more equitable way of going about the procedure of elucidation."

"So getting back to our most difficult situation. Not that all this information isn't really interesting, but we have been pummeled by Mother Nature for over a year now, all our friends and most of our animals have either died, disappeared or we don't know what and frankly I want to keep on learning about you but we need to figure out what to do next." Jinny voice stretched thin over the auditory link.

'You have brought some of your pets with you I think, *n'est pas?* How are they faring?" Oscáre questioned them as if Jinny hadn't spoken.

Morna answered his question telling of the group's internment, subsequent escape facilitated by their pets and discovery that no one seemed to be left in their decimated homes.

Euroswydd, Mort, Reiki Clowne and Oscáre looked somberly at each other at the conclusion of her narrative. Interment camps had been set up in strategic spots to facilitate humane termination and ease of assimilation by planet Threa. Only those decreed unfit for transplantation had been left there.

"We have no desire to harm anything. If we have done so it has been in a desperation spurred on by our need to survive. We just want to be able to find a place to call home. I think I speak for all of us when I say we've had enough stress and striving to last several lifetimes." Lileas said. "We're scared; we don't know what's causing the destruction on the Surface and we don't know if it will end and if it does whether there will be any habitable lands. If we stay in this Cavern system will it be safe or will this eventually be destroyed?

How will we find food? You say you aren't the ones with the UFO's and weird shapes that have been sighted on our Planet . . . so what of them? I guess I could go on like this forever but we just don't know what to do anymore. We're scared; that's the bottom line, and we don't know what to do next."

Again the Caretakers looked at each other. Euroswydd spoke at last, "We don't know quite what to tell you. We don't know how long these Upheavals are to last either. Perhaps since you seem to be safe at the moment you should try and live where you are for the time being." Euroswydd peered down through his glasses at the Threans hanging on his every word, "Might I ask, however, that you not fiddle with the equipment. While it doesn't have anything to do with what's happening on the Surface it could expose you to things that are best left alone. Now I know that my saying that peaks all of your curiosities but believe me you aren't emotionally equipped to deal with the repercussions of some of the knowledge contained in those computers. Let's give ourselves time to mull this all over. You may disconnect using your remote control devices if you so wish."

"OK." Jinny gasped out motioning for her fellow Threans to use their remote controls and disconnect the signal.

65.

"So what does everybody think?" she asked as soon as they were alone.

Hans eagerly grabbed the shell, "They don't seem antagonistic but I don't think they're telling us everything about themselves or their knowledge of what's been happening. They may have this noninterventionist credo but I get the feeling that they are doing more than merely watching what's occurring on this Planet."

Now clutching the shell Morna agreed, "I wonder though if they are right in saying that we shouldn't explore more into this electronic machinery than we already have. Sometimes treading where one's been warned not to go makes sense."

"Yeah, where would our world have been if the curious hadn't sought to create and learn more than what was already perceived? We wouldn't have advanced as far as we did."

"True Hans, but in 'advancing' in the way that we as a race did we may have precipitated the destruction of our very own Planet . . . our world. Somebody or something doesn't want us to continue to pursue the path we've been on. It's uninhabitable and while we seem to have escaped so far with our lives will we be able to continue?" Lileas interjected, "The only reason we have electronic equipment to use right now is because the Extraterrestrials left it here. Everything else, other than what we managed to salvage has been destroyed."

"All this *fascinating* philosophical speculation aside WHAT ARE WE GOING TO DO NOW?" as he uttered each word Derek's voice rose in pitch and intensity. "You know that bit about being scared? Well I am and I don't like that feeling. I don't think we can just sit around and wait for *something* to happen. We need to be more proactive; let's insist they help us."

"Look we're totally out of our depth here. These are Beings from another planet, Universe . . . who knows. We have no real concept for what's out there or what wonders and/or dangers exist that are probably way beyond our scope to even envision much less deal with." Mab said. "I think we should tread as if on egg shells and do our best to not offend them in any way. I certainly don't think we can demand anything of them."

"AgggHHH." Throwing his hands in the air Derek garbled his frustrated disgust before marching out of the room.

"I don't think we should make demands of these Beings but by the same token I don't want to loose touch with them. Let's do as they suggested and think up questions and comments that we can present to them the next time we communicate. It's amazing what can be said if it's done in a careful, polite, nonconfrontational manner. What do you say?"

Five heads shook in slow agreement to Jinny's suggestion.

66.

I'm transfixed by the enormity of it all Jinny wrote in her journal. The idea of sentient advanced life forms from another planet is speculation no more. We've spoken with some! Somehow that feat makes the past months seem all but inconsequential. Of course some of that comes from having spent time away from the actual zone of demise, cocooned miles below the Surface of a hitherto nurturing Planet.

We've communicated verbally and easily with these Beings and they seem extremely compassionate, albeit in their own way. I realize that the Threan version of compassion would have necessitated our group being saved from their problems, the scenario being similar to a knight in shining armor arriving on horseback, and displaying powerful control sweeping the distressed maiden away from impending doom. These Beings version of compassion seems to revolve around the concept of caring. Caring doesn't always mean running to the rescue but it does mean possessing the ability to understand and empathize when another living Being is distressed. They certainly didn't present themselves as know it all deities, exemplifying the heavy handed way so many of our kind do.

Of course I wish they would rescue us from our current predicament but we're one small group on one small planet in what I'm beginning to realize is a sizable conglomeration of habitable spheres and other 'heavenly bodies' for want of a better way of describing whatever is out there in Outer Space. Hindsight is 20/20.

Somehow I have the sneaking suspicion that the root cause of the occurrences on the Surface is the result of our negligence in caring for our Planet. Warnings were shouted from mountaintops, disappearing rainforests, asphalt smothered paradises, sludge clogged waterways, not to mention the constant reminders of depleting natural resources like the protective ozone layer, and oil as well as the increase in planetary temperatures. The decades before the final siege of natural catastrophic occurrences rent our land the severity and frequency of major storms, earthquakes, temperature extremes, rapid changes in climatic norms in all its various forms plagued those insistent on ignoring them. Yes, there were safe regions, such as the one that my companions and I hailed from that had been under the protection of atmospheric converters but even those marvels of Threan ingenuity had been working less and less effectively prior to finally succumbing to the severity of our Planet's Upheavals.

This line of thought leads me to another question—is our Planet manufactured or did she come to be through natural selection and evolution or is it a combination of both? When I say manufactured I ponder within the realm of a God or Goddess or Beings from another Universe, Planet, whatever, that put in motion the formation of this Planet— the coming together of the right ingredients, temperatures et cetera to bring about her inception. I don't think she is mechanical in spite of the ease with which the catastrophic Upheavals could then be explained.

Could or would the Aliens tired of seeing their creation ruined perhaps beyond repair press a button, flip a switch and *voila* . . . back to the drawing board? My instincts and words spoken in our conversation with the Beings leads me to the conclusion that this Planet contains a life thread which while manifested throughout my life is presented in such a way that my limited Threan brainpower or lack of experience has rendered it all but impossible for me to envision this Planet as a living Being. Oh yes I have always understood the parameters of life as being something 'familiar' to me. Whether that be mammalian, amphibious, insecticidal, plant or so on. And I understand the theories, supported by much fact, that when substances viewed by the Planet as noxious are present in overly large amounts, imbalance occurs. As with any complex structure once the system of checks and balances is disturbed the integrity of that structure suffers and with continued barrage suffers quite severely. I always assumed that the problems would be taken care of, or that they would resolve themselves in time without my quality of life being compromised. After all the problems were so long standing, everyone cried foul and maintained that all was doomed in a very few years, but those years always passed and doom remained dangling threateningly just out of reach. If the events of the last couple of years are any reliable indication, doom ceased to dangle.

Well that's it for now. I'm going to get some sleep.

67.

"Time is running out. The group cannot remain in stasis much longer." The words insinuated themselves into his sleeping consciousness.

"But what of the agreed upon plan to beguile them with benevolence? They were all thrilled with me and my sandwiches yesterday." Was this a dream or a real conversation he wondered to himself. Pariah had never interrupted his sleep before and just yesterday they'd agreed on the plan of action he'd initiated by being pleasant, helpful and surprising his fellow Threans with food.

"Strategy must be revamped. The dangers are increasing." The words a conscious impression preceding returned vacancy of unconsciousness.

68.

"Their presence is quite problematic *oui*?" Oscáre addressed Euroswydd directly while including the others with an encompassing wave of his hooves. "They know of our existence and that they had been deemed unworthy of the transplantation. Can we just let them work the things out for themselves or can we justify the breaking of the pact with Threa and interfering?"

Euroswydd shook his head, "Technically we should cut off ties, letting them fend for themselves but I don't see this as such a black and white situation. And we can't be sure they won't activate the computers and cause some damage that way."

"They found the Satellite Station to begin with! We didn't initiate any of this. We simply pursued the signals in our capacity as Caretakers."

"You're right Reiki Clowne," Mort said slowly, thinking out loud, "This incident falls into the category Threans refer to as 'the exception that proves the rule'."

'True, we haven't done anything to precipitate this but the question is what to do now? In order for Threa's plan to reach the effective completion there cannot be any Threans on the Planet with any acquaintanceship of Extraterrestrials, electronics or any other accoutrements of the 'modern', 'developed' world, much less any that were deemed unworthy of the life extension. If the Threanoids do wind up recurring they must start and hopefully remain within the standards of the term 'indigenous'. In other words native participants in the balanced environmental community, respectful of the natural homeostatic way of things." Oscáre pointed out. "I think we will have to wait for the Planet to cleanse herself and then transport them from this place to another."

"Sounds reasonable but what about their memories of these events and what if they manage to interfere with this Planet's attempts at a return to health?" Mort asked. "Do we tell them what's going on and try and get them to remain stationary or do we just hope for the best?"

Euroswydd replied to them all, "Again, we don't have complete control in this situation since there are other personalities and mindsets involved. They claim to believe that we are not involved in the Upheavals occurring on their Planet but they do know that we are from Outer Space as they term it. Perhaps we can try and persuade them to stay in the Cave system until this is all over with and promise that we will take care of them at that time. Maybe not tell them that we're thinking of transporting them off the Planet to another one, but imply that they will be safe and sound. Let them know that we will be instrumental in that safety . . . maybe that will keep them from getting into trouble and still allow us to keep our agreement with Threa. Keep in mind we can watch and listen to them through the video cam the Extremophiles set up."

"If we follow that policy we should still be within our capacity as Caretakers and by removing them to another Planet we will be in keeping with our agreement with Mother Threa." Mort filled his pipe.

"Yes, but what about the fact that they'd been slated for destruction? The others we transplanted all practiced ethical environmental behavior. Threans do have the capacity to learn lessons and change habits but we don't know if these seven have or can do that." Reiki Clowne reminded them now standing in between the screen and his companions.

"True enough but I'll bet by the time we are ready to transport them off, if they even continue to survive we'll have a much better idea of how they feel about things. Perhaps they have acquired an enlightened point of view after living on the Surface during the Upheavals. We can subtly 'teach' them more while they are waiting for the Cleansings to be completed." Euroswydd's glasses slid down with his nod.

"Ah, *mon ami* this is the hard part for the four of us. We will have to watch the Threans and not interfere with their activities even if it looks like they will take the plunge into the death. It is so difficult to watch others if they are undergoing the agonies *n'est pas*? Compassion and executing the correct actions can be at odds with each other."

"Yes, dear Oscáre that is so true. We must remember our teachings and not get too caught up in the possible emotional hardships or our vibrations will slow and lessen our capacity to effectively take care of these Caverns. Whatever these Threans do or have done it was their own decision to do so. As we might not want to see another living Being suffer in any way we are not responsible. They may be just fine until Threa is done and lest we not forget these seven were slated for absorption after much testing. " Reiki Clowne never liked to see his Oscáre upset.

"He's right you know, let's not go and borrow trouble since it might never happen. And let's also not fall into Threan emotional traps, we must remember who we are at all times." Mort's attempt at sternness dissolved his companions with laughter.

"Mort don't get your bones in a tizz. We know you are perhaps the softest heart among us. Seriousness we accept but sternness just isn't you." Euroswydd consoled. "I think it's time for us to take a break before meeting back here in a few hours, let's say 0400. We should also keep an eye on the monitor connected to the video cam, just in case."

"I've set up the recording device so that we can replay anything of worth back if that's OK with you. We can be sure we don't miss anything this way and if need be show them that they shouldn't take us lightly if that ever becomes an issue."

"Thank you Mort, that sounds perfect." And with that Euroswydd's screen darkened. Mort remained glued to the screen for the next few hours until Oscáre and Reiki Clowne reentered the Chamber, just in time for their meeting.

Desire needles logic
To give way
And enjoy

16

ABYSS BECKONING

69.

The water's ripples sealed as they eased downward. The submersible, its name a mystery until the code of the Alien's marking was cracked, had a cockpit the size of a four seater biplane. Muted grey black with markings reminiscent of a seal or squid— blotches of lighter color lingering amidst stretches of dark—in shape resembling a sizable manta ray minus the tail but replete with central core body and wings that on the submersible could retract and extend to gracefully flex up and down propelling it through the water. Those inhabitants of the sea calmed by the "beast's" outward appearance failed to detect the two sets of non aquatic eyes peering through tiny portholes scattered along the hull. Embellishing on its appearance as a native of the depths the portholes relinquished their view of the outside realm through a colored hue tinged to represent safety features similar to those found on living Beings. Meant to confuse prospective predators these Beings sport eyes, ears and mouths in profusion, some the real thing, others representations strategically placed to baffle and intimidate.

Peering at the array of lights and switches before her Morna said, "Everything seems to be working OK, we've got air, ambient temperatures seem to be holding steady and it's rather like driving an electric car, no engine noise but I can tell we're moving." Looking at Orla framed against a greenish-yellow hued porthole she pointed, "Look at that!" Orla turned to see a sperm whale pass slowly by on its tranquil, steady downward glide. "Wow, I thought they were extinct. And we were right next to one. Too bad we can't take pictures."

"I'm sure we could if we only knew how, but that'll have to be another day. Hey what's all that coming towards us?" Orla pointed through a different porthole at a school of fish whose individual members exhibited characteristics dissimilar to Surface dwellers. One's exceptionally large mouth seemed propped open and what could only be described, in Threan terms of recognition, as a fishing line extending from the head with a bit of bioluminescent bait tantalizingly bobbed just an inch beyond the forehead. Others had exaggerated teeth and/or jaws, one looked to have a hatchet for a mouth, and one lent credence to the ancient tales of deep sea dragons. The two inhabitants of the submersible, forgetting to breath, stared wide eyed at the ensemble peering just as raptly at the submersible. The undersea Beings generated light patterns reminiscent of the pre-dawn fire glows at a hot air balloon festival. Producing flames at varying intervals the dark skies fill with giant glowing specks of balloon shaped amber light. The aquatic colors varied from greens, yellows, blues to reds and even a rather muted burnt orange glow. As one they turned swarming away into blackness.

"Let's see if we can follow them. Maybe we can learn something." Morna's eyes gleaming she allowed fingers to caress the controls.

"Hey, careful what you touch there, we don't know what everything is attached to." Oral cautioned grabbing her friend's hands. "I want to follow them as much as you do but I don't want to be stuck out here unable to breath or wind up running into something or exploding or who knows what!"

"I think I'm getting the hang of this. I used to go down in the little submarines at the Naval Station on days they allowed the public to visit. I'd pretend that everything was cute, safe and just for our protection. I really felt comfortable in those things; they were so easy to operate. A lever here, a switch there and swoosh, off we'd go. Anyway no harm done and we seem to be moving at a good clip now." Indeed the decreased visibility did seem in direct proportion to the increased speed with which the submersible sliced through the waters.

"We're wooshing not swooshing. This reminds me of the wakes created by surface craft propelled at high speeds or being submerged in a freshly poured glass of soda. It's like it's happening down here and we're moving right through it and at the same time it's staying with us. I suppose you're going to tell me you can slow or stop this thing if we need to?"

"Yeah, I'll just do the reverse of everything I just did." Orla's glaring silence brought a smile to Morna's face. "Don't worry, it'll work." And so saying she prompted a red then blue light to brighten at the touch of her fingers and the submersible slowed to a drift. The perception of being suspended, held in place by a miasma of particles, intensified with the activation of the floodlights.

Floodlights perhaps too harsh a description as it elicits sensations of harsh, glaringly revealing rays depicting stark, razor sharp differentiation in black and white. The light emitting from the submersible glowed rather than sliced, enhancing dulcet color hues, illuminating the masses of tiny life forms busily going about their daily tasks. A sharp contrast to the prevailing perceptions pre-Upheaval Threans level of familiarity would have decreed this cloudy world—a welter of polluting, toxic scum.

"How far down do you think we are?" Orla asked staring questioningly at the controls and gauges. "I really wish I could understand what they're telling us; it might as well be chicken scratch."

"I think I have some of it figured out; I'll bet that one," pointing to a gauge replete with lines and slopes, "has something to do with depth and the position of the submarine. Look there's a little pinprick of color there and it doesn't seem to be moving. I think that's us. I've been so busy looking out I didn't notice what happened to that dot when we were going so fast before." The dot moved in tandem with the ship as she caused it to move downwards before leveling off, "Yeah that's what this gauge shows."

"Not forward motion, just up and down."

"Seems so." Both returned to watching the world beyond the portholes. The inhabitants seemed oblivious to the guest in their midst. Eels with enormous mouths, isopods their multiple short thread like legs swirling, hagfish whose large voluptuous bodies dwarfed their small pinheads, an eel maneuvering as though rowing, all initially seeming to be nothing more than flashing or steady lights until their physical forms defined within the glow emanating from the submersible.

"This is really something. Who'd have thought there would be such a complex of Beings living down here. The pressure must be incredible, not to mention the cold and dark." Orla paused, peering out into the depths pointing at some darker shapes silhouetted by the light, "It almost looks as though there are mountains or something over there."

"We have more visitors." Several sea Beings circled the submersible occasionally touching it with a fin or nudging with a mouth.

"It's as though we're the Alien creature and they're the natives wondering what or who we are."

"We are." Morna watched with as much trepidation and interest as the natives of the area. "Oops, what's happening now?" The sea Beings, two resembling rays, one a swordfish, two sea turtles, two different kinds of sharks—one reminiscent of a nurse shark—and several squid of varying sizes surrounded the submersible. They maneuvered the vessel between them then propelled it forward.

"Shouldn't we do something, start the engines, try to get away from them?" Orla questioned, wide-eyed staring out.

"No, I want to see where they take us. We can't stay in this vessel forever and it's almost as if they're being careful to not harm us. Let's see where this goes." Morna and Orla allowed themselves to be escorted through the inky black water and eventually guided through a transparent wall which seemed to melt around them then reform as each shape passed. Depositing the submersible with its port side resting on a rocky promontory their captors backed off, staying close enough to observe. After a short interval individuals left various bits of food, a pile of various seaweeds and unidentifiable bits and pieces growing on the rocky ledge before their bow.

"I don't think they realize we're here; they think the vessel is a living creature that they've never seen before and they're trying to feed it." Morna's awed voice contained hills and valleys of air and sound.

"Could be, so what do we do? Stay here until they get tired of us or make some move ourselves? What say we maneuver to the surface or at least try heading up. It looks lighter than before we passed through the barrier; maybe we're in some sort of inland sea like the cave we found this thing in. My legs are cramped and it would be nice to get some fresh air."

"Orla you make me laugh sometimes, here we are, somewhere at the bottom of the sea, and you want space and fresh air." Morna shook her head, "Do you have any idea the import of this? And do we really want to take the chance of antagonizing them by doing something they might misinterpret?"

"Yes, I'm fascinated and no I don't want them to see us as a threat but I think we have to take some initiative here. They're watching us to see what we're going to do. Let's do something. We can't stay in here forever."

"OK, let's see what happens." And so saying Morna moved the rod and pressed the button for power. The submersible rose a couple of feet until water flowing off its upper body splashed to the surface now several feet below. "Look you're right, we were very near the surface." Within moments they crunched onto the sandy, pebble strewn shore.

The aquatic group of observers followed the vessel to the shoreline moving back a few feet when, as they perceived it, the Being opened its blowhole and extended forth appendages which detached from the main body. These appendages moved about as if by some form of remote control navigating towards the water's edge.

70.

"Is it dividing? Giving birth? Getting its defense systems ready to retaliate? I'm not sure this was such a good idea." One of the rays said, his winged fins barely undulating in the water.

"And now's definitely the time to come to that realization!" observed a shark.

"Actually they don't look any more threatening than the Vessel they arrived in. They seem to be rather tentative don't you think?" one of the sea turtles said watching Orla and Morna treading lightly around on the sand, taking in their surroundings between glances in the direction of the water and its punctuating decoration of fins and dorsal mounds.

"You know I get the feeling that each side is watching the other trying to figure out what to do next." Morna seemed to be looking for answers in the rocks as she picked pebbles up, rolling them in her fingers before staring intently at each one. "It's almost as if we're in some sort of holding pen. I wonder if we're part of a scientific experiment or discovery. Maybe this has something to do with the Aliens that look like toys. What'dya think?"

"Maybe, maybe not. Let's secure the submersible and try communicating with these creatures. Hey where'd they go?" Unbroken by fin or bump the water's surface extended smoothly into invisibility.

"Well, that's eerie, let's keep looking around and see what we can find." Morna looked back down at the pebbles in her hand. "This is interesting material, it seems to be a mixture of serpentinized periodotites and gabbros, rocks that usually make up the deeper layers of the oceanic crust. Oh don't look at me like that. I took a course in geology. I do know what I'm talking about. It's really old, old rock and it's really cool that we're here. It's not something the average person generally stumbles across."

"It's not like anything has been normal lately." Orla reminded. "You know I'm not seeing any way out of this place. There are no openings of any kind in these walls. And even if I wanted to get back in that thing," waving at the submersible, "we don't know how that clear barrier in the water works. You may be right, we may be in some sort of holding pen."

"Greetings." Grinding their heels in the gravelly substrate they pivoted to see Oscáre, Reiki Clowne and Mort.

"You're real." Off balance both gaped, stunned.

Smiling Reiki Clowne held up his knitted hands in greeting, "Yes, we're very real. And we mean you no harm so please relax. That you are here presents something of a problem but we will work out the end results in due time."

"END RESULTS! That doesn't sound very comforting." Orla's voice came out a high pitched vehement challenge.

"Perhaps *mon ami* has used the indelicate wording. We don't mean end results to connote anything terrible. We ask that you come with us to the Chamber we spoke to you from a couple of days ago. There we can communicate with your friends to let them know you are safe . . . they have been quite worried about you and you will also meet with Euroswydd. Are there just the two of you? Well then if we are all gathered please come with Reiki Clowne *est moi.* Mort will you follow after making sure that the vessel and everything else is secure?" Offering the two no choice or time to question the matter of accompanying them, Oscáre and Reiki Clowne ushered the two Threans through the opening in the rock.

Their upward journey through the Cavernous "High Rise" afforded the Threans as Euroswydd later punned in his report, "the guided tour". Periodically their eyes locked in one with the other before rotating to the next revelation.

71.

Stopping before an entryway Oscáre grandly extended his left front leg inviting them into the Monitor Chamber. "It's just as we saw it on the screen." Morna said her eyes sweeping the Chamber.

While maintaining a neutral aura Reiki Clowne chuckled a little, "You really didn't quite believe you were talking to us did you?"

"It's like when you see something or hear about it but until the reality of the issue becomes three dimensional it doesn't quite sink in. When that happens it can be very unsettling."

"Is there any chance we can talk to our friends . . . let them know we're OK?" Morna's voice gathered strength with each utterance.

"But of course, we are scheduled to speak with them in the few minutes. The timing is perfect." Oscáre pointed to two chairs directly in front of the monitor. "If you would like to sit in those two seats you can talk to them as soon as they come on. But first we would like to introduce you to Euroswydd." This last as Euroswydd's screen filled with the old donkey's image. "Euroswydd I'd like you to make the acquaintance of Morna and Orla, two of the party of Threans that have relocated into the Satellite Cavern." then looking significantly at Euroswydd, *"deux pas trios."*

"Pleasure to meet you, don't worry I'm not a threat. I'm located in a different Universe so I'm coming to you via this screen." Euroswydd said as the two women stepped back.

"It's not that we're scared of you it's just that, well, this is all happening a bit fast. I think I'll take that seat now." Orla finished rather weakly and moving to the chairs they both sat down. "Thank you." This to Oscáre who served them herb iced tea and a little snack of crackers and pâte made from herbs and seaweeds topped with a goat cheese. Color returned to their faces as the monitor in front of them gradually changed from black to blank blue before revealing their friends anxiously peering at their screen.

"Look there they are," Lileas pointed, "how did you get there? Are you alright? We've been worried sick."

"We're both fine. We found a small submarine and were just going to take it a little ways to see how it worked and if we could find something useful and the next thing we knew we were being herded into this place."

"You haven't been hurt in any way have you?" Jinny's head took over the screen eyes scanning her friends.

"We're fine; they've even fed us. I've no idea what it is but it's delicious. If these Beings do everything else the way they prepare food I want to learn all I can. You should see this place it's huge." Morna and Orla answered simultaneously creating an overall jumble.

Retreating from the field of view the Caretakers allowed the two women privacy to relate their exploits and for the separated Threan groups to catch up on events. Those Threans still in the Satellite Cavern had spent their time conjecturing on where and how their friends had disappeared and while wanting to finding it hard to trust the figures that came to them on the screen in the Chamber's wall. Outwardly they'd been polite but underneath it all, and when they thought the Caretakers couldn't hear them they'd discussed the possibility of a direct correlation between their friends' disappearance and the existence of the Extraterrestrials. Of course it had been two days before they realized anything was amiss since it had been agreed that Morna and Orla's exploratory trip be an overnighter.

From the Casyoans perspective the submersible's launch had mandated the physical meeting of the two groups. The aquatic Beings of the depths unable to positively identify what creature they'd found and perturbed by its erratic behavior had decided to rescue and deposit the submersible safely within the confines of Euroswydd's Caverns. As guardians of all that reposed within the confines of the Chambers it was incumbent on the Caretakers to appear before the Threans and escort them through its intricacies to prevent further negative repercussions.

"I'm glad we've been able to calm their fears about Morna and Orla's disappearance but that still doesn't answer the question of where the one they call Derek is. Their being here opens up yet another can of worms." Euroswydd talked quietly to his fellow Caretakers.

"We can no longer be mere observers. They've actually found us and the two that arrived today in the submersible witnessed a sophistication of technology beyond their wildest dreams, although I'm sure they don't realize the full extent just yet. And of course there are other questions to be answered."

"I know Mort, we're dammed if we do and dammed if we don't." Euroswydd shook his head, "All I can think to do is bring the ones still in the Satellite Cavern here and put them all in their own contained environment with the means to survive until Threa is done with her cleansing then transport them somewhere."

"We do need to have them somewhere where we can keep an eye on them. But as for how to approach the situation in the long term, they were sent to the Interment Camps, something done only after much consideration. Where could we safely transplant them? The situation is different now that they will be under our direct tutelage. How will we know if they could be safely sent away to another planet?"

"I don't have the answer to that right now Reiki Clowne. First things first, let's get them here then we'll figure out what to do after the Cleansings are done."

"Agreed."

"I do have the question to ask. How will we get them here? We can't allow the other two to go back to fetch them." Oscáre whispered.

"I don't think they could figure out how to get back even if we encouraged it. Remember they were basically transported here, at least the final leg of their journey." Mort added, "Anyway it's way too dangerous to let them go anywhere now. Who knows what Threa has coming up on her agenda. They were fortunate getting here without getting caught up in her ministrations. She must have been between episodes or working elsewhere. We can only hope for such an eventuality if more trips are going to be made back and forth. We're going to have to be candid with these Threans and hope they understand. They might even have some viable suggestions."

72.

"Suggestions about what?" Morna and Orla as well as the faces on the screen were all looking at the Casyoans.

"We are discussing the situation."

"What *situation* are you referring to? You seem nice but the reality is we're in the clutches of Beings that say they're from a different Universe. Our planet is being destroyed by forces we can't identify much less overwhelm and you four act as though we're the problem!" Arms folded across her chest lips puffed, eyes slits, Mab's entire being challenged the Casyoans.

"True enough, we each have the personal perspectives regarding this situation. As such it is one that requires the utmost of the delicate handling," and looking at Mab while waving his front hooves to include them all, "by everyone, *tout les* persons involved. We should sit down and relax while we relate a few of the facts that you don't know yet, perhaps that will help increase the confidence."

The Caretakers shared the basics of what was occurring up on the Planet's Surface, the fact that Threans had been transferred off the Planet to other living accommodations and the difficulties posed by the unexpected appearances of these Threans and their having discovered the Satellite Station. Glossing over the aspects of choosing certain Threans to be transported leaving the rest to be participants in the Planet's cleansing/recycling procedures they instead emphasized the importance of not doing anything that would impede that process or the natural evolution needing to occur once the process was completed.

"So what do you suggest we do? Stay here? What if that area starts to fall apart? From what you say your present location is the only safe place on the Planet right now. There must be some way of figuring out how to get to you. Maybe we can find another submersible." Jinny spoke as the others nodded in agreement.

"I doubt there's more lying about; can you build something from the detritus yourselves? Something that would be like a small submarine and could get you to these Caverns?" Mort asked filling his pipe.

"None of us has that kind of knowledge and I don't know of any materials that would be usable for such a thing. There's no other machinery here except the computer and monitor electronics in this room. It's as though everything but this was cleaned away when this station closed or was abandoned or whatever." Hans' voice came into the Cavern heavy with depression.

Euroswydd spoke up. "We don't think it's a good idea for you to stay where you are but were hoping you might have a solution other than transporting the small submersible back and forth. However since that appears to be our only option let's ask the aquatic cultures to help in this venture."

"That could work. We'd have to send out word through the aquatic communications line that we are looking for volunteers for this mission. And make sure they understand the risks involved. This is going to be a lot more complicated than getting the video cam to the Satellite Station." Mort mused, the smaller more frequent puffs popping from his pipe mimicking the increased intensification of his thought processes.

"Video cam to the Satellite Station?" And once told Jinny shook her head. "That's amazing. Is it going to be possible to meet or at least view these Beings?"

"I'm sure that can be arranged but for the time being let's concentrate on getting you safely here. We will contact you when we have further details. In the meantime please remain as and where you are. Thank you." Euroswydd's commanding voice broached no argument as the communication signal disconnected.

"Where's Derek? I forgot all about him while we were talking to them but I haven't seen him for several days. I know we thought he'd gone with Morna and Orla and just not told us but that's obviously not it." Mab looked around as if expecting him to pop up from behind a computer.

"I don't know and right now I just don't care. It's peaceful around here with him gone. I'm sure he's OK; people like him always are. It's the others around them that suffer. And there's plenty of food for him in those storage chambers at Ambrosia Lake." Silently, eyebrows raised Lileas, Jinny and Mab exchanged looks as Hans strode out of the Chamber.

73.

A profuse enveloping ooze incrementally changing shape moved about the perimeter of the orb sitting in the Satellite Station's Monitor

Chamber. The dark form writhed beneath the maelstrom sporadically visible through the swath of colors.

Just beyond cognitive reach
The echo of fear beckons
Cuckolding those in need

17

HOVERING STAGE RIGHT

74.

Several days later, preparations complete, all was in readiness. Giant squid would support and propel while sperm whales—between breathes at the surface—provided most of the accelerating power. Once the trek along the bottom reached the Northern Temperate Continent's Coastal Shelf large rays would lift the submersible to the entrance of the Satellite Caverns. The aquatic conveyor belt would follow a route laid out by the Extremophiles.

The submersible with its limited carrying capacity needed transportation for several round trips further adding to the danger of successful mission completion as well as necessitating a numerous band of volunteers. Extremophiles and other Beings not able to help with actual physical transportation had eagerly offered their services as lookouts and scouts, communications between the various groups to be facilitated by the smaller aquatic Beings. Entire schools of fish waited in the waters to, as one, dance between those needing information. Eels electrified with anticipation awaited their turn to signal. In the shallower regions where shellfish abound, the eyes of the scallop would keep watch for possible troubles as well as the messengers that would tell them of impending arrivals.

Navigation within the Satellite Cavern area would be done by those aquatic cave dwellers adept at living in cave waters where visibility is, at best, limited.

"I've given the submersible a thorough going over, the environmental controls and such are in perfect condition. I've taken the liberty of disconnecting much of the control panel as I don't want anything to get touched accidentally or on the off chance that they decide they want to pilot the thing. The communication devices are working so if by some strange happenstance they do need to navigate themselves they will be able to on our instructions." Mort relayed to Euroswydd during their private meeting.

"Thank you Mort"

"I'm still puzzled by the existence of this submersible. It shouldn't have been left by the inland sea. According to our records none of our submersibles were left there. And some of the controls on this are configured differently than I would have expected." Mort continued shaking his head, "something about this is nagging at me but I can't put my finger on what."

"Configured differently?" Euroswydd cocked his head brown eyes peering quizzically at his friend over the top of his glasses.

"While I was checking and disconnecting I found electronics configured in a different pattern than our engineers followed during the time period they assembled this Complex. The mechanics of the submersible are set up in a way that was acceptable in the recent past but has since been improved upon."

"Couldn't it be as simple as an old piece of equipment being utilized because it could get the job—whatever that might have been—done and then been an unfortunate careless mistake when the crews left?"

"I suppose. But I think we should look into our records of the submersibles used during the construction period. As I said, something's nagging at me and I'd be happier if it went away." Mort said tapping out a tiny wad of blackened dottle into his bony palm.

"I will have those records checked." Euroswydd promised. "For the time being though let's join Morna and Orla and get this show on the road or should I say afloat!"

75.

There was great excitement in the Monitor Chamber. Morna and Orla, all smiles, were talking to their friends still in the Satellite Chamber and the visual link to the Observation Panel had been turned on showing a group of Extremophiles, sperm whales and giant squid waiting to begin the first leg of their journey.

"Are you all ready?" questioned Reiki Clowne as he spread his arms out, waving knitted hands.

"*Bonne Voyage,* we will monitor your journey and see you when you reach the Satellite Station. Swim with safety and our blessings." Oscáre waved a brilliantly chartreuse scarf as the first conveyance team, submersible in tow, disappeared from view.

"How long will it take them to reach us?" Lileas asked. "What with everything else going on I forgot to ask."

"Barring the unforeseen problem, within the week . . . do you agree Mort?" Oscáre said turning to face his friend.

"Yes, I believe that's about right."

"Wouldn't it be faster to show us how to use the controls and let us get there the way Morna and Orla did?" Hans asked. "It's going to take at least two weeks to a make single round trip. It seems like forever."

"We have deemed that this is the safest route and means to get you all here in one piece. It was sheer luck that, at the speed they were going, your companions didn't run into a force that blew them to smithereens." Mort explained. "Going through the water as fast as they did if Threa had been moving the waters or a hurricane had been occurring the force of both the energy of the natural event meeting the force of the energy propelling the submersible forward would have caused it to implode."

"Ah, something like when a train traveling at the speed of sound meets an automobile traveling ninety miles an hour . . . there's almost nothing left but a pile of scrap metal. However if the train goes five miles an hour and the car, two, it's just a fender bender." Jinny loved explaining concepts through comparison.

"Yes, by keeping the submersible safely with the Beings that have been dealing and quite successfully I might add, with Threa's self ministration and by moving at a slow pace which affords you the ability to move out of the range of danger instead of rushing headlong into it we believe we stand an excellent chance of completing a successful operation." Euroswydd declared. "And anyway what's the rush. Sit back, relax and read a book or two. Clearly life hasn't been all that easy for you of late. Enjoy a little break while you can."

Laughing the Threans looked at each other. Being stressed and always on one's toes had become so engrained they were at a loss when the burdens were lifted.

With a chuckle and shake of her head Jinny said, "OK, we'll try and adapt to a calmer lifestyle. Thank you for all your help."

"Don't thank us just yet, the transferal operation has barely begun. We will, as we've been doing, leave the com links open so that you and your companions here can communicate whenever you wish. But for now we must get on with the daily tasks of running this Station." The Caretakers nodded at the Threans dispersing to their various tasks. The video cam transported and installed by the Extremophiles was on and sending images through to a receiving unit that the Threans in Euroswydd's Caverns weren't cognizant of.

The next few days passed without incident. The journey being taken by the submersible and transporters continued apace or afin as the Caretakers were wont to say. With decreasing frequency as time went on but still at least once a day a contingent of fish swarmed up to the Cavern reporting the travelers' progress, the increased time between reports merely a function of overall distance. Day Five found the conveyance group in sharply decreasing depths buffeted by strong disturbances originating not only above the Surface of the water but below as well. During the journey they'd experienced some negligible ripple effects of Surface storms and one heart pumping incident when the submersible slipped momentarily out of the conveying squid's clasp. Having gotten a bit lax in their wariness the incident served as more of a reminder of possibilities than anything else. On the sixth day the whales and squid relinquished their charge to the rays who transported it to the species of the shallows.

Consisting of hammerhead sharks swimming in unison side by side the conveyance team held the pod on their front protrusions. They were escorted by dolphins—a truce having been called in light of the circumstances—as well as a bevy of well wishers. By the end of the sixth day the inner cave dwellers were maneuvering it through the labyrinth leading to the internal sea.

"There it is." Jinny exclaimed as the submersible appeared, slicing its way through the slate grey water on its way to the shore. With a concerted swish from escorting fins it crunched against the shoreline. "Thank you." She called to the Beings disappearing back into the darkness. They would wait until given the signal that the submersible was filled and ready to begin its return journey before reappearing. Most cave creatures are rather small, some no more than a few inches long, few larger than a foot. Literally hundreds of these Beings had banded together to transport the submersible. Resembling their external dwelling counterparts in body shape only these aquatic cave dwellers lacked pigment and functional eyes, relying on the increased development of other survival mechanisms such as hearing and touch.

"So I guess we pack up and ship out." Hans was already grabbing the packages set out by the water's edge. It had been decided that he would take the first trip across with several of the larger animals. Not having any tranquilizers at hand at the Satellite Station and purely as a precautionary measure—the idea of one of the pets experiencing hydrophobia, bathyphobia or claustrophobia in that small submersible alarmed one and all, pets included—Oscáre had sent some of his herbs—valerian, hops, linden, lavender and chamomile—along with instructions on their use.

In very short order—not more than a couple of hours—the submersible was filled with food, water, as well as the donkey, dogs, cats and birds. As if by magic a contingent of aquatic cave dwellers rose to signal that they were ready to escort the loaded submersible on the first leg of its return voyage.

After waving Hans and the pets on their way Jinny, Lileas and Mab looked at each other.

"You know he's been missing over a week. Now that Hans has gone maybe we should do something about it."

"Mab's right, Hans felt he was off somewhere sulking, trying to get us worried but he's never been gone for more than a couple of hours." Lileas spoke to Jinny still watching the spot where the submersible had become nothing more than a convergence of iron grey surface ripples shook her head, "I don't know what to do about him. He's been nothing but a nuisance but he's still part of our family. I'd like to find him and at least give him the opportunity to come with us. There is the other side of the coin too. He may be hurt and need our help. Although I just don't feel that to be the case I do have a rather negative feeling whose origin I can't put my finger on." Sighing she looked at Mab and Lileas, "I really hate when I get these feelings. I never seem to get enough information to do anything specific, just enough to make me feel that something's amiss."

76.

Within the All Seeing Chamber the orb's interior colors writhed while on surrounding table screens a slow, molasses oozing of pinks, oranges, and light reds welled up. A low pitched all encompassing *thrummmmm* vibrated. As if pulled by the increasing volume Derek passed through the entryway stopping before the display. Eyelids and shoulders twitching as if shivering or sleeping, he flicked some switches before exiting the room. Heading left his slow, measured steps faded down a tunnel whose terminus came after several hundred feet.

In repose once again the ball and screens roused no suspicions when Jinny next entered the ASC.

77.

"Something is definitely going on but what? I'm glad you left that video cam on." Euroswydd spoke after seeing the tape of Derek in the All Seeing Chamber. "To the best of my knowledge none of the orbs installed as part of Monitor Chamber mechanics have ever demonstrated such variant color and vibrational swathes. And that man looked as though he was drugged or hypnotized or perhaps being remotely controlled."

Mort wreathed in tobacco smoke spoke slowly, thinking aloud, "I think there's some other presence on this Planet and I don't think they're Threan. After seeing this video it makes sense that the submersible that shouldn't have been there was and that it would be configured in a different way."

"Well it doesn't appear to be anybody from Casyo the vibrations are too slow." Reiki Clowne said.

"Maybe, maybe not . . . there have been a scattered few who haven't grown to their potential. Some of them have left and gone elsewhere and then of course there are those destined to live their lives in the Recycle Zone. The submersible was, according to Mort, one of ours albeit from a previous era."

"Hmmm. I thought that once you were consigned to spending the specific lifetime in the Recycle Zone that you couldn't exit?" Oscáre twirling the tips of his mustachio looked at his three companions.

"That's the idea of course but there have been escapees over the years. Few and far between but nevertheless some have managed to squeeze out."

"Ah *mon dieu*. How will we figure out who or what these Beings are? First the Threans and now this."

"Jinny, Mab and Lileas are waiting for the report." Reiki Clowne motioned towards the screen where the three women were waiting to speak.

"Well then let's talk to them and get back to this afterwards." Euroswydd turned to the screen smiling.

"You four looked very serious, is anything wrong?" Mab couldn't get the words out fast enough once the com connection was enabled.

"Oh *non*, everything is fine with the submersible."

"By the way," began Mort, "have any of you heard from that friend of yours that disappeared?'

"No, and now that Hans is on his way to you we have been trying to figure out what we should do. We don't know whether to try and find him or leave without him." Jinny looked closely at the Caretakers. "Why do you suddenly bring him up? You've not asked about him before."

"We don't want to have any loose ends. He's a rather volatile individual isn't he?" Reiki Clowne replied.

The connection between the Satellite Station and Euroswydd's Caverns fell notably quiet, the three women looking at one another then back at the Caretakers.

"How do you know that? Have you seen him, do you know where he is? He hasn't been around here for days. Hans was just glad he wasn't around but we are thinking we should try and locate him. You know, give him a chance to come with us . . . at least make sure he's OK." Jinny explained.

"No we don't know where he is right now. As Reiki Clowne said we don't want any loose ends, or cannons wandering about. I'm sure he'll be fine." Euroswydd bowed his head to the three anxiously glued to their screen. "For now we must return to the upkeep of the Complex. We'll talk again soon, give you a progress report on Hans's voyage." Nodding at Mort to disconnect the signal Euroswydd bid his friends a quick *adieu* as a meeting of the Elders he was expected to attend had already started.

"I must admit to the feelings of perturbation regarding the disappearance of this young Threan." Oscáre commented as the three headed out the entryway.

"Me too, but let's do as Euroswydd suggested and make sure everything is OK within this Complex." Reiki Clowne put his glasses in their case before returning Mort's departing wave.

"Ah *oui,* lately I feel there is always the something dangling in the wings waiting to spring forth. *Quelle* surprise!"

Mysterious personalities are clarified in their reactivity.

18

PERCEIVED ASYLUM

78.

The illumination slowed then reversed its nightly dimming as Derek rose, stretching before beginning his short trek back to the All Seeing Chamber. Approaching the smaller, horizontal table screens surrounding the orb he activated several switches prompting the swirl of colors. Placing his hands on first one then another, then another the colors permeated through his palms before disappearing into the bulge of his lower arms, his reflected image disappearing from the now deadened black screens.

Fifteen minutes later he entered the Living Chamber.

"Hey, what the Hell . . . oh hi . . . where have you been?" Jinny stared sleepy eyed up at the black eyed rigid faced man standing over her. "Why are you in my cubbyhole? Don't touch me!" as she grabbed his wrist removing his hand from her naked forearm. The release was accompanied by the resounding *thwack* of suction breaking.

Appearing behind Derek, Lileas was unable to stem the downward plunge of her hammer. Springing from the kneeling position the blow imposed he shoved her aside, jostling Mab before nothing but fading sandal slaps on rock affirmed the reality of his fleeting materialization.

"Did you see his eyes? They looked like solid black marbles. What did he do to your arm?" Lileas held Jinny's forearm as if displaying a trophy while Mab looked closely at the raised circular blemish, "I've seen marks like that before on people who'd been bitten by ticks carrying Lyme Disease. How do you feel?"

"Startled. I can't imagine why he gripped my arm. He looked so strange. Not like himself at all. Do you think he's gone psychotic?"

"Certainly seems that way. But that doesn't explain how he could make such a mark on your arm just by putting his hand on it." Lileas now rubbing it with calendula salve. "Does this hurt?"

"No, if I didn't see it I wouldn't even know it was there. How much longer 'til we're due to speak with The Caretakers?"

"Why, are you just going to tell them what's happened? What if they are the cause of this too?"

"I know, I know but we have to figure out a way of finding out . . . Morna and Orla are in their Complex and Hans and the animals are in the submersible headed there. We have to talk to them."

79.

"But the Krell haven't been an influence on Casyo for mivtees. What makes you think they're the cause of this?" Reiki Clowne asked Mort, Oscáre and Euroswydd at their hastily convened meeting following the viewing of Derek's actions in the ASC.

"They vibrate at such a slow rate that they're unable to shape shift into multiple forms the way those of us capable of faster vibrations are. When not on Casyo they've always had to take over the forms inherent to the planet they've assaulted in order to survive. It would explain what we've just seen and why the one the Threans call Derek has been missing." Euroswydd sighed before continuing. "One thing to keep in mind is that the Krell seek out those with ambivalent or negative dispositions. Only those that are weak or have been weakened in some way allow the Krell to invade and take over. Having become separated from the neutral state such individuals unconsciously grant them asylum by presenting a condition of duality. Threans had a saying, 'united we stand divided we fall' and while they were referring to causes involving difference of opinion the saying aptly describes this physical manifestation. When the two main forces of energy, positive and negative, are bound together harmoniously healthy balance prevails. A lack of balance between the two creates a weakened system open for attack and conquering."

"Perhaps the Krell were in the process of taking over the Threans on this Planet when we intervened with the Internments and Threa began the Cleansings? Maybe *un petit peu* of the Krell managed to escape their Threan forms and are 'hiding out' looking for the new forms to embody and/or a way off the Planet?" Oscáre's shirt billowed as he paced back and forth, front hooves clasped behind his back.

"It's certainly possible, and given the conditions of this Planet and the actions of the majority of Threans they'd probably been there a long time. I think we've stumbled on a bigger problem than having these Threans with us. Apparently they weren't embodied with Krell—if that's indeed what's going on—but Derek has now been compromised." Mort watched the now empty ASC on their screen, "I wonder if those three Threans have grown and matured during their time on the Surface after the Upheavals began."

"They certainly resisted Derek's attempts to pass on the Krell Entities into their systems, or at least the one called Jinny did. Could we have made a mistake in sending them to the Internment Camps?" Reiki Clowne's body language personified anxiety, knitted hands clasped together.

"We should talk with those women right away. They must be made aware of the possible danger and that we are not the cause." Euroswydd sighed, "This is a grave dilemma whether our hypothesis is correct or not." And turning to Mort, "Please activate their screen and let them know we wish to speak."

"That's the signal they want to talk with us." Jinny said to Lileas and Mab as a series of loud beeps shrilled through the Satellite Station.

"Yeah, and it's the middle of the night . . . do you think there's a problem with the submersible? Or that they know something's happened here?" Lileas spoke tentatively.

"Well . . . there's only one way to find out." Jinny said striding towards the ASC.

80.

"So you're the good Aliens and they're the Bad? When do we get to see the Ugly?" Jinny asked Euroswydd after the Caretakers explained their theory of Krell presence.

"Ah . . . according to an old Threan saying 'Beauty is in the Eye of the Beholder'." Euroswydd bantered back with a smile.

"Don't you realize the seriousness of this situation? Just because you're safe and sound on your planet or wherever you are we are dealing with a lot of things going on around here not the least of which is the weather on the Surface of our Planet!" Mab erupted.

"We are *tres* cognizant of the problems. Euroswydd is not making light of the situation but merely trying to relieve some of the tension that we all feel. Allowing the tension and stress to take over will only make things worse." Oscáre jumped in to explain before Euroswydd could get a word out.

"So what do we do now?" Jinny asked.

"We continue with the planned transferal of you and your things keeping a weather eye peeled for danger. We don't know how many Krell individuals are using Derek as their base but no matter how many or few they cannot remain within him for long." Reiki Clowne explained, "Only one Krell can live within an individual for any length of time—usually the time span of the individual accosted."

"OK but what if the Krell as you call them aren't the cause of this? What then?"

Euroswydd cleared his throat, nodding his head up and down once before answering, "Of course we don't know for sure but there are factors that point to this being Krell engendered. The submersible left at the inland sea, the deteriorating behavior of the Threans over time, the apparent ability of these Beings to use our electronic equipment, and my instinctual feelings about this. Not necessarily very scientific I know but faith is something considered to be very important by you Threans and we would ask that you have some faith in our abilities to discern issues." Stopping he looked at the women for a few moments. When they did nothing but silently stare back he continued, "If it's not the Krell it seems highly probable that whatever Beings are perpetrating this are similar in mindset and actions to the Krell. The religious sect on Threa giving credence to the falsehood of there being an actual Hell with an all evil powerful overseer named Satan while being overly dramatic and highly inaccurate nonetheless hit upon the truism that there are always Beings who, for whatever reasons—hormonal, societal handling, maladjusted perception issues, persecution to name a few possibilities—can't maintain even an approximation of a functional balance between negative and positive. Such individuals live an existence governed by fear and aren't able to exhibit beneficial life qualities."

"It will be over a week probably more before the submersible can be back to pick you up. You will have to be on guard for his attacks." Mort looked at his three companions then back to the Screen. "What kind of weapons do you have?"

"Some knives, a hammer or two, an ax . . . ." Lileas spoke slowly. "But I don't think I can do anything really bad to Derek, I haven't exactly been a fan of his but he's a living Being and he's been with us for over a year."

Euroswydd's team glanced at each other before Euroswydd answered. "You may find that he's your friend Derek in appearance only. The Krell take over the mind and soul of their 'host' changing his/her way of thinking to theirs. Many of your serial killers have blamed their actions on 'voices in the head' telling them what to do. It's possible that they were the voices of the Krell. It could also be that they were the victims of other mental aberrations and psychoses however now that we are aware that the Krell are probably on this Planet—and we don't know for how long—it's possible they were responsible for at least some of the voices."

Depression lacing her tone Jinny voiced what all three were thinking, "OK. Now I'm curious . . . some people were taken off this Planet before the Upheavals began and some were left. I assume that those who were left were chosen for recycling because they didn't pass the squeaky clean test?" She paused, no one moved, "So the assumption is that we seven weren't considered worthy of transplantation. According to your judgment criteria that doesn't say much for any of our characters. Does that mean we are all possibly susceptible to Derek's advances?"

"Well we don't believe you to be since you fought him off but we still don't know about you or you." Reiki Clowne nodded at Mab then Lileas. "It's also conceivable that you've learned and grown in the time you've spent on the Surface surviving through the Upheavals. These are very delicate circumstances and we don't want any of you to panic or be suspicious of us or each other.

"No I would imagine you don't. Why on Threa should we believe you? How do we know that you're not trying to trick us?"

"Why go to all the trouble Mab? If we wanted to do you harm or even just capture you we could have easily just left you there instead of involving ourselves and many of the sea dwellers in this transportation project." Euroswydd's eyebrows raised. "I think even the most suspicious Being would have to admit that telling you about the Krell and putting you all on your guard would be counterproductive for us."

"I suppose." Mab agreed sullenly.

"And we could go on talking forever about what ifs and might have beens but the bottom line is we have to trust somebody and so far you four seem the most likely prospects. We'll gather whatever might work as a weapon and oh . . ." Lileas peered at them all, "if we do have to knock out or kill Derek what will happen to the Entities in him?"

"Knocking him out won't do much if they don't feel they can infiltrate your defenses but if he is killed the ones that escape before he draws his last breath will be desperate for the new quarters. Those that fail to escape before he dies will also have met with their demise." Oscáre told them. "We will leave you to your preparations and we will be on our guard. Remember these Beings can only infiltrate if you allow them. Physical dealings with the body of Derek are another matter."

'Thanks for the warning. Talk to you later." Jinny motioned to her friends and they moved away from the screen's range.

81.

"So what do you think of the Krell theory?"

"It sounds like the stuff of science fiction books but seems rational enough to me." Lileas shook her head, laughing a bit. "Did you just hear me? I said that Alien Beings taking over our bodies is a rational explanation and I actually believe it to be a possibility. I don't know whether I'm losing my mind or expanding it. What next?"

"That's what we have to be on the lookout for. I guess we'll have to sleep in shifts until the submersible returns." Jinny looked at Mab whose head was cocked as though listening for something. "What?"

"I don't know, maybe I'm just being paranoid but I thought I heard the clanking of chains just outside this Chamber." Back to her companions she now blocked the entryway, head swiveling, "Nothing seems to be moving around though. I guess it's nothing." She disappeared in the direction of the Living Chamber followed by Lileas and Jinny both looking cautiously about.

"Well I certainly didn't sleep well last night I might as well have taken all the guarding shifts." Jinny yawned hugely, her eyelids determinedly insisting on protecting their charges, dropping each time she endeavored to lift them. Clenching a mug of steaming coffee each woman faced a pot of oatmeal congealing on the stove's heating ring. A series of loud explosions followed by the gushing of water transplanted them to the entryway.

"What was that?" Lileas clipped out, eyes bulging down the empty tunnel. The normal quietude of the Satellite Station pervaded.

"I wonder if the Upheavals are having an effect on the structural integrity of these Chambers. Should we investigate?" Mab questioned white knuckled still clenching her mug.

"No, I think we should stay where we are unless something obvious happens to make it seem unsafe. We need to be able to communicate with Euroswydd's Caverns and we need to be able to get to where the submersible can pick us up and we don't know if it's not some type of trap." Jinny pointed out.

"Yeah, agreed. What'll we do if things start falling apart here?" Mab patted at the walls as if testing for solidity.

"Report to the Aliens and hopefully they'll have something to suggest. Until or if such an eventuality presents itself let's stay close to one another, something we should do anyway in case Derek or his friends try anything. And let's not go anywhere except the ASC and the Living Chamber." Lileas and Mab nodded at Jinny as in silent tandem the trio returned to the cooking stove.

The rest of the day passed uneventfully but the following morning each related hearing sounds of wailing and what could only be described as the metal grinding against metal type of creaking during their individual watches. Nothing had been visibly amiss despite the fact that the sounds seemed to emanate from the Chambers they were inhabiting.

"What's your take on all this vibrational stuff they were talking about?" Lileas asked Jinny and Mab about halfway through their second day of waiting for the submersible.

"Well I know that molecules vibrate and musicians play in rhythms and sometimes I can feel the vibrations through my feet but I never really thought of living Beings as vibrating energy. Maybe it has something to do with how their bodies manifest, you know because they're from another planet."

"Could be Mab could be. I've read some of what was considered wacky literature that's been written about vibrational energy. At least it was considered wacky when it pertained to anything other than something we could use to our advantage like electrons bouncing about producing electricity to power our electronics. When it got to a discussion of Beings the vibrational aspects were only given credence by certain scientists and those considered 'radical' spiritualists. Interestingly enough what Euroswydd, Oscáre, Reiki Clowne and Mort told us ties in with a lot of those spiritual teachings. There's no mention of Krell but there is of negativity overpowering causing fear pervasion resulting in and facilitating expansion leading to slower vibrational levels. The situational compounding is very similar."

"Well then if you have all the answers Jinny what does this all mean?"

"I obviously don't have all the answers Mab I'm just saying that this vibrational thing may not be so alien to us Threans as we might think. The principles have been available to us and as a group we ignored it probably because we were indoctrinated into another mindset. We closed our minds and didn't allow for expansion into another realm or aspect of reality." A gurgle focused them on Lileas who suddenly pale, her eyes luminous pools of color, was clasping her neck with both hands.

"I . . . can't . . . breathe."

Leaping to her side, Jinny pried Lileas's hands from her neck revealing purple, reddish finger length welts. Mab helped lower her to a prone position on the Cavern floor. Both held her arms by her sides until they stopped straining upwards.

Gulping in air Lileas's color slowly returned to normal. "I'm fine now."

"You were chocking yourself; you had to have been. As soon as Jinny removed your hands you were able to breath." Mab said looking all around.

Looking down at her hands Lileas just shook her head.

82.

"This is getting really scary. And I didn't see Derek at all. Do you think he or his Krell friends were responsible for this?" Jinny asked Euroswydd after a quickly called meeting.

"I've no doubt although I'm not sure how since he wasn't in the Chamber as far as you could tell."

"I wonder if the Krell have developed the way to either make their host invisible or at least appear to be invisible?" Oscáre offered his eyebrows crinkled in perturbation.

"It would certainly appear that way. Or it may be that these entities aren't the Krell but the same form of mindset from another planet with different behavioral modes." Euroswydd shook his head back and forth, "I just have the gut feeling that they are the Krell but I suppose this is all a rather mute point right now. Anyway," he looked directly at the three frightened women, "you must continue as you have been and try to act in a most positive manner. Although I know it's very difficult you must not think or give much attention to fear. Any negatives on your part may be seen as an opening for the Krell or whatever they are to try and enter your bodies."

"Yes, if Lileas had managed to choke herself to unconsciousness she would have been available for them to take over." Reiki Clowne said.

"Just because I was unconscious? That didn't work with Jinny."

"Not simply because you would have been unconscious but because they were able to infiltrate your mind enough to make you do life threatening damage to yourself. Under normal circumstances you would never have tried to choke yourself would you?" Euroswydd paused.

"Of course not. I guess I see where you're going with this. They spotted some sign of negativity or weakness in me and it was all they needed to attempt a coup."

"*Exactment mon ami.* You are all under the tremendous amount of the stress and as such are much more susceptible to giving in."

"Oscáre's right and we may have underestimated their prowess when it comes to this sort of thing. It's been many mitvee's since we've rubbed shoulders with the Krell and they may have refined and upgraded their techniques." Mort said refilling his pipe.

"So the 'weapons' we have aren't going to be much use against this threat are they?" Mab asked.

"Maybe, maybe not. These Beings will try everything they can to chip away at each of your psyches. You'll have to be on guard every moment and we strongly advise you stay with each other at all times." Reiki Clowne emanated severity, not an easy accomplishment for him. "If you can think of yourselves as a unit, for the time being at least, you can emit a unified mental front that should help you get through the next few days until the submersible returns."

"OK, I guess it's all we can do." Jinny sighed.

"Do you think they will make it without being compromised?" Mort asked Euroswydd after the connection between the two groups was severed.

"I hope so. They've been tougher than we would have expected so far, maybe they can overcome this too."

"What do we do if they don't? After all we can't have Krell in the Caverns with all the saved life."

Sighing heavily Euroswydd turned to face Oscáre, "We would have to consider how best to neutralize the issue."

"Ah . . . *oui*." Silently pensive the three exited the Chamber.

Efforts taken to shed parental blunders
Oftentimes engender self perpetuating behavioral extensions

19

INSIDIOUS ANONYMITY

83.

Within a fortnight of the Krell revelation the submersible again broke water in the subterranean sea, this time near the end of the women's sleep cycle. Initially unaware of the submersible's arrival, within minutes of Oscáre's transmission they'd thrown themselves and their prepacked belongings aboard, the hatch clanging shut.

In spite of the conspicuous absence of a tangible enemy efforts to sabotage had continued. The previous week had been smattered with gut quivering reverberations, goose pimpling ephemeral touches felt as wispy tentacles dancing across their skin and the ever present crippling of tension.

Mab had been the next target. Passing time working on deciphering the runes she'd fallen suddenly to the floor of the ASC enveloped in an orange tinged amorphous cloud. After pulling her from the mass before completing its transformation into the stiff outer husk of a cocoon or chrysalis—it vanished as soon as they reached in to grab Mab—in similar fashion to keeping a drug overdose victim from passing out Jinny and Lileas had walked her about and talked, forcing her to respond to their comments until she returned to herself. The entire process had taken several hours and frightened them to the point of wanting to sit together in a huddled, impenetrable, immovable circle until rescue arrived. Persuaded by the Caretakers that nothing would suit the Krell more they'd forced themselves to continue going about their daily tasks, whistling and chatting to bring up their spirits and increase the difficulty of subjugation.

While fringe peculiarities—sounds, lights and sensations—continued, no more outward attempts were made against any of the women before the submersible reappeared. Speculation regarding Derek's whereabouts included his having gone to Ambrosia Lake, perhaps for no other reason than the need of nutrition. Another hypothesis was the hope engendered possibility that the Beings inhabiting his body were prompting him to look for more easily obtainable Beings in which to plant themselves. Perhaps they'd felt there might be others left on the Surface to be recycled in the Cleansings who had survived the Upheavals just as Derek and his Threan companions had. These other survivors might seem more accessible to the Krell, and unwarned of impending takeover probably easier targets than Jinny, Mab and Lileas all of whom had now been approached and managed to thwart their advances.

84.

As the submersible and its cargo made its last voyage to Euroswydd's Caverns the Caretakers continued monitoring the Satellite Cavern area visible through the video cam, hoping as well for auditory information from those areas beyond its scope. Not wanting to clue Derek or the Krell to their continued watchful presence they didn't activate any of the screens.

"I don't understand why Derek didn't make some sort of a move. Now that the three women are on their way here he's lost his chance to infiltrate." Mort mused.

"Maybe, maybe not. We can't be absolutely sure the Krell haven't entered one or more of those women, although it wouldn't appear so. Also we don't know for sure if there aren't other Threans that survived. After all these did," a quick head bob moving his glasses to a more comfortable position on the bridge of his muzzle Euroswydd continued, "and quite frankly we can't be one hundred percent positive he didn't get onto the submersible somehow . . . we are going to have to make sure these Threans aren't allowed to be without escort when they're anywhere in these Caverns except their Chambers."

"Can't we confine them in their own little Environment?"

"Yes, but remember Oscáre, the others are here voluntarily. These Threans, particularly if infiltrated by the Krell, may not submit to being confined."

"Ah *oui, mon ami c'est vrai.* Perhaps Mort you can use your engineering prowess in order to fashion the contrivance to keep them from causing the problems?"

"I think something can be arranged." Smoke rose in sharp, rapid sequence from the bowl of his pipe.

85.

Although glued to the portholes the physical passage out of the Satellite Cavern was palpably nothing more than a myriad of tiny whirlpools gyrating around the hull, ripples disappearing into the inky blackness. Once transported through the darkness of the catacombs the waiting group of hammerheads continued through the lighted surface waters downward and forward, leaving the Northern Temperate Continent's Coastal Shelf behind. Finally held in the grasp of the giant squid the enormous tranquility of the deep sea pervaded the anxiety of the cabin releasing the three from their vigil.

"We're certainly not out of the woods yet but at least we're on our way. Look at those suckers will you, they make me feel safer than I've felt in a while." Her voice shrill and reedy Lileas settled in between two sleeping bags. "I just may get the first sound sleep I've had in ages."

Shortly after Lileas woke up from that first restful sleep she'd enjoyed in ages the three women noticed a marked and increasing chill in the cabin's atmosphere. Initial twinges of concern quickly gave way to feelings of euphoria and hilarity, Mab commenting that she didn't know what was happening but since none of them exhibited any negative symptoms such as headache or nausea why not just enjoy the sensation. They each felt as though they'd enjoyed a few stiff drinks and were the more relaxed for them and when was the last time they'd laughed so heartily and lengthily?

One and all ooohhed, and aaahhhed when the outside of the hull lit up the surrounding waters with a brief but intense fiery red, yellow glow. None noticed the sudden withdrawal of supporting tentacles as the submersible plunged downward. The ensuing bumps and bangs equated with the exhilarating release of a carnival ride were greeted with squeals of enjoyment.

86.

They came to themselves muffled in motionless black.

"Hey watch where you put your hand that's my nose you just squashed!" Mab exclaimed.

"Sorry, I can't see a thing. Are we still in the submersible? I've never experienced such complete darkness before, there's absolutely no light anywhere. I've no concept of up or down. What happened?" Lileas's voice a reedy, querulous gush palpated in the all pervasive blackness.

"We're still in the submersible but I don't think it's moving. I don't remember much except feeling euphoric and disjointed as though I'd had too many drinks and all I wanted to do was fall asleep. Do you think there's something wrong with the air mixture?" Jinny's voice incrementally changed locations. "I can't see anything out the portholes."

"Well it seems to be fine right now. I remember feeling drunk too and cold, although the temperature is comfortable now." Lileas' voice declared before continuing, her voice taking on the hesitant tone of someone trying to draw back the details of a fuzzy dream from wherever those details go as soon as one wakes up. "I remember someone, I think it was you Jinny telling Mab that submarines don't have thermostats the way houses did so we couldn't just turn it up to get warm."

"Yeah, and I kind of remember feeling as though there was a tug of war going on in my head, half of me wanting to just curl up and sleep and the other half struggling to keep awake until we figured out a way to get the atmosphere in here back to normal." Jinny's voice expressed puzzlement.

"What's happened to our escorts? Aren't they supposed to be taking care of us?"

"Well Mab I'd say it's a good guess that something unexpected happened to them or they wouldn't have just left us here." Jinny's voice faced Mab's.

"Or maybe those Caretakers are really out to get us and they set this whole thing up just to get rid of us. Who's going to know where we are and come rescue us?"

"Oh shut up Mab," Lileas's voice had recovered some of its customary strength, "you're always the first to distrust these days. I can't imagine why the Aliens would go to so much trouble to get some of us to their Complex and dump the rest of us in the depths of the ocean to perish. I think a more likely scenario involves Derek's inhabitants having somehow or other managed to sabotage our journey and I'll bet that we're the object of a rescue effort even as we speak."

"We seem to have replaced one problematic issue with another. We have control over our minds and bodies but now we're at the bottom of the ocean or some close approximation abandoned by our transports." Lileas's voice was sharp, slicing through the darkness. "Aaaggh, I keep trying to look out the port holes as if I'm going to see something. Old habits are hard to break."

"Uh huh," Jinny stared at the control panel using the weak glow from a flashlight, "I don't know why these communication devices don't work. Euroswydd specifically said they'd kept them connected in case we needed to get in touch."

"Maybe something broke when we got dropped down here.'

"I guess," sighing Jinny moved to look out a porthole before laughing and sitting down, "you're right, habit is hard to break. Even if a squid or something were on his/her way we couldn't see it until it wrapped around us."

"Maybe we should be careful how often we use the flashlight in case of an emergency. We don't want whatever powers it to run out and with no power available we don't have any way of recharging the battery pack, if that's even what runs it." Mab suggested.

"I agree that not overusing it is a good idea but I can't imagine more of an emergency than right now. If they don't find us soon, if they're even looking for us, we may well succumb to something Derek and his Krell friends dream up. I still think whatever brought us to this position was caused by them."

"You're probably right Lileas. Jinny you're so big on feelings about circumstances . . . got any helpful vibes to share with us about these?" The sharp edge in Mab's voice bordered on the sarcastic.

"I wish but when I'm stressed I don't seem to be able to get them the way I can when I'm relaxed. I'm not sure that we can do anything except wait until we're found, or something happens."

87.

Strident sirens filled the air in Euroswydd's Caverns as Mort, Reiki Clowne and Oscáre dashed to the Monitor Room. Having just retired for the night Reiki Clowne and Oscáre were in boxers while Mort although never clothed seemed undressed without his pipe.

"Lionel." Greeted Reiki Clowne as the three stopped before the screen. Euroswydd's image now joined by that of a grey stuffed elephant—only his head, ears, trunk and upper torso encased in a navy blue t-shirt were visible—looked gravely back.

"Greetings to all of you. It's unfortunate that these can't be happier circumstances but I suggest we don't stand on ceremony but let me get to the crux of the reason why I'm here. We've not got time to waste." The three Caretakers silently bowed as one.

"Another one!" Hans voice gasped behind them.

"Yes, this is Lionel a Multi-Dimensional Philosopher from Casyo. Please give him your undivided attention. There is no time to waste." Euroswydd's voice broached no argument from the three Threans now looming rigidly behind the Caretakers.

Taking a moment to look closely at each Threan Lionel spoke in the clipped cadence of British aristocracy circa 1900's—Threan time—, "In my capacity of Multi-Dimensional Philosopher I often visit planes of existence other than the one we are presently interacting within. As Beings of swift vibrations all Casyoans have this ability but my adeptness is a bit more finely honed as it is my life's calling. I offer this brief explanation to you Threans," Lionel bowed twirling his trunk upward, "so that you will give full credence to what I have to tell you." Pausing briefly, when no reaction evinced he continued. "In a nutshell, and know that I don't have a pinpointed location to give you; I have received information that the voyage of the submersible has been compromised."

"What specifics can you give us?" Mort's fingers worked as though filling an invisible pipe.

"I believe the Krell—yes the problematic Beings are the Krell and they've added to their repertoire of tricks since we Casyoans had direct dealings with them. Anyway these Krell have taken over Derek and rendered him invisible to the Threan women. He snuck aboard the submersible, waited until they were away from the Coast then implemented their plan."

"Plan?" Orla's voice trembled.

"Yes, my dear, plan. In order to lower Jinny, Lileas and Mab's defenses Derek has manipulated the pressure and temperature controls of the submersible creating optimal conditions for nitrogen narcosis to compromise you friends."

"Oh *mon dieu* they could die of such high levels of this nitrogen gas in the bloodstream!"

"Yes Oscáre they could but I think the main issue here is the Krell taking them over. Remember they need live bodies." Euroswydd replied. Hans, glaring at Euroswydd, mumbled a barely discernable, "How comforting."

"Actually Hans it is comforting, if they are alive there is hope for their safety and continued life." Drawing in a breath, lowering his trunk and staring intently from his screen Lionel continued, "Since neither Derek, the Krell, the women or apparently any of the aquatic Beings know where the submersible is, as I've said, I'm not able to pinpoint their location. The Krell have presumably picked a point far enough away from these Caverns that even the fastest swimmers won't be able to get here in time to let us know details once they do have details to relate. Something was done to the conveyance swimmers between checkpoints to close their consciousnesses because I can't get any readings from them."

"OK. So what *can* we do." Morna's voice reverberating vehemence took over the Chamber.

"We can gather together and send a specific message or in this case series of messages to the women in the submersible. We need to enable them to fix whatever has gone awry with the equipment that controls the pressure and temperature and perhaps even the mixture of gases they're breathing. We also need to encourage them in keeping the Krell at bay and not allowing their personal inner sanctums to be compromised by encouraging wakefulness. And we must do this as quickly as possible." Lionel nodded at Euroswydd who added.

"We need to present a unified and concerted persona in order to infiltrate their consciousness and influence their actions. In case you think this is all a bunch of hooey that we are making up scientific experiments were actually conducted on Threa to evaluate the efficacy of what was termed then as 'praying' and 'belief' and it was found to be an authentic means to bring about change."

"So what exactly is Nitrogen Narcosis?" Hans questioned.

"When pressures on the outside of a body increase the partial gases within the body expand so that interior and exterior are equal. When breathing in compressed gases from an atmospheric supplying system such as that found in this particular submersible—we've since developed more proficient systems because of the negative issues that can result—the ensuing increase in nitrogen within the bodily system brings on symptoms and behavior mimicking a drunken state."

"Imagine having consumed several of your Threan dry martinis." Lionel interjected.

"Yeah I'd feel very happy but totally unable to function with any kind of normal discrimination. How, even if our consciousnesses can connect with theirs would any of them be able to figure out how to reset the pressure and temperature much less still have the dexterity to perform whatever manipulations might be necessary to bring the changes about?"

"We will need to send great encouragement for believing that they are capable of doing what must be done. It's amazing the power of the mind, even when artificially altered. It will not be just us here, we will have the help of Beings from other planets in other galaxies."

"I think the time for discussion is *fini.* We should get to this task of helping." Oscáre straightened his boxers with a tight smile, "It is most fortunate that dress is not important for this exercise or we would lose more minutes." A tight burst of laughter loosened them slightly before Lionel gave final instructions.

"All please concentrate on the same concept . . . overcoming the nullifying effects of the nitrogen narcosis and restoring the interior of the cabin to more conducive pressure and temperature levels. I will leave Euroswydd here with you as I am going to organize the participants from other worlds. You may begin now if you wish." Lionel turned moving beyond the screen's range.

"Well are we all ready then? I would suggest finding comfortable seating. We will be at this until we know it's OK to stop." Euroswydd's head swiveled giving each his undivided attention for a moment before continuing. The three Caretakers, veterans to such group efforts, seated themselves in their chairs drawing in deep breathes of relaxation and concentration.

"I realize that this is all new to you three," he addressed the Threans, "so please don't be upset if I offer some instructions that may help you to better free your minds of extraneous thoughts and focus on the task at hand."

"Please . . . ." Orla murmured as the others nodded setting themselves up for long term sitting comfort.

"Initially we are going to work on relaxation to clear the mind and allow your body to be a noninvasive factor. Please breathe in through your nose only and then out through your mouth. Pay attention only to your breathing. Once you've done that for a few breathes you'll find your body starting to relax and its functions not the usual invasive consideration in your consciousness." He waited a few minutes watching as the Threan bodies gradually relaxed before intoning the concepts they needed to get across to Jinny, Lileas and Mab.

Silence curiously amplified by the thrumming of the Complex's sedate machinery held sway for several hours.

88.

"Are you sure." Reiki Clowne questioned an exhausted reddish featured cusk.

"Yes, I spoke with the squid herself. The submersible just seemed to burst into flames. Her suckers suffered the most damage. They are quite red and sore and she can't really use her tentacles without flinching. But from the coordinates she gave we sent down a search team and they have located the submersible."

"But no one has approached it yet."

"No, we're afraid to. We don't know if the Krell have it still or what. We thought we should let you know and have you decide what the next best step should be."

"Thank you, go and rest you've done well."

"You don't want me to carry some message back?"

"No, you look worn out. We'll send someone else." Reiki Clowne smiled watching the relieved expression on the cusk's face as she swam off.

"We will have to find out if the group encouragement worked *n'est pas?* Someone must go and see who is in control of the submersible." Oscáre voiced the thoughts of all gathered in the Observation Chamber.

"How will we know whether the Krell were successful or not in taking over our friends?" Orla questioned.

"I believe that if there had been a successful takeover the submersible would be operating by now. Because it's still apparently resting on the ocean's floor it's my feeling that they managed to stay themselves but that for some reason the communication devices aren't working and they haven't been able to get hold of us." Euroswydd finished with a smile.

"Or they could be dead."

"Before jumping to the unfounded, bleak conclusions let's send emissaries to the location and ascertain the facts, until then there can only be the conjecture."

"I agree with Oscáre; let's go find out. If they're OK then we can get them back here and figure out what happened and if Derek is within the submersible or what." Mort pressed several buttons and several species of swift swimming bottom dwelling fish appeared. Turning to Euroswydd who nodded Mort continued, "Thank you for volunteering. Please let us know as soon as you can what the situation is. I see you have the radio attached firmly," and indeed a tiny radio unit was strapped to a scup. "good, we'll await your first communication." Waving fins the school swam away.

Swirling unrecognized about us,
The very thing we most necessarily seek out.

20

WHO WOULD HAVE THOUGHT

89.

The submersible discharged three disheveled, relieved women, glad to be reunited with their companions.

"I've never been so glad to be in a cave before! I'm not sure I'll be persuaded to leave any time soon, if ever." Lileas declared backhanding moisture from her eyes. "And would you believe it, the best most welcoming sight I've *ever* seen were those long squid tentacles wrapping themselves around the submersible."

"Yeah I have to admit I never thought I'd feel relieved being the recipient of such an embrace. Although I must admit to being almost as relieved when all those fish swam up to the sub and peered at us through the portholes. I've never seen a fish do a high five with a fin before. It's a good thing the aquatic Beings of the depths carry their own lights with them or we might not have realized they were there." Jinny released from simultaneously hugging Hans, Morna and Orla looked curiously at Mort, Reiki Clowne and Oscáre standing politely out of the way rather than intrude on the Threans' reunion.

"You really do look like 'toys' if you'll excuse my saying so. I don't mean it as any kind of slam so please don't take it that way." She walked towards them her right hand outstretched in greeting.

"Oh no, we don't take umbrage with such phraseology. As you know we purposefully emulated these physical manifestations in order to better interact with the Threan environments and now you bipedal Threans." Euroswydd spoke from his screen as she bent over to shake hands with each of the three. "No signs of anything suspicious during the second half of your trip following the rescue from the ledge?"

"No, nothing. You don't suppose Derek and the Krell swam away or died on board do you?" Mab sounded hopeful.

"Most likely they are back in some sort of stasis similar to when you first arrived in the Satellite Complex. What they have done with Derek's body I can't even begin to guess at."

Jinny turned to face Mort as he spoke to them, "You mean you think they've disposed of him in some way?" her voice reverberated horror.

"No not necessarily, remember they could—and we believe it's possible due to their numerous presence within his body—focus all their combined energies blurring his physical parameters making him invisible and able to move about without his material presence being physically felt. Also remember that this is no longer your acquaintance Derek as you once knew him. His very Being has been compromised and I can't imagine there is any returning to what he was before takeover."

"But you said there was a chance for Threans to change. You said we could have learned and changed over the past months." Jinny interrupted sweeping her hand encompassing the other five Threans.

"*Absolument*, change without the invasion of the Krell is quite possible. However once the Krell have taken over the bipedal forms all is lost. They do not relinquish their host and certainly with the many Krell we believe are within the body you used to know as Derek there cannot be any vestige of the previous inhabitant."

Clearing his throat Reiki Clowne took over as Oscáre paused, "Derek suffered emotional trauma meted out by his parents and that damage was compounded by the continued ill treatment he was subjected to during the rest of his formative years. Unfortunately he didn't run into someone or ones who believed in him the way Hans did." He paused as they all looked at a now red faced Hans shaking his head as if to deny a charge of some sort.

"It is true is it not that you never speak of your father because he deeply resented your close resemblance to your mother? The woman left your father when you were just three. That in large measure your intolerance for Derek's behavior stemmed from the fact that you felt he should have 'gotten over' his emotional hurt?" Reiki Clowne continued gently.

"Who are you to go prying into my personal affairs? And how could you get that information anyway?"

"We checked records of Threans from our files and found yours, as well as everybody else's. We are not trying to be invasive but in order to follow the fairest most equitable path in this situation we need all the information on you six that we can get. Perhaps if the rest of your friends were more familiar with the circumstances surrounding your retrieval from the 'frying pan' they might be better able to guard themselves from the Krell in the future. This applies to you as well, not to mention being able to better deal with the demise of Derek and his body." Euroswydd interjected.

"Fine whatever, I guess it really doesn't matter who knows what now anyway." Hans shrugged and sat down.

Reiki Clowne continued, the ball at the end of his knitted hat bobbing as he included each listener in the story, "Using Hans as an emotional punching bag his father vented his anger, frustration and loss pummeling his son's psyche into a bruised and battered emotional pulp. Knowing first hand the power of positive reinforcement Mab," he swept his knitted hand towards Mab red ink staining her neck before rising upwards in patching swatches on her face, "whose supportive family had been instrumental in helping her overcome the initial educational difficulties resulting from her being dyslexic, always tried to make up for his lack of parental encouragement. Hans had someone who cared and supported him no matter what and Derek did not. Look at the differences in their ultimate integrity. Each Threan is born with the capacity to handle equally the negatives and positives in life. If they are balanced there are no problems, if not, well I guess the results are obvious to one and all."

"You mean there can be an overabundance of the positive?" Morna looked skeptical.

"Ah *oui, bein sur*. Those displaying the unhealthy amount of the positive attributes fall into the descriptive categories familiarly described on Threa as the better than thous, the goody two shoes, the all knowing et cetera." Oscáre rubbed his left ear absently, "While these Threans don't outwardly disobey any laws of the society or the Universe they are intolerable. Both intolerable to be around for any length of time and intolerant of everybody and everything they see, hear, and know about."

"They say 'adversity builds character' but there does have to be a reason for it to build a good character." Laughter greeted Euroswydd's pronouncement easing the tension. "Good I'm glad to see things on a lighter note. We've all been through a lot these past few weeks and I think it's time to, what's the phrase? 'Chill out' a bit." Turning to Orla, "Would you three who have been living here like to take your companions to their new home?" Then addressing Jinny, Lileas and Mab directly, "There are things we will have to look into and discuss soon but for now why don't you go get cleaned up, eat some and get some rest. We are going to go over the submersible after we put it into a quarantine area. Maybe we will have some answers for you by tomorrow."

Jinny her eyes twinkling asked, "We're not actually going to be 'chilled out' are we? I can only speak for myself of course but I've had enough chill for quite some time."

"Ah, a sense of humor . . . always an admirable quality. No, the Environment you will be living in has thermostatic control," A smile wreathed Euroswydd's face at Mab's exclaimed, "Good."

"So what exactly did happen to us in that sub? We felt weird, then as if we were the rope in a tug of war. Frankly I don't think any of us knows exactly when in all this milieu we settled onto that ledge near the bottom." Lileas looked from her friends already ensconced in the undersea Caverns to the Caretakers eyebrows cocked. "Do we have any idea if there was a successful coup on the part of these Beings in taking over our bodies?"

Ignoring that last part of her question Euroswydd relayed the theory of nitrogen narcosis, extreme hull temperatures and invisible Krell. The three women's faces a study he explained how the numerous Galactic Entities had managed, through mass concentration on the same message to help Jinny, Lileas and Mab overcome the effects of their gaseous poisoning enabling them to bring the atmospheric conditions in the sub back to measurements ensuring optimal physical and mental functions.

"I've heard the theories and hypothesis that such concentrated thinking could engender such results but wow." Reverently Lileas shook her head.

"Ah *oui*, the power of the positive thought magnified by galaxies of inhabitants. *C'est magnifice*!" Oscáre front hooves folded before his chest bowed.

"How did the sea creatures find us?" Jinny asked.

"A lot of swimming and searching through the areas surrounding the projected path across the ocean." Euroswydd answered. "Once the submersible was located volunteers investigated, found you were alive and then the squid took over transporting you here. We think the period of time after you were poisoned when you felt as though you were being pulled in two different directions was the time we were sending the galactic group message. Even though you don't remember any details somehow or other you must have managed to correct the situation."

"Couldn't the Krell have taken over and set everything right?" Mab asked tentatively.

"Sure, but we think they would have had the capability of getting the submersible running again. It was theirs; they would be familiar with its operational mechanics waiting for us to find and transport doesn't seem like a very likely scenario if they had been successful in takeover." Mort interposed.

"Well it's time we were off then." Declared a suddenly bustling Orla herding her fellow Threans away from the docking area.

The Four Caretakers remained silent as Hans, Orla and Morna led the way to the Environment planned by Mort and executed by the Caretaking team to safely house the six Threans.

90.

"So my friends what do you think?" Euroswydd questioned. "Orla certainly didn't want that conversation to continue."

"No, but I can't say that I blame her; there are a seemingly endless amount of scenario's regarding whether the Krell were successful in taking over their minds and bodies or not. The more we all dwell on the possibility the more fear engendered reactionary issues will plague these Caverns. I tend to doubt they are compromised but I don't know about that submersible. He could be in there somewhere or his physical remains might have been somehow absorbed and the Krell integrated into the equipment of the sub in similar fashion to their technique of using the monitors in the Satellite Station." Mort looked at the outer hull as if within resided the plague of the ages. "I think we'd better get it into the quarantine area then no one will be touching or any nearer to it than the remote controlled 'arms' we'll use to do the examination."

"Agreed. What about that orb? It seemed to play an integral part in their scheme in the Satellite Complex but it hasn't moved since the last three women left." Reiki Clowne sighed putting his two knitted hands together.

"I've actually discussed that with Lionel and he hypothesized that the orb contained the majority of Krellians who'd escaped their Threan hosts before recycling. He feels that the Krell employed the type of round glass orb Threans used to leave in their gardens for decoration and imbued it with the essences from their no longer viable hosts. As many of them entered as they could while the rest settled into the screens close by, the orb containing the administrative center. Lionel feels the Krellian agenda involved resurrection from the orb and screens into surviving Threans when the time was right, using her or him as a means of temporary transport while searching for new hosts. Something either went awry with their plan or they saw their opportunity when the Threans stumbled over the Complex."

"My that's quite something. The Krell really have come up with some new tricks of their trade haven't they?" Mort neglected to pull on his pipe, merely holding it between skeletal fingers. "Does that mean they might be trying to hold onto Derek's molecules or matter in some seemingly innocuous form to facilitate their eventual reappearance?"

"Seems a likely scenario based on their recent history. The other thing to keep in mind is that lots of Krell obviously met their demise, were broken down then recycled into healthy matter when the Upheavals first began. They're not indestructible; it's possible the trip in the submersible was more than their systems could handle. The energy expenditure required to keep Derek invisible might have debilitated them to the point of nonexistence. Even banded together in a common cause they would need to recoup their energies at some point. It's unknown how long they could keep up the charade before having to take a break."

"So then what of the body of Derek?"

"I don't know Oscáre. Maybe our investigation will clarify that." Euroswydd nodded at them all, "I look forward to our next time together but for now I must run. 'Break a leg' getting the submersible safely into the quarantine area!" Although his screen darkened his gleeful chuckling notes cascaded across the audio connection a few moments more.

Gritting his pipe stem between his teeth Mort pulled down a lever revealing an opening in the rock below the waterline. With a swoosh the submersible whisked into the cavity below their feet.

"Time to do a little metallic grabbing," he said with a grin, "anyone coming to join me in the hunt?"

"I think both of us will help you."

"*Oui,* I would not miss this for the world."

91.

Each seated himself in a swivel chair, thrusting hands and lower arms into encasing sealed gloves extending beyond the safety glass into the quarantine area before turning on the viewing screens. Manipulators moved the 'arms' and 'fingers' of the metallic probes used to examine the submersible and place recording—visual and auditory—devices inside as well as throughout the pool. When they were done the submersible rested on a ledge above the water line every porthole emptied of glass and the hatch detached.

"Well so far nothing worthy of note. I think I will leave you and continue with the other tasks that call for my attention."

"Me too." Reiki Clowne looked at Mort, "I think we've done all we can for the time being. Are you going to join us?"

"I believe so. They've either eluded us or we will see some evidence on these recording devices." Nodding and smiling, "My bones are tired; I think I'll go see how our new inhabitants are doing."

The three Caretakers carefully sealed off the quarantine area, including the Manipulator Chamber before humming and light stepping their way to the upper reaches of the Caverns. For a time no movement registered on the digital receptors of the recording devices, then the submersible slipped off the ledge, the slate grey water spilling in until filled it sank to the bottom of the quarantine pool.

Look within for the guiding light
Stocked by outward clues
Heightened perception
Should you invite them to

21

SETTLING IN

92.

"There does seem to be hope for their recovery. I just wish the location of Derek's form and/or the Krell were known." Oscáre nodded at Euroswydd. "I think your idea for *le fête ete une tres bonne idée*. It is the polite, considerate way to thank everyone and there are the other possibilities to consider as well."

"Yes, I agree with Oscáre." Reiki Clowne spoke while typing. "We should tell them soon."

"We need to fill them in on recent events from our end as well. They must be getting curious," Mort said, "although they haven't signaled us and seem to be enjoying their reunion and new home."

Euroswydd ended the meeting as Reiki Clowne finished typing the invitations.

"We'd like to invite you to a celebration/thank you gathering for all the Beings involved with the mission to find and then bring you to safety." Euroswydd formally nodded towards each of the six Threans now holding typewritten invitations. "Those who can't attend, for instance the Beings living within the cave systems of the Satellite Complex, will be provided with the means to celebrate in their own habitats." Euroswydd spoke to a meeting of the Caretakers and Threans several days after the arrival of the three women.

"A party! I barely remember what it's like to enjoy such an event." Lileas twirled, mirroring the excitement glowing from the five other nodding Threan faces. "Who'd have thought that being here so far below the Surface, actually at the bottom of the ocean with you Casyoans, would seem more like home than we've felt since, well it seems like forever."

Having been left to their own devices to acclimate this was the first interaction between the two groups since the Threans' reunion. Mort had set the weather conditions in the Threan Environment to mimic a Northern Temperate Continental spring, perfect for reconstituting threadbare mental and physical constitutions.

Temperatures hovered in the 70's during the day, dropping into the upper 40's or lower 50's at night, humidity levels only sporadically higher than 35 percent. Frequent gentle rains coaxed the yearly metamorphosis of stark silhouettes into light green billowing promises of vitality. Grass grew thick beneath their exploring feet, maturing buds, forsythia, lilac, crabapple and cherries perfumed the air. Shelter from the promised full gamut of seasons and resulting conditions existed in the form of a structure complete with kitchen, library, living and dining room, den, bathrooms, and bedrooms. Pantries and storage areas replete with nutritional fare supplied their every eating and drinking need. Built into a hillock from 'green' materials it exemplified environmentally conscious housing. Morna expressing a desire to live there forever suggested naming it Shangri La.

Unbeknownst to them the Caretakers continually recorded the Threans' activities, not in the interest of invasiveness, but in order to glean necessary information. Upon reading each of the sixes dossier the reason for Interment had become clear. One and all had displayed a lack of adequate knowledge and level of respect for living Beings and nurturing, noninvasive interactions. Through no fault of their own and they would have vehemently protested such a judgmental assessment of their natures had the suggestion been put to them, these behavioral characteristic had delegated them to recycling. Ignorant of the full ramifications of their negligent actions or as in some cases lack of action they were the deceptively innocuous type of Beings. The most disturbing aspect the fact that if asked all would have said they had acted in accordance with their deep respect for the Threan Environment and the living Beings housed therein. Threan life had progressed so far from anything non-contrived that few actually had a reality based concept of what sentient and natural interactions really were. Most Threans, as mirrored by the sixes behavior before the Upheavals, did what they could to act responsibly within their limited understanding when it was convenient and only to the extent mandated by law. Their actions didn't stem from a deep rooted, kinship with the vibrancy of the living world around them, in part because by the time they were born so much of it was gone. They had lived in a sheltered Threan created protective zone.

In the interest of keeping such lack of perception from continuing through the transferred Threans and pervading another society it had been decided that they be recycled. Their molecular constituents of better use in helping Threa rebuild than anything else. Naturally each displayed a variety of personal peculiarities and/or negative habits which although threatening on a personal interactive level weren't part of the deciding equation. While a plus, adroitness within the realm of personal relations isn't a necessary contributing component to the ideology of being respectful of life and surroundings. All bipedal forms have some behavioral aspect or other in need of modification.

One of the most notable sophistications of Casyoans and others of similar ilk is their cognizance and adherence to the ideology of transposition. The premise states that all living Beings are capable of making mistakes. That predilection in and of itself should not be considered the negative attribute. Failure to recognize that all are proficient at facilitating errors, judging worth based on behavioral expectations impossible to fulfill, contributing to misconceptions and not being open to relieving knowledge and subsequent change are the actual negative stumbling blocks. Being stifled and closed doesn't allow for the relieving bending and swaying with the prevailing forces of life necessary for a soul to learn, strengthen and grow. Rather like a physical body staying in homeostasis there needs to be constant flux and adaptation—within moderation's parameters.

Prolonged imbalance results in increased repercussions and so on and so forth until the negativity becomes overwhelming, as was the case on Threa.

All six of the Threans had been viewed by the Casyoans as sincere in their wish to do no harm. However their points of reference being so far from the mark they had been consistently perpetrating damage. At the time of the original judgment the opportunity for teaching had passed. Present circumstances offered a second chance.

Surviving on the Surface through the Upheavals seemed to have brought about realization and change in their perceptions. However reverting to ones tried and true behavior patterns when the causes of severe angst and stress are no longer mitigating factors is a well recognized bipedal trait. Once things return to 'normal' and life becomes easy it's the rarity when all the promises and changed mindsets viewed as specific to those times of emergency aren't tossed to the winds. These Threans had to be cognizant of their misguided beliefs and willing to learn the truth.

It had been decided to discourage the Threans from dwelling on the possibility of Derek and the Krell alive and loose within the Complex as it decreased their chances of exhibiting overtly paranoid and/or delusional behavior. This approach, it was hoped, would allow the Casyoans the best possible chance of an accurate insight into the caliber of the Threans as they lived and interacted in their Environment. Left to their own devices as much as feasible—Oscáre had pointed out with a chuckle, ironically adhering to the Casyoans policy of non-involvement—the Threans would have ample opportunity to reveal their true colors. Barring more unforeseen happenstance character analysis would be completed well before Threa finished the Cleansing and Restoration process.

The issue of other Threans having survived on the Surface was briefly touched upon then dismissed. Euroswydd's pointing out that there wasn't anything they could or should do as per their agreement with Threa unless more signals were heard put an end to any conjecture.

"We have to trust that Threa is able to take care of her needs in this without our interference. These seven may have been the only ones. After all the process was set up to be as compassionate and efficient as possible. It's doubtful there are more up there."

So far the main focus of the Threans attention was exploring. They seemed most astonished and delighted in their first exposure to a completely natural, healthily interacting environment, the type of which had once abounded on Threa. While reveling in the new sensations, not the least of which was the lifting of stress, occasionally one or the other was seen watching their companions closely. No overt displays of paranoia evidenced and they ate, slept and seemed to draw healing sustenance from their surroundings.

93.

"They seem to be settling in well. We recorded this just a few hours ago." Mort explained to Euroswydd at a meeting of the Caretakers.

"Do you think they can hear us?" Mab asked looking around their Environment. "They've been nothing but kind to us but I still don't think they completely trust us."

"Yeah they've got us locked up in here don't they? At least we can't get out without calling them and asking for someone to come and undo the doorway." Orla walked over to the clear entryway. Pushing the membrane it stretched, puckering out in the shape of her hand but didn't break. Previous attempts to release the membrane's diaphanous molecular structure had met with similar results.

"I think we're going to have to wait this one out. I can't say that I blame them for being careful. They're here to protect the sanctity of this Planet's attempts to heal and return to a healthier existence." Jinny smiled thinking her five other friends gave the impression of resting on fallen fluff gifted from the billowing clouds above instead of cherry blossom petals coaxed down from the trees by the previous night's rain. "From their point of view we should be viewed with suspicion. We were left on the Planet's Surface to be reintegrated as little bits and pieces, apparently the Krell have taken over Derek and possibly one or more of us. Those Krell could be waiting in dormancy, like those animals I've heard about living in deserts. They could stay in stasis for years waiting for enough moisture to wake up, reproduce, do a little dance, make a little love then recoup in dormancy."

"You mean waiting within us, ready to leap forward and do their thing? I'm not sure I like that idea." Morna frowned looking down at herself.

"Or they may be dead, or they may be dormant somewhere else, there's just no way of knowing. I don't think we should dwell on it in any event. Just know that they may be around waiting to take advantage of a weak moment on any of our parts." Hans contributed.

"Is that what your feelings are telling you?" Lileas peered closely at Hans before turning to Jinny, "And what about you? Getting any feelings or hints about any or all of this?"

"I'm feeling that we should enjoy and learn all we can about healthy natural interactions from watching what goes on in this Environment we're lucky enough to be living in. Learning new things is always fun. None of us has had the opportunity to live in such a place, and yet for millennium our Planet looked and behaved just like this. Perhaps as the Caretakers said we can leave here and go help others to realize before it's too late."

"I don't feel any particular negativity and would like to keep it that way. The Caretakers said it could be a long time before the Upheavals end. Let's just take it one day at a time for now. I'm going for a walk anyone want to come with?" After a brief hesitation Mab followed in Hans' wake.

"You know we're just trying to make sure we don't get into more trouble than we were on the Surface."

Hans turned, "I know. But there's nothing to be gained from conjecture. They've provided us with everything we could possibly want and we have to wait here anyway. The Caretakers are probably suspicious of us and frankly I get the feeling that we're all watching each other just a bit more closely than before there was a possibility of Krell inhabiting one or more of us."

"It's kind of hard not to, given everything that's happened."

"Yeah, well time will tell." Hans strode towards the woods, "Coming?" trailed over his shoulder. Mab ran to catch up.

"So should we stop talking about the possibilities and enjoy what we've got for the moment?" Lileas eventually broke the silent concentration of watching them diminish, "What do you think Jinny?"

"Enjoy, learn and be on the lookout for anything odd." As that was met with peals of laughter, "OK, OK, I know everything's been odd lately. But you know what I mean. If one of us seems to be acting out of character, if the Caretakers do something that doesn't seem in our best interests . . . I don't know exactly just *something*."

"There really isn't anything else we can do is there? Might as well enjoy the benevolence. I tell you one thing though. I'm not going to waste anything here. This place is way too beautiful to mess up." Orla pointed at a mother doe with two white spotted fawns grazing on the ankle high meadow grass stretching beyond the cherry trees. Its far horizon edged by the woods enveloping Hans and Mab. "That's just spectacular and it's real not some historical video recounting."

94.

"Yes a party. We all deserve a bit of relaxation and it might do you six good to see the full extent of cooperative networking amongst Beings of all persuasions—aquatic and terrestrial Threan as well as Extra Terrestrial." Euroswydd smiled at the six. "Nothing was spared in these operations just as nothing is being spared in facilitating Threa's recovery and ultimate return to viability. Perhaps you can carry the ideologies you've been exposed to and spread them to other communities heading along the destructive highway the people of your Planet traveled."

"You mean enlighten others and perhaps keep them from destroying their home? Does this sort of thing happen a lot?" Jinny looked perplexedly at the Casyoans, "You know it's going to take some getting used to this idea of being a fairly inconsequential inhabited planet among hundreds."

"Each group with a mindset such as yours feels themselves to be the proverbial unique center of the universe. Actually the expanse of interactive worlds is so extensive it isn't within the powers of your Threan mind to comprehend. The Universes extend into infinity as your minds know it with all variation on the dimension/plane reality that your Threan minds have been able to process. Suffice it to say there's a tremendous lot more 'out there' than you've ever realized and even recognizing that it will take time for your minds to be able to grasp the new concepts necessary for full conceptual realization. And you're not inconsequential. If you were we wouldn't be going to all this trouble. All life forms are unique individualistic parts contributing to the makeup of the whole. Even the minutest part out of whack has a negative effect on the entire system. That you might be able to help us in our quest to keep homeostasis throughout the Quadrants is quite an honor." Mort explained.

Shaking her head Jinny, "I feel totally overwhelmed. Maybe we could be allowed to live here for a while and let this all sink in. I can only speak for myself but I feel I have a lot to learn before I could even consider being effective in helping someone else understand."

"*Certainment*, we are not wanting to rush you into the decision of any kind. Merely letting you know of the possibilities for your future. And none of this will be possible until Threa is done with the ministrations." Oscáre brushed his shirt into aligned submission. "You have been through the travails terrible and for the immediate moment should be looking forward to the party rather than eventualities that will not transpire for many of your months to come."

"Has there been any news, sign, anything to do with Derek and the Krell?" Lileas asked.

"There's been nothing suspicious on the Surface or within these Caverns outside the parameters of the quarantine area." Mort said. "As you know nothing has registered on the recording devices to rouse any alarm and except for the daily checks the submersible and the quarantine area are without activity."

"So the existence or demise of Derek and/or the Krell is a complete mystery?" Hans questioned, eyebrows raised.

"You could look at it that way however, we are all alerted to the possibility of problems and if they are still in existence and if somewhere in this Complex they must be exhausted to the point of not being able to move about. The entire Complex is under careful, constant scrutiny and should anything suspicious occur the alarms will sound immediately. Let's talk party!"

95.

The celebration lasted a twelve hour—Threan increments—time span and extended beyond the inner cave complex to the watery depths. All able to attend whether sea dwellers or terrestrial feasted, shared tales, made new friends and enjoyed good company. Musical interludes provided by the Extremophiles as well as various Cavern dwellers graced the event. The Extremophiles revealed their talents within the theatrical genre putting on a live performance of their most popular musical, *Pluming on Currents,* for live viewing by all in attendance and recorded for later viewing by those not able to be. Oscáre catered a veritable feast and as promised those unable to attend were provided with the means to enjoy their own celebrations in their preferred ambient conditions. The dance recital further captivated the audience's rapt attention as aquatic life both within and without the Caverns swam in gracefully choreographed, synchronous harmony, bioluminescent displays akin to fireworks enhancing the event finale.

Reiki Clowne, Mort and Oscáre, the Threans' escorts after the party, smiled at the sounds of contentment coming through the membrane entryway securing the Threan Environment. Six arms waved a brief *adieu* to the Caretaking three before pleasantly tired the Threans called it a night or more accurately a very early morning.

"They certainly know how to throw a party." Murmured Lileas pushing the front door open.

Muffled yeah's, sure do's, and goodnight's yawned in reply as each ascended to their second story bedrooms.

I feel peaceful just as I used to before all the troubles began mused Jinny dropping neatly folded clothes on the desk chair before arranging herself under the covers. Are there really worlds where positive and negative aspects balance each other out? And the connotations attached to those words seem unnecessary. The way the Casyoans explained them they're simply two halves of a whole and whenever there's a major imbalance there's a problem rectifiable by correction and returning to balance. Admittedly the simplified version but still. I wonder if becoming more attuned to natural rhythms and processes will help me be better able to understand the inner messages I get. Sighing into sleep her thoughts slowed and within minutes nothing save the whispering whistles, snores and rhythmic breathing of the soundly sleeping joined with the occasional rustling of a night creature going about her/his business.

96.

"I would be more comfortable if we knew what's happened to Derek and the Krell within him. It's as though they disappeared into thin air." Reiki Clowne spoke to Euroswydd, Oscáre and Mort at the convened meeting several days after the party. "But everything is copasetic for the time being." Pausing he cocked his head meeting Euroswydd's eye, hat pompom bobbing. "The Threans are ensconced in their new home. All seems to have settled down as it was before the unidentified signals."

Chuckling Euroswydd said, "I see you've been studying colloquialisms too."

"I couldn't let you be the only one toying with them." At which all four burst into laughter.

"I wonder if they're on the Surface somewhere; you would think we'd have seen some sign if he'd stowed away somehow on the submersible unless the Krell have adapted to survival in water. It's not been moved from its landing spot on the bottom of the quarantine tank." Mort's pipe emitted billowing clouds of white grey tinged smoke as he settled back in his chair. "Nothing has shown up on the video cam in the Satellite Complex. We will make sure to continue monitoring everywhere . . . but for now I am glad to be returning to a quieter life. She will be at this for many months to come."

"Yes, and in spite of being in the Caverns I'm confident we can find out the true personalities of our new guests. They seem quite content to stay within the confines of the Environment you created for them. I thank you all for your help with this unexpected development." Euroswydd nodded to them all before sighing, "I must leave you now and go to a meeting with the Voting Entities. They want to know all about what's been going on." He chuckled, "I think they're enjoying the intrigue."

"*A biento mon ami* we look forward to hearing how the meeting goes. For now I will be joining my little Reiki Clowne and Mort in playing for the Tropical Rainforest Environment. We have not been able to for so long. It will be good to get back to the more normal rhythm." Oscáre waved at Euroswydd as the screen went dark.

They left the Monitor Chamber humming as one with two softly tapping drums to the measure of Mort's guitar string stroking.

97.

Betraying nothing droplets coalesce. Amoeboid parameters incrementally enlarge within crevasses of microscopic space surrounding the pebbles upon which the submersible had rested. Nothing registered on the finely tuned recorders pausing a millisecond before shrugging digital dismissal of an insinuated tic.

EPILOGUE

A slight twist of the lever shortened light years of distance to inconsequential. Springing in to fill the viewing screen swatches in hues of white, blue, brown and green pulsated about her periphery. Vitality glowed through the viewing scope.

"Elva's tucked in." Gilead's voice wafted over her left shoulder. "She never woke, just curled under the covers." Refusing to miss any of the tale or have it spread over several nights, Elva had not allowed the final relinquishment to sleep—lodging her head against her grandmother's shoulder—until the last word had been uttered.

"What are you looking at?" and upon setting his eyes to the viewer. "Ah Threa, she still looks as though everything's going OK." In tandem with his mother's nod of agreement he yawned, stretching his arms upward, "I'm going to bed myself are you coming in?"

"Not right now. Sleep tight." Having picked up her journal her pen was already skimming across the paper.

Elva is old enough to grasp the nuances and importance of the past, the generic past as well as her personal heritage. It's an essential means of survival handing down lessons gleaned from strife rather than focusing solely on the resulting accolades. Truly meaningful victories don't result from conflict, battles fought and won through grand gestures and force but by more subtle means. Mahatma Gandhi said "an eye for an eye and a whole civilization goes blind" which couldn't have more aptly put into one phrase the inception of the decay that led the eventual need for Threa to go through the Upheavals. The Threans wanted control—at all costs—and as a result lost their world to poisoning of the heart, soul, mind and environment. I've witnessed countless scenarios in my helping other planets avoid the ravages that nearly destroyed planet Threa and succeeded in destroying cultural Threankind whose problems stemmed from the disregard and trivialization of the past.

Only cognizance of past lapses in judgment can stem repetitive behavior. Those societies that lose respect for their elders—alive and passed—are the ones that tend to move inexorably towards oblivion. The further a major societal cataclysm recedes in time the less of an impact it carries unless there is appreciation for historical relevance and the acquired wisdom of the elders. Building on a foundation of previously acquired and continually respected knowledge is a sign of health.

Rather than reducing past events to boring, antiquated episodes retained briefly for scholastic's sake but employing them—for example—as entertaining bedtime stories much as historians in pre-writing days told tales during feasts, times of celebration and classroom groupings, history and lessons can be effectively and meaningfully passed from generation to generation. The past must be related in a way that keeps it alive and vibrant instead of something dusted off and paid homage to by hierophants and others of similar ilk.

While all six of us learned tremendously sojourning in Euroswydd's Caverns only Lileas and I continued traveling to needy planets and peoples after being transported to our present home planet of Aibi. It's just a hop, skip and a jump—on an interplanetary transport—from Casyo. Having become dear friends and valued family members visiting the Caretakers is always an eagerly anticipated pleasure.

I'd been correct in thinking that increasing knowledge of nature's rhythms would open the floodgates of my, as Threan's termed it, "psychic powers". While more in tune than I could understand at the time of the Upheavals my discernment capabilities weren't developed enough to allow for comprehension. With the helpful guidance of all the Caretakers and Reiki Clowne in particular I'm now fully in touch with my heightened sensitivity levels to the rhythms vibrating in the Universe.

Of course being "psychic" had nothing to do with the partial messages. There really are no such abilities as Threans defined them. They felt there was some sort of mystic or occult forces and perhaps on their level of perception there was. To all of us the great "out there" was a mystery and traditionally mysteries controlled by unseen forces were considered supernatural, magical phenomenon. In reality all that transpired had nothing to do with magic, deities or any such thing. It was merely a function of misunderstanding the perception of other planes/dimensions and existences. Threans and as it happens others on other planets having the same sensibilities but living in less developed circumstances than the Caretakers never fully understood the messages they were receiving. Those that did receive limited enlightenment were stereotypically perceived as wackoes, gods, and/or possessed depending on how they presented themselves and the prevailing mindsets of the times they inhabited.

Anyway, Lileas and I have spent many years traveling within the various galactic systems helping to awaken the perceptions of other cultures. As emissaries for the Casyoan Council of Elders most specifically Euroswydd, Reiki Clowne, Oscáre Tarjáy , Mort, and Lionel who had over the years become an integral part of the Caretaking team, we taught by example and/or lecture depending on circumstances and needs. Oftentimes the Caretakers would assume forms least likely to arouse panic amongst the groups allowing for a smoother introduction. Hans and Mab settled down together, raised a family of their own and counseled from Aibi. Orla and Morna settled on different planets and after several decades we all lost touch with one another. Some things are just meant to fade away.

My son, Gilead, is not biological but chosen. Rescued from a planet in crisis he was one of the few enlightened ones. Our instantaneous bond strengthens with time's passage. To this day it never ceases to amaze me how certain individuals seem to be birthed on their planet with a different mindset than the majority. Actually I think more are born than are realized but their insights bludgeoned by societal pressures never have a chance to blossom. Few Beings want to be seen as different and when given the choice of struggling against the tide or being able to relax and be one of the accepted choose the latter. Many simply forget their childish—as they perceived it—thoughts and "grow up". Fortunately Gilead was one of those few who, sticking to his guns, was taken from oppression at age twelve following our arrival on his planet to supervise the same type of judgments that had been passed on Threa before the Upheavals. He'd displayed impressive fortitude.

With the arrival of Elva we (Lileas and I) ceased our constant traveling and contentedly settled down on Aibi. After all the traveling it's been nice to be in one place more often than not. Our present capacity as consultants enables us to enjoy a more sedate but no less stimulating lifestyle. Research and exploration through technology, preparing ways and means of continuing the teachings and ministrations of those like Euroswydd, Oscáre Tarjáy, Reiki Clowne, Mort, Lionel and the rest of the Casyoan Elders fills our hours with crucial activities. Interacting with and teaching Elva is no less important.

Both Lileas and I hope to pass on as many lessons as we can to Elva and any other children Gilead and Morticia have. Both of them picked up much from us. Gilead of course being gifted and splitting his formative years between traveling with us when possible and living on Casyo with the Caretakers when it wasn't has been able to teach much to Morticia and is passing it all to their children. They are both schoolteachers for which I couldn't be prouder and more pleased. Next to parental figures—not necessarily biological—teachers are the most instrumental sculptors of a child's life. To be under the tutelage of ones in tune with the nuances of the Universal Rhythms is an exceptional bonus.

Of Derek and the Krell there have been no overt signs. It's possible that they've been the root cause of many a planet's backward slide towards chaos but even though nearly a century has passed since those days on Threa there is no way to state anything with surety regarding them. Negativity, or perhaps more accurately phrased factors leading to imbalance, can be that way. The only means to keep it from flourishing is through awareness of the possibilities and maintaining balance between the two forces.

One of my favorite sayings, I think Oscáre first quoted it to me is, "sow your seeds in fertile ground bestowing nothing but peacefully harmonious nurturing. From time to time remember to stand back and watch the expansion of your horizons."

Closing her journal Jinny leaned back in the chair face uplifted to the star emblazoned night sky.

APPENDIX

FRENCH TO ENGLISH

A bientôt – so long

A tout a leur – see you later, bye-bye

Absolument – absolutely

Bien sur – absolutely, but of course, sure

Bonjour – hello

Bonne – good

Ça va? – how're you doing? everything OK?

Certainment – certainly

C'est – it's

C'est magnifique – it's magnificent

C'est vraie – that's right

Common Ça va? – how are you?

Ete - is

Fête – party

Fini – finished

Idée – idea

Impossible – impossible

Incroyable – incredible

Merci – thanks

Mon ami – my friend

Mon dieu – oh dear

Monsieur – sir, Mr.

N'est pas – isn't it

Non – no

Oui – yes

Quelle – what a

Trente – thirty

Un feat – a feat

Vraiment – that's right, ok

CASYON RUNIC ALPHABET

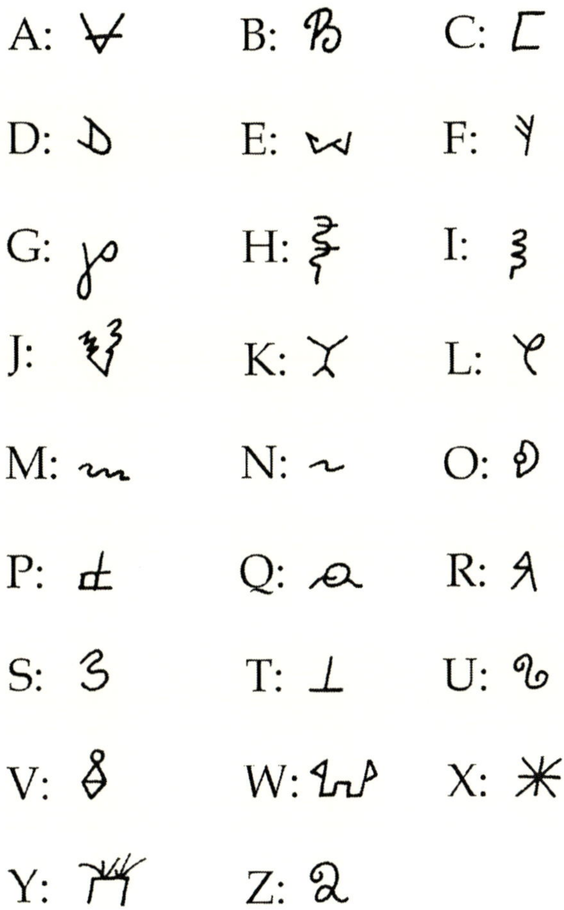

question mark

exclamation mark

period

Printed in the United States
201229BV00003B/151-171/P

9 780615 188409